New York Times Bestselling Authors

Vivian Arend
Elle Kennedy

Love is a Battlefield

DreamMakers

Vivian Arend
Elle Kennedy

This is a work of fiction. Names, characters, places, and incidents either are the product of the author's imagination or are used fictitiously, and any resemblance to any persons, living or dead, business establishments, events, or locales is entirely coincidental

Love is a Battlefield
Copyright © 2014 by Vivian Arend & Elle Kennedy
ISBN: 978-1-500323-16-5
Edited by Jennifer Miller
Cover by Amanda Nicole White
Proofed by Sharon Muha

First print publication: July 2014

Dedication

We're so thankful to have an awesome team to help us put these books together. Jennifer Miller, Sharon Muha, Nicole Snyder—we really couldn't do it without you.

And from Viv to Elle—since I got to see the final document after you, I'm sneaking this in. Hee! Thank you for stalking me and telling me we'd be BFF. You were right. The past couple years have been a blast, and writing with you makes me very happy. Looking forward to more HEA.

Chapter One

THE STREET front was empty as Jack Hunter parked his Aston Martin near the front door of DreamMakers Inc. The music from the party he'd just left still pulsed in his veins, and he hummed along with the tune stuck on repeat in his brain, clicking open his trunk to pull out the enormous box filled with mostly full bottles of leftover booze.

Normally at the end of a party, remaining stock belonged to the clients who'd purchased it. In this case the party had been for one of their own, which meant the leftovers were going to refill the office liquor cabinet.

Jack grinned. When he and his best friend, Parker Wilson, had established DreamMakers it had been gamble. They'd wanted to capitalize on the skills they'd gained as soldiers while enjoying life to the max. The fact the company had become wildly successful didn't suck.

He put his shoulder to the door, balancing the heavy box with one arm as he coded in the security key. After years of serving overseas as a Ranger, it felt strange to be home. Still watching his back, and the backs of his partners, only no longer against a foreign danger.

The security system flickered from armed to standby, and he moved quickly to get under shelter as rain began to fall.

Inside the office, he moved rapidly through the darkness, familiar with every inch of space. To his right their secretary's desk stood vigil near the front door, a half-dozen comfortable waiting chairs lining the wall across from it. Didi had left her radio on low—no matter how many times he and the guys teased her, they couldn't convince the older woman to shut things off at night. And considering how much work she did, none of the three partners was prepared to call her up on the carpet for something as minor as leaving her music playing night and day.

He shut off the radio, then headed to the staff area at the back of the building, past the center corridor where they each had an office. He and Dean Colter pretended to work in theirs. Parker Wilson actually had a desk and chairs in his office space, his open door revealing impeccable military neatness in every organized inch.

Jack wasn't so much into the office furniture and filing cabinets. He had a couch. It worked fine for the rare times he was in the building.

DreamMakers organized dates for the people who couldn't coordinate enthusiastic enough romantic gestures on their own. In the beginning, their work had been one hundred percent reaching out to confused and desperate friends. The guys who needed some major groveling to get themselves off their ladies' shit-lists, but over the past three years the company's reputation had grown.

It wasn't just about getting their fellow man out of trouble anymore. Now they helped anyone who needed some direction in planning a romantic date or kickass celebration.

Jack paced the hallway, the sneakers he'd changed into after leaving the party landing silently on the laminate flooring. He made it all the way to the staff room/kitchen area and froze.

A light shone by the sink. That in itself wasn't enough to make him blink. No, it was the light and the dusty backpack lying on the counter that shoved his suspicions into high gear.

He set the box in his hands on the floor, checking around carefully as he reached for the corner cupboard and silently pulled out the gun stashed there. Didi constantly teased the men about the strategically placed weapons in the office, and their reply was always the same—Rangers for life. You could take the man outta the army, but you couldn't take the army outta the man.

Gun in hand, Jack eased into the corner to prepare himself for anything. A quick peek behind the freestanding barrier by the back exit revealed a worn pair of shoes left outside the bathroom door.

Someone appeared to have entered the building, and unless they were currently strolling the streets of San Francisco in bare feet, they had to still be around. And from the size of the shoes, his mystery person was a whole lot smaller than him.

He'd already seen into all but three of the rooms, and one of those was rapidly eliminated as Jack cautiously poked his head around the corner to discover an empty bathroom.

The towel hanging on the rack was still damp, but other than that there was no sign of his intruder. Which left one of two places.

He paced silently down the hall to stand outside Dean's office, cocking his head toward the door. Nothing. Nothing but silence so thick it made his ears buzz. He was reaching for the doorknob when a low murmur jerked him from his task.

Someone in the building, less than ten feet away. Somewhere behind the door that led to Jack's domain.

Maybe he should've called for backup, but Parker and his sweetheart Lynn had just left the party, and while Jack knew his friend wouldn't hesitate for even a moment before dropping everything, he could handle this one on his own.

As for Dean, the man was undoubtedly by this time buried deep in bed with at least two women. It required an emergency on par with a nuclear attack before Jack would dream of interrupting his evening.

He steadied his gun hand, then twisted the doorknob exactly right to avoid letting it squeak. He pushed on the wood, letting the heavy surface swing away from him. There were no curtains on his window, and outside the streetlights illuminated the area. Cool blue light shone in and revealed the entire room. Jack glanced quickly for his target.

4

His basketball hoop was mounted on one wall. A heavy bag hung in the corner. The rest of his kit was laid over an exercise bench beside the school lockers he'd found to store stuff in. To his right, directly below the window, was the leather couch he'd inherited from his dad, the only thing he'd gotten besides the Aston Martin.

And on the couch, where he definitely had not left anything, was a small bump covered with the blanket that usually hung over the back of the nearby chair. The blanket he'd picked up one wild weekend in Mexico on a road trip with Parker back when they were still in high school.

The size of the lump confirmed his guess that the vagabond visitor wouldn't present too much danger, unless they were armed. And the way they were lying on the couch, facing toward the back, no way they could get off a shot if Jack incapacitated them first.

All his calculations took less than three seconds before he was across the room, landing on top of his uninvited guest. A grunt of pain escaped the stranger as Jack used his full weight to pin down his target and render him—or her—immobile.

His fingers easily circled delicate wrists—either a child or a woman—and he instinctively eased off to avoid causing any damage.

"Don't move. Don't do anything, or you'll hurt yourself," he warned.

The body under him wiggled, the motion barely registering on his bulk. The groaning escalated, turning into a string of creative and anatomically impossible curses. A feminine voice, definitely.

His suspicions were confirmed when she flipped her head, long black hair whipping past his face as she snapped her teeth at him. "Jack? What are you doing? Get the hell off me."

A feminine voice, yes, but more than that, a familiar feminine voice. Jack was already scrambling to his feet as he responded. "Pepper? Is that you?"

She moaned as she rolled to her back. "God, I don't know. What the hell time is it?"

"Oh-three-hundred."

"Holy ravioli, are you pointing a gun at me? You maniac!"

Stifling a groan, he tucked the weapon in his waistband with the safety clicked on, then backed to the doorway and flipped on the overhead light. "Jesus, Pepper. Why on earth are you here?"

She'd pulled herself to a seated position, elbows resting on her knees, head cradled in her hands. She swayed as she sat there, and Jack rushed across the room to brace his hands on her shoulders and steady her. "You okay?"

Her shoulders lifted then relaxed as an enormous sigh escaped her. "Nobody was supposed to be here tonight."

She steadfastly looked at the floor, and Jack's suspicions rose. "Why didn't you come to Lynn and Parker's party? And when did you get back into town? And why are you—?"

Pepper lifted her head, and his questions vanished as a jolt of anger struck him hard in the gut.

Her right eye was partially closed, shades of blue and purple tinting the area all around it. A long, partially healed scratch ran from her cheek up into her hair. Hair that was obviously dyed, because when he'd seen her last she'd had her brilliant red locks piled high

6

in a ponytail, her whole body vibrating with life and excitement.

Now she looked beaten and defeated, not at all like the energetic, enthusiastic pain in the ass he'd known while they were growing up.

"Who the hell did this to you?" Jack asked as he reached to cup her cheek gently. He traced his thumb over the cut.

"Doesn't matter." Her big green eyes tightened with pain as she adjusted position.

His earlier flash of anger returned, and he didn't even bother to restrain his frustration. "What do you mean it doesn't matter? Pepper, you've been MIA for the last two months, and you finally show up looking like someone's taken a two-by-four to you. Bullshit on it not mattering. I want to know exactly what happened. And don't think that Parker is gonna—"

"Don't." The word shot out like a bullet. "You can't tell him. Or my mom and dad."

She pulled back, and his hand fell away. From the way she was moving, the bruises on her face weren't the only ones she carried.

His blood was boiling.

She'd been like an irritating little sister, tagging along uninvited behind him and Parker, at least when they were in high school. Later, when he and Parker had signed up for the army and their ventures home had become far less frequent, her presence in his life had changed. She was no longer annoying, no longer constantly trying to get into their things.

Her wild forays into his life had brought a different sensation to his gut. Something that made him uncomfortable, something he couldn't quite put his finger on.

But in spite of the discomfort, no way in hell was she going to get away with not telling him the details. He'd take care of her whether she wanted him to or not.

He sat back on his heels and stared at her. She stared back, a storm of defiance rising in her expression.

"How do you think you're going to keep this from them?" Jack demanded. He gestured toward her bruises. "Parker's gonna take one look at you and be ready to go on a manhunt."

"I'm not going home. Not until this is gone." She fluttered her hand in front of her face. "And I can put on makeup."

She was waking up, becoming more alert with every passing moment. Jack admired how swiftly she'd gone from sound asleep to ready to do mental battle with him. And that was in spite of the fact that he'd recently crushed her under him on the couch.

The thought disturbed him. Made him feel guilty, which he shoved aside to concentrate on the current issue. "No amount of makeup is going to hide anything right, and you can't sleep here in the DreamMakers office without getting caught."

"I'm going to find a hotel tomorrow. It was too late tonight, and I was worried that if I tried to check in…"

She broke eye contact with him, and for a second Jack wondered if this was even more serious than it looked at first. "Pepper. I want to know, and I want to know now. Is there some bastard out there who needs killing? Or did you already do it?"

She jerked in surprise, turning back to face him. "Oh, no. It was nothing like that." She made a face, adjusting position as she ran a cautious hand over her ribs. "I can honestly say that it was ninety percent an accident."

That still meant ten percent someone else was to blame for her being hurt, and Jack's protective instincts kicked into overdrive. He knew better than to follow that line of thought with her, though. Pushing the issue at this moment wouldn't get him anywhere.

She'd been smart enough to realize if she had attempted to check into a hotel someone would've asked some tough questions. Now it was Jack doing the asking, and he wasn't going to allow her to say no.

But first he'd need to get her to a place where he had the upper hand. He stood, towering over her, thinking it through. The only solution he could think of that didn't involve Parker or her parents was pretty simple.

"Get your stuff. You're coming home with me."

Her jaw dropped slightly in disbelief. "Excuse me?"

He tugged the blanket from her hands and tossed it back onto the couch. "You heard me. Grab your things and let's go. Unless you want to be here when the office opens in the morning. That would be a great way to stop Parker from finding out you're back in town and that someone's been using you as a punching bag."

She shot to her feet, a frown building in her expression, but the instant she got vertical she swayed violently. Once again Jack reached out to steady her, catching hold of her arms. She cringed as he made contact, and he let go quickly, swearing as he jerked the sleeve of her T-shirt over her shoulder.

A massive blue bruise covered her arm from elbow to shoulder. "Jesus, Pepper."

"If you don't mind, I don't need to be manhandled."

9

"No, but it looks like you need a keeper. Get your things and don't argue."

She shrugged out of his grasp, stomping past him and down the hallway to where her bag sat. He followed hard on her heels, clenching his teeth to stop from saying anything more.

As she slipped on her sneakers, Jack glanced around to make sure all signs of her presence were gone. At some point, he'd tell his best friend what he'd done, but this wasn't the moment.

He ignored that little sense of impending doom that hovered over him as they left the office, resetting the security system. "You knew the access codes."

"Parker told me a long time ago, and they were still the same. Good thing you guys never went into security. You'd suck." She plopped into the passenger seat of his car, for the first time looking something other than annoyed. "Nice wheels. I didn't expect something like this from you, Jackjack."

Another shot of anger, this time not at all associated with anything to do with her. "It was my Dad's."

He stepped on the gas, cranking the music up to discourage her from saying anything else. They had too much to talk about, but at that moment he didn't want to say a single thing.

THE NIGHT wasn't proceeding like she'd expected, and the entire drive from her brother's office to Jack's apartment, Pepper appreciated the gap in conversation.

It gave her time to really consider what she was going to tell him.

The truth?

Well, at least part of it. That was the only option, because the best lies were always based on truth.

No way in hell would she admit *all* the details. Not to the man who probably figured she was still a virgin, and besides, he'd probably go and spill the beans to her brother. Which was all kinds of wrong.

Jack's sphinx imitation continued until he tossed his keys on the sideboard just inside his apartment door. "Bathroom is down the hall on the left, guest room is the next door toward the back. Sleep as long as you want. The office isn't open until noon tomorrow, so I'll be around in the morning, and we can talk then."

It wasn't the brightest idea she'd ever had, but he was so damned cocky and bossy she couldn't help but argue. "What if I don't want to talk to you in the morning?"

Jack stopped in the middle of pacing away from her, then turned back with darkness in his eyes. Man, she'd forgotten how deadly those dark chocolate eyes could look. Normally they twinkled with humor—well, when his gaze was directed at someone other than her. For some reason, she seemed to bring out his intense side.

Also known as his annoying caveman asshole side.

"Go to bed, little girl. You really don't want to push me right now."

His snide dismissal stung. "Really?"

"Really. Because if you don't want to talk, first I'm going to find out exactly how far those bruises go, even if it means I have to strip you like a toddler who's fallen into a mud puddle. And I won't give a damn how little you like it."

She paused, working for control. "You wouldn't dare."

He shrugged. "It wouldn't be the first time I had to rescue you, and this is a whole lot more serious than you taking a tumble into some dirty water wearing your good clothes."

Then he stood there, waiting for her to make a decision. Waiting for her to push him one more time. "You are the most irritating, overbearing, bullheaded, stupid bastard."

"Agreed. Now get your ass to bed before I change my mind about this entire thing and send you home."

They stared each other down again. Pepper was tempted to ruffle his feathers some more, but truth was, she was too damn exhausted for any further verbal sparring, so she decided to let Jack win.

This time.

"Fine." She tilted her head. "Can you give me something to sleep in? I don't want to soil Jack Hunter's sacred sheets with my dirty traveling clothes."

A muscle in his jaw twitched. "I'll grab you a T-shirt."

She trailed after him toward the hallway, too tired to pay much attention to her surroundings. Then again, she probably wasn't missing much. Knowing Jack, the whole apartment was furnished with beanbag chairs and decorated with framed headshots of his cocky self.

His cocky, *attractive* self. Just because the man was a major pain in the butt didn't mean she couldn't acknowledge his hotness. Six feet tall, rock-hard bod, chiseled features—Jack Hunter was hot with a capital

VIVIAN AREND & ELLE KENNEDY

everything. Growing up, she'd seen countless girls throw themselves at him, though how any of them had stomached his God's-gift-to-the-world attitude, she had no clue.

Maybe he made up for it in bed? Naah, she doubted it. If the guy *wasn't* a selfish lover, she'd eat her hat.

Jack stopped at the second door and left her in the hall as he popped in to find her a shirt. He returned a moment later and thrust out his hand. "Here. Now go to bed."

She accepted the faded gray T-shirt. "Thank you, Master. I shall retire to my quarters and see you on the morrow."

He raked a hand through his sandy-blond hair and muttered something under his breath.

"What was that?" she said sweetly.

His jaw tensed. "I was just saying your hippie parents really should've reconsidered their no-spanking stance."

Pepper smirked at him. "Wow. You wanna spank me, Jackjack? Dirty boy."

Something crossed his expression, a flicker of...holy Ryan Seacrest, was that *heat?*

It was very rare for Pepper to be caught off guard, but for a moment, she was rendered speechless. The thought that Jack Hunter—*Jack Hunter*—could feel even the teeniest smidgen of lust in her presence—her, *Pepper Wilson*—was downright mind-boggling. He'd never treated her like anything other than a pesky kid sister, and was as possessive and protective as Parker when it came to keeping her in line. Jack was a grumpy, prickly stick-in-the-mud. He was the bane of her existence, and she was the bane of his. That was how it'd always been.

She must have imagined that lustful glimmer in his eyes. Two months of traveling in a cramped car with four other people had clearly made her go insane.

"I swear to God, Pepper, if you don't go to bed in the next two seconds, I'll—"

"Take a chill pill," she cut in, sighing dramatically. "I'm going, all right?" With that, she strode off toward the last door in the hall, tossing a saccharine look over her shoulder. "Nighty-night, Jackjack."

When she was alone in the bedroom, she collapsed, her carefree bravado snuffed out like a wet candle. God, she was tired. And sore. And, frankly, still pissed off. What had started off as a fun cross-country road trip with her fellow college grads had ended with a bang. And not the good kind of bang, where people ended up sweaty and sated.

Nope, it was the kind of bang that left her looking like a reject from a Jean-Claude Van Damme street-fighting movie.

Her plan to come home like the prodigal daughter and greet her folks and Parker with hugs and kisses had been shot to hell. Jack was right—her brother would go on a murder spree once he saw her face, and her parents would never let her leave their house again. Which interfered with her *other* plan, the one that involved finding her own place and living a life where she wasn't being babied by everyone.

Sighing, Pepper changed into the shirt Jack had given her. The soft fabric swallowed her entire body and hung past her knees, making her feel like an orphan girl who'd been taken in by a gentle giant. Except...Jack, gentle? Ha. She'd pay money to see that.

Well, if she had any money. Her savings account was pitiful since she'd refused to take out any school loans. Her parents had fronted the tuition costs, but Pepper had paid her own expenses and residence fees by waitressing at a diner back in Chicago. She didn't like owing anyone anything, and she had every intention of paying her parents back the first chance she got.

But right now...sleep was the only item on her agenda. Tomorrow she'd call Kendra and arrange to pick up the belongings she'd abandoned at their campsite. And then she'd suck it up and let Jack lecture her for a while.

And after that? Time to take charge of her life, and woe to anyone who screwed around with her plans for the future. This was one girl who'd seen the light, and she had no intention of lying down and letting anyone walk over her ever again.

Chapter Two

THE AROMA of cooking bacon lured Pepper from her restless slumber. Groaning, she checked the alarm clock on the night table, saw that it was eight o'clock, and groaned a whole bunch more.

Damn that man. *Sleep as long as you want,* he'd said.

Sure, like that was even remotely possible when he was taunting her with the delicious smell of bacon. He *knew* she'd give up her firstborn if a lifetime supply of bacon was on the table.

Jerk.

She heaved herself out of bed. Stretched her arms over her head and instantly regretted it when a jolt of pain shot through her ribcage. She hadn't gotten the official word that anything was broken since she hadn't

16

seen a doctor, but her ribs were either broken or really badly bruised. Maybe a hot shower would help.

She moaned the second the thought entered her head. Washing up at Parker's office yesterday hadn't done more than knock off the surface dirt. Being immersed in steamy hot water sounded like heaven at the moment.

Hot shower. *Then* bacon.

The guest room didn't have a private bath, so she padded barefoot toward the hall bathroom. She tossed Jack's oversized T-shirt on the towel rack and a moment later was purring happily as blistering moisture slid down her aching body.

She wasn't sure how long she stood there under the spray, but it must've been a while because suddenly Jack pounded on the door.

"Get out before you drain the hot water, Candy Cane!" came his muffled voice. "I haven't taken my shower yet."

Candy Cane. It irked her that he still used the juvenile nickname. Even Parker had stopped calling her that a long time ago. Like, once she'd turned eight.

"I mean it, you brat! Shower time's over," he shouted.

Just to annoy him, Pepper counted out two full minutes before stepping from the stall. Once the rush of water stopped, she could clearly hear Jack mumbling expletives in the hall.

"Stop lurking behind the door," she called as she grabbed a towel off the rack, her borrowed T-shirt tumbling to the floor before she could catch it. "It's creepy."

His receding footsteps involved some stomping, and she grinned. Needling Jack was so damn easy. Didn't hurt that she happened to be so damn good at it.

She bent over to retrieve the T-shirt, then realized it was soaked thanks to her dripping-wet hair and the fact that she'd now as good as used it as a bathroom mat. Ah well. Who needed a shirt? She secured the towel tighter over her breasts and left the bathroom, heading for the small kitchen at the other end of the apartment.

When she walked in, she found Jack at the counter, sulking over a plate of scrambled eggs and bacon. His head lifted at her approach, and he gaped.

"What the fuck, Pepper? Put some clothes on."

"I don't have anything that's clean." She sauntered to the eat-in breakfast counter and plopped onto a stool, making sure the towel didn't ride too high up her thighs.

"What about the T-shirt I lent you?" he said suspiciously.

"It's on the bathroom floor and it got all wet. *Oooh*— can I have some of this yogurt?"

A disgruntled noise rumbled from him. "Four years of living on your own and you didn't learn to pick up after yourself?" He leaned forward on his stool and swatted her hand before she could grab the plastic yogurt cup. "Dream on. This is the last peach one in the pack. It's mine."

"But I'm the guest," she protested.

"You're not a guest." He smirked as he peeled off the foil yogurt lid. "You're a hostage."

Pepper narrowed her eyes. "What the hell does that mean?"

"It means you're not taking a step outside this apartment until you tell me what happened to you."

So. They were doing this right out of the gate, apparently. She'd hoped to have some coffee in her system before the interrogation began, but she should've known Jack's patience wouldn't last that long.

With a sigh, she reached for the second breakfast plate on the counter and pinched a strip of bacon in her fingertips, ignoring the cutlery he'd laid out for her. "Look, it's really not a big deal," she said between bites. "I fell down a hill."

Silence.

And more silence.

"It's true," she insisted when sheer disbelief flickered in his eyes.

"You fell down a hill," he echoed.

"Feel free to make fun of me for it." Her tone was gracious. "It was pretty fucking stupid on my part, so I deserve to be laughed at."

His expression was stone-cold serious. "Does it look like I'm laughing?"

She swallowed another bite, then reached for her fork to spear into some scrambled eggs. "I get it. You don't believe me. But it's the honest-to-God truth. It happened the night before last. We were all drinking—"

"Who's *we*?"

"Me and the friends I was road-tripping with."

Jack shoveled a spoonful of yogurt into his mouth, then set down the container. "What are their names?"

"Oh, come on, are you serious—?"

"Names."

An irritated breath flew out. "Kendra—she's a friend of mine. We lived in the same dorm. Dirk and Ben, also from our dorm. And Adam from my digital media class."

"I see." Jack swept a hand over his stubble-covered chin. "Just so I'm straight on everything—Dirk, Ben, and Adam are all female, right?"

Pepper snorted. "Do those names *sound* female?"

He cursed loudly. "You were on a road trip with three dudes? *Three dudes?*"

"Yep, three dudes. With penises and everything."

"Pepper."

"Jack."

He frowned. "Pepper."

"*Jack.*" Her annoyance levels snapped into high alert. "Will you wipe that disapproving look off your face? I'm a grown-up. I'm allowed to go camping with my friends, female *or* male. And you, Jackjack, are not my father, my brother, or my protector. Got it?"

His sharp gaze studied her face. "Did one of the guys rough you up?"

"No. I told you, it was my own stupidity." She paused, deciding to offer another piece of the truth. "Dirk and Adam roughed *each other* up, okay? There was this silly misunderstanding, everyone was drunk, and the guys got all up in each other's faces. I foolishly stepped in the middle to try to break them apart, and accidentally took a fist to the eye." She gestured to her shiner. "That's how I got this."

Jack's jaw went so tight she was surprised it didn't snap right off his face. "One of those bastards *hit* you?"

"By *accident*. They were both horrified afterwards, and that's what ended the fight. I was pissed at both of them for acting like such fucktards, so I went for a walk to cool off, tripped over a rock, and took a not-so-fun tumble down a hill." She offered a glum look. "It sucked."

There. She'd given him ninety-five percent of the truth. The other five percent? Well, that was none of his damn business.

Jack went quiet, his contemplative expression telling her that he was going over the details of her story in that caveman head of his.

"I believe you," he finally said.

"Hot *dog*! Gee, thank you *so* much. I can live out the rest of my life knowing Jack the Magnificent believes I'm not a liar." Rolling her eyes, she jabbed a finger at his abandoned yogurt. "I swear to God, if you don't finish that in the next three seconds, I'm taking it."

He sighed, drawing her attention to his muscular chest. The black wifebeater he wore was so tight it outlined every last ripple on his washboard stomach, and his bare arms were equally ripped, heavy forearms resting on the counter.

"Fine, it's all yours," he grumbled. "I've lost my appetite anyway."

With a broad smile, she snatched the yogurt and polished it off while Jack sat across from her scowling the whole time.

Three more bacon strips and two cups of coffee later, she hopped off the stool, adjusting the bottom of her towel with one hand as she carried her plate to the sink.

She was about to rinse it off when something buzzed. Jack's cell phone, sitting on the counter next to the sink.

"Oooh, you have a text message from—" she peered at the screen, "—*Charlene*. Here, let me read it to you in my best Charlene voice."

Jack raced to intercept her, but Pepper had his phone in her hand before he could.

"*Hey, sugar, dinner at my place tonight?*" Pepper said in her breathiest voice.

"Gimme that," Jack snapped.

She held the phone out of his reach. "Charlene sounds real nice, *sugar.* Is she your girlfriend?"

"No." His voice was terse.

"Fuck buddy, then?"

"None of your damn business," he ground out. "Now hand over the frickin' phone."

Laughing, Pepper tossed him the BlackBerry. But she'd forgotten about her current attire, and by thrusting her arm out like that, she'd caused the top of her towel to come loose.

A second later, the terrycloth dropped to the kitchen floor.

NAKED.

Very, very naked.

His best friend's little sister was naked.

In the back of his mind, it occurred to him that he might've just penned a very nice haiku, but Jack was too busy seeing Pepper naked to count all the syllables and find out.

Hollywood SFX invaded his kitchen and time slowed down, which was good because he couldn't decide where to look first. Even as his gaze caressed Pepper's astonishingly full rack, he knew he wasn't *supposed* to be looking in the first place.

Only there didn't seem to be a way to stop himself. He tried, he really did, but she had nipples. Pale pink

22

ones, like candy floss, with teeny little points rising up that would be perfect for catching between his teeth as her sweetness invaded his system.

And she had hips—his gaze jumped to take advantage before his conscience won the current fight it was waging with his libido—and she was curvy enough to trigger instantaneous fantasies about stroking his palms over the luscious surface before digging his fingers in as he moved her over him.

Between her legs, red curls were trimmed into a heart, the point at the bottom aimed like an arrow toward a clean-shaven pussy...

...and *that* was the final fucking straw.

Time whooshed back to full speed so rapidly Jack got lightheaded. Something slammed into his chest before falling to the floor with a clatter. He wasn't sure if he deliberately moved forward, or if it was the head rush that knocked him off his feet. Either way, he ended up damn near diving for the towel, grabbing it the same instant Pepper knelt, her fingers catching hold of his.

His head snapped up, and he came eye to eye with her breasts, her rapid breathing making them move mesmerizingly before him. Like a snake charmer, pulling him nearer and nearer until he was far too tempted to do something very un-big-brotherly.

Pepper jerked the fabric from him, shooting to her feet and tucking the fabric against her torso. "I'm capable of picking up my own towel," she snapped. "Your phone is behind you. *Charlene* is waiting for an answer."

He wasn't going to allow her to distract him. Jack's mouth had gone dry, but now that Pepper was mostly covered up again he was able to concentrate. And it wasn't the sexually tantalizing assault on his system that had sent all his instincts into overdrive. "Stop right there," he ordered.

"What? I'm going to get dressed. Thanks for breakfast." Pepper clutched the top of the towel with one hand, the other behind her back, probably trying to keep a bit of the material over her ass.

Her very *fine* ass—far finer than he wanted to admit, but right now?

"Let me see," he snapped, closing in on her.

She pressed the towel harder to her chest. "Didn't you get enough of an eyeful already? Jerk. You could have looked away or something."

No, he really couldn't have, but he wasn't going to argue. "If you don't let me check your bruises, I'm driving you straight to the clinic."

Pepper's gaze narrowed. "You poke any of them like you used to do when I was little…"

He didn't let her finish. Just caught hold of her arm and turned her, slipping the towel aside and this time focusing on the damage to her pale skin. Mostly managing to ignore the sensation that moved through his fingers and arm like an electric shock at the feel of her under his fingers as he checked her hip and side.

She wiggled as if wanting the entire thing over with. "See? Only bruises—shit, *ouch*."

He'd pressed his palm over her ribs where a particularly spectacular green and purple splotch had formed. "It's bigger than my damn hand. How are the ribs?"

"Don't touch—" She sucked in a quick gasp as he traced his fingers along the edge where her ribs met the dip to her stomach. Her curses cut off abruptly, and he glanced up to discover she had locked her teeth together,

24

staring straight ahead as if her life depended on not making a sound.

Damn stubborn woman. "You might have cracked a couple of them."

"Maybe."

Her obstinate attitude was beginning to piss him off. "You don't think you should get checked out?"

She laughed, an abrupt sound. It still sent his heartbeat dancing for some stupid reason.

"Tell me, Jack. The last time you and Parker did something stupid like, oh, let's say, kiteboarding without ever having tried it before. Did you go and get your booboos checked after?"

"That's different—"

"Because you're all big and strong and a dude, and I'm a delicate little female flower." Pepper turned away from him, separating his hand from where he'd forgotten it rested on her stomach.

Bullshit he'd forgotten.

And bullshit on her argument. "You have a black eye, busted ribs, and bruises from head to toe. I'm worried, okay? Suck it up, Pepper Wilson. You'll just have to put up with me giving a shit if you're hurt or not."

That stopped her short, and a faint flush hit her cheeks, this time apparently not from wanting to throw something at him. "Aww. That was sweet. But really, I'll be fine." She wrinkled her nose. "Although, can I borrow some more clothes? I'll do laundry today, but until I do, I'm down to towels."

God. "I'll find you something."

Like five minutes ago, because if he had to watch her walk around his place for much longer... He grabbed his phone off the floor. "You're staying for a few days?"

By the time he turned back she had the towel firmly in position. He wasn't sure how to feel about the disappointment in his gut.

Pepper strolled through his living room, the bottom edge of the towel nearly exposing her butt.

"If you don't mind." She glanced over at him as if she'd just remembered something vital. "Oh no."

"What?"

"Charlene. Your sugary dinner date."

"She's not my..." Jack let his denial fall away. He wasn't even sure what to call the woman. One-night stand that kept going on way too long?

Pepper wouldn't drop it. "Am I in the way? Because I can totally be out of here by this afternoon."

"No. You're staying." He said it with a lot more force than he'd intended, and her brows rose. "Charlene's just a friend. Nothing serious."

"No sleepovers then?"

She was going to kill him. Or he was going to kill her. "My sleepover situation is nothing you need to worry about, okay? Stick around for a few days, get your feet under you. If you're healing fine in a couple days I'll stop ragging on you to see a doctor."

"Deal." Her utter delight in his seeming to cave went beyond pleasure, sliding over the line into revelry in pulling one over on him. "I've got a list of things I need to look into, jobs and stuff. I'll even do the dishes and tidy up to pay for my keep."

She was still gloating when he handed her a pile of clothes he'd salvaged from his dresser and pointed her back down the hall to the guest room.

His tormenter might have vanished behind the door, but her smirk followed him. All the way back to the bathroom and into the shower where the heater had somehow managed to pull together a faint bit of power so the water wasn't icy cold.

Jack stood under the full-on spray, letting the water smack him in the face.

He was a fool. And a shit. And all kinds of bastard. Because no matter how much he tried, the only thing filling his head were images of Pepper standing naked in front of him. And not thoughts of her dyed black hair— dye covering the gorgeous color he remembered far too vividly considering she was supposed to have never been on his radar. Not thoughts of the injuries she had— although he'd love to punch the crap out of both the guys who'd been around when she got hurt. Little shits for not taking care of her better.

But even as he tried to muster up brotherly indignation, he found his hand wrapped around his cock, his body refusing to see Pepper as anything less than the sexy-as-fuck woman that she was. He gave in to temptation, soaping his body and his hands, leaning toward the showerhead and letting the sharp spikes of cooling spray stab him like punishment for what he was about to do.

Because he was totally going to do it—stroke off to images of her.

To the thought of slipping his hand higher, off her stomach where earlier his thumb had barely brushed the underside of her breasts. All the way up until he'd filled his palms with the heavy weight of those perfect tits. Her nipples would rub his palms, the tiny tips like spears into his flesh.

Or maybe he'd slip his hand downward, over the—for fuck's sake, she had a *heart* on her mound—and to where her pussy was waiting for him to touch her. He'd taste her, pushing her against the wall and swinging her leg over his shoulder so he could dive in and feast until she couldn't stand.

Jack tightened his grip, picturing Pepper giving him sass. Tossing her head as she leaned over the back of the couch, the edge of the towel riding up and exposing her ass. Her attitude drove him crazy, but it also *drove him crazy.*

He pumped his fist around his shaft, circling the head on each upstroke, smart enough to know he'd never be able to slow down. No taking time to savor or draw out the fantasy. His balls tightened, and as he thrust his hips forward, driving his cock deep into his dream woman, he came, seed hotter than the shower water exploding out to coat his fingers as he pumped another half-dozen strokes.

The door creaked open and Pepper stormed in. The real one, not the one he'd just fucked in his head.

"You got an extra toothbrush in here?"

"Pepper!" He jerked his back toward her, presenting his ass to the glass shower wall. He was still gasping for air after his brains had leaked out when he came, but he was coherent enough to know he didn't want her spotting him with his dick in his fist.

"Oops, forgot. So used to the dorm set-up. I'll wait until you're done."

She was out again, the door closing with a definite click, but Jack kept cursing. Pepper, himself, the entire fucking universe.

The water had grown icy cold, but the urge remained to start all over. Or better yet, start all over, and this time, not make it a fantasy. He'd actually take her and turn her world upside down.

Christ.

What the hell was he going to do?

Jack cut off the water and shoved aside the shower curtain, staring into the barely fogged-up mirror. Accusation stared back that he couldn't turn away from. He had no right to be fantasizing about the woman, or at least not until he'd dealt with a shit-ton of other issues first.

Now if his body would just get the message to wait, things would be fine.

Parker

SOMETHING WAS up.

Parker eyed his best friend with suspicion. For the past week he could have sworn that Jack had something on his mind. They'd been through a lot over the years, and the currently distracted man wasn't himself.

Of course, Parker wasn't the most alert these days, either—he'd admit it. Moving in with the love of his life had given him a new perspective, and having Lynn around 24/7 was distracting in all the best ways.

Still, he needed to stay alert and keep the business end of things rolling. Which meant now, with both his partners in the room, he was looking at a long list of assignments and wondering how on earth they were going to get through them on time.

And that was without Jack being a distracted fool.

"Are you sure everything's okay?" he asked again.

Jack snapped to attention, guiltily turning away from where he'd been shredding the edge of a brochure. His lips twisted into a smile, but a far more fake one than the joker usually wore. "Of course. Everything's fine."

"Because if you need some time off, you've got it coming. You and Dean both." Even though he had no idea how they'd finish all the work without everyone on board.

"Time off? What's that?" Dean quipped, tipping his chair back and rocking on two legs. "All we do around here is work, work, work."

"Ha," Jack retorted. "You seem to have skipped the parts of your agenda where you fuck around with half the population of San Francisco."

"Half plus a little," Dean said with a smile. "Female population outnumbers the male by one percent." He rolled his eyes. "Anyway, you're one to talk—at least I'm not fucking around with a client."

For a second Parker thought Dean had been talking to him—after all, he *had* hooked up with Lynn after her slimy ex had tried to hire DreamMakers for her—but then he realized Dean's gray eyes were directed at Jack.

Who just shrugged. "Charlene and I aren't sleeping together anymore. Things kinda fizzled."

Parker nodded. That made one item on the agenda easier to deal with. "Good, because now that she hired us to plan her folks' anniversary party, it'd be a conflict of interest if you were still seeing her." After Parker's own borderline blip on the unethical radar, he wanted to avoid any potential headaches when it came to their business. Charlene Halliwell's parents were paying DreamMakers a fortune to help arrange their fiftieth

31

anniversary gala celebration, and he didn't want to risk losing a major influx of cash all because Jack couldn't keep his pants zipped.

"Don't worry, it's over." Jack's tone was vague, but there was nothing disingenuous about his expression, which told Parker that his partner had indeed called it off with the busty Charlene.

Didi's voice crackled out of the intercom on his desk just then, announcing their ten o'clock appointment had arrived. With the stack of upcoming jobs overflowing on Parker's desk, they'd decided it was time to hire a few extra employees. They'd set aside the morning to interview candidates, and Parker was seriously hoping at least some of them would be a good fit.

"Who are we seeing first?" Dean asked. "Please tell me it's Colby Warden. Now that you're all googly-eyed over Lynn, I need another wingman, and Colby would be perfect for the job."

Parker grinned as he thought about the man they'd met years ago during Hell Week, but he wasn't hiring anyone just so Dean could have a partner for his escapades. "Naah, Colby is coming in later. First up is—" he glanced at the list in his hand, "—Gillian Reyes. Second lieutenant, sniper, served in the 11th Regiment, stationed at Fort Irwin."

That intel finally broke through Jack's fog. "The Blackhorse Regiment?" he said, naming the deadly unit that had been involved in multiple global conflicts. "She must be one tough mofo."

"She is," Parker confirmed, remembering the conversation he'd had with his old unit's CO, who'd told Parker they'd be "total morons" not to hire her. But no matter how highly recommended she came, he wasn't making any decisions until he met the woman for himself.

A moment later, the office door swung open and Didi appeared in the doorway. With her teased blonde hair, layers of makeup, and bright, skintight clothing, their receptionist looked like she'd walked off the set of *The Real Housewives*. Despite her flashy appearance, the woman had a heart of gold, and all their clients loved her.

"Miss Reyes, your ten o'clock," Didi introduced. She gestured to the woman beside her, then disappeared.

Leaving all three men to gape at the newcomer, who turned out to be...

Well, *hot*.

Like seriously hot. So tall she could only be described as statuesque, with shoulder-length brown-black hair, bottomless dark eyes, and curves galore. Parker was a happily in love man, but not even he could deny that Gillian was goddamn stunning.

In his armchair, Dean blinked rapidly, as if he'd just wandered into heaven and bumped into a bona-fide angel.

"Hi. I'm Gillian." The gorgeous woman extended a hand even as she raised a questioning brow at the trio of silent men.

Dean blinked again. Then shot to his feet and blurted out two awestricken words.

"You're hired."

Chapter Three

"HOLY HELL, Peps, I didn't realize it was that bad!" Kendra Lewis looked horrified as she swept her gaze over Pepper's face and bare arms. The bruises were fading at a rapid pace, but a bluish-green tinge continued to mar her skin, especially under her eye.

Pepper sucked on her milkshake straw, welcoming the cool burst of strawberry on her taste buds. Kendra and the boys had finally made it to San Francisco, and the two women were meeting at an ice cream parlor a few blocks from Jack's apartment so Kendra could drop off the suitcases Pepper had left behind. Fortunately, she'd come alone, though apparently Adam had begged to tag along.

Pepper had no desire to see that jerk. Thanks to him, not only had her dream night gone up in flames—and not the good kind—but then she'd gotten into a fight with a hill. And the hill won.

"Trust me, it was a lot worse a week ago," she told her friend. "I can finally breathe without shooting pains going through my ribs."

"Fuckin' Adam," Kendra muttered. "I had no idea he was such a nutcase. Is he still texting you like crazy?"

"Oh yeah." She swallowed her annoyance as she thought of all the messages she had to delete from her phone on a daily basis.

Please, Penny, call me back! I'm so sorry, Penny—I didn't mean to freak out like that.

The only saving grace about the situation was that Adam wouldn't be able to track her down at her folks' place when she finally headed back there tonight. Pepper had enrolled in college as Penny Wilson, after enduring years of belittlement about her real name. Her parents were both comic book artists, and they'd had the *brilliant* idea of naming their children after their favorite comics characters. Parker had lucked out. At least his namesake, Peter Parker, was totally normal. But to name a child after Pepper Potts?

Sometimes she wondered if her parents had done it on purpose, almost like they'd known she'd end up being a pain in the ass and had preemptively decided to punish her.

Although she'd told some of her classmates, like Kendra, her real name, Adam only knew her as Penny Wilson, and this past week he'd texted *Penny* so much, and so often, that Jack had started to notice. Luckily,

Pepper had found a surefire way to distract him from asking too many questions.

Turned out all she had to do to get Jack to back off? Flash a little skin.

Yup, who would've thunk it. She'd known that Jack was a horndog, but she'd figured his one-track mind hadn't applied to her. That first morning, when her towel had fallen off, she'd realized how wrong she'd been. Jack Hunter might not like her, but he liked *women*, and she happened to possess a couple things that were bound to trigger his lust—boobs, a nice ass, and no qualms about using either against him.

So if her neckline sagged a *little* too low in the middle of one of his lectures? Oops. Or if she *happened* to drop something and slowly bent over to retrieve it just as he asked who kept texting her?

Oops again.

She'd been toying with the man all week, and she had to admit, it was kind of fun. The only thing better than verbally demolishing Jack Hunter was watching his eyes glaze over every time she sauntered around in something skimpy.

And the best part was knowing he would never act on his lust. He might notice her very womanly attributes, but he still viewed her as a kid. She knew he didn't *really* want her, which was fine by her. She didn't want him, either. He was annoying. And always on her case. If they ever wound up in bed, he'd probably scold her the whole time and list all the things she was doing wrong.

So...no, thank you.

"Well, don't worry, I gave him a piece of my mind on the drive back." Kendra's voice jerked her from her thoughts. "I told him he's not allowed to go near you ever again."

The memory of Adam's enraged brown eyes floated into Pepper's head, making her uneasy. "Let's hope he listens to you."

"Are you still planning on moving back home?" Kendra asked as she brought a spoonful of chocolate-banana ice cream to her lips.

Pepper nodded. "I'm heading there later. I think I've overstayed my welcome at Jack's. If I stay even a day longer, he might murder me."

Kendra flashed a grin. "When do I get to meet him?"

"Never, if you're lucky. Trust me, Jackjack is a grumpy bastard. He wouldn't know fun if it hit him in the face, and all he ever does is order me around."

"I like 'em grumpy, and I like being ordered around. Alpha men are super sexy."

Pepper strongly disagreed, at least about the ordering-around part. She'd spent her entire life fighting for her independence, but no matter how hard she tried, her family viewed her as an immature brat who needed a good scolding. Her father still saw her as "his little girl"—hell, he'd almost gone into cardiac arrest when she'd brought her first boyfriend home.

Parker was even worse. He was insanely overprotective, acting like she wouldn't survive a day in this world without his assistance. She still remembered the time she'd gotten her learner's permit—she'd been bouncing up and down with glee, only to have her excitement shatter when Parker informed her she wasn't "responsible enough" to operate a motor vehicle by herself.

Needless to say, she was very glad he'd seemed to lose the complete control freak gene while she was gone. He'd still tried bossing her around even from the opposite side of the country, but the attempts faded quicker. Still, she wasn't looking forward to seeing her big brother today. When she'd called earlier to tell him she was back in town, he'd reverted to his old unwanted norm and demanded she come to his office. Supposedly he had something important to discuss with her, but with Parker, that meant another lecture.

She made a mental note to throw on a cardigan and put some makeup on her face to cover up her lingering bruises before she went over there. If Parker saw her like this, it definitely wouldn't go over well.

"Anyway, I hate to milkshake and run, but I should go," she told her friend. "I rented a car for the day and I only have it until nine o'clock, and I have a ton of stuff to do."

"Dinner and drinks once you get settled?" Kendra asked as they left the little table at the ice cream parlor's outdoor patio.

"Absolutely." Pepper leaned in for a quick hug, then picked up her suitcases and winked at her friend. "We'll go cruising for some hotties. Two months on the road with Adam and the others really soured me on college boys."

Kendra sighed. "Yeah, me too. Call me next week-ish and we'll figure something out."

The two women parted ways on the sidewalk, Kendra heading for the sedan right at the curb, while Pepper lugged her suitcases toward the end of the block, where she'd parked her sporty red rental.

She reached the car just in time to see a parking cop slide a ticket under her windshield wiper.

"Oh no!" She dashed over, desperation shooting through her. "I'm here, officer! Please don't give me a ticket!"

The cop turned to face her, and for a second she was taken aback by how handsome he was. Wavy black hair, tanned skin, rockin' bod. He was the most attractive parking cop she'd ever seen in her life.

"I'm sorry, Miss, but your meter ran out." His voice was deep and husky, and not at all apologetic. "Got no choice but to ticket you."

She bit her lip, torn between arguing and accepting her punishment like a grown-up. After a beat, she decided that picking a fight with a cop was *not* the way to go.

"I understand." She let out a breath. "I didn't think I'd need more than thirty minutes, but I guess I was wrong."

Surprise crept into his tone. "That's it?"

She frowned. "What?"

"You're not going to scream at me? Kick me? Accuse me of being in cahoots with the devil for having the *audacity* to write you up?"

It was too easy to offer a grin in response. "Oh my. I take it that happens to you a lot?"

"You wouldn't believe how often." He lifted the sexy Aviators off the bridge of his nose to reveal his eyes.

Very nice eyes. Dark brown, with flecks of gold around the pupils. "I want to sympathize, I really do," she said with another grin. "But you're the enemy, and I don't make friends with enemies."

He laughed. "Yeah? Well, you're the perp, and I don't make friends with perps."

"Well, then. Obviously we can never be friends." She clicked the car remote, walked around to stow her suitcases in the trunk, then headed back to retrieve the ticket.

The cop intercepted her hand, swiping the paper before she could grasp it. "You know what? I don't think you need this. I'm in a good mood today."

Her lips twitched. "Really? Why's that?"

"Because I'm about to ask a very pretty girl out to dinner, and I don't want to start things off on a bad note."

Pepper raised her eyebrows. "I see."

In a flash, Sexy Cop tore up the ticket, then held out his hand. "I'm Billy."

Billy? What grown man still went by Billy? You'd think he'd start using Bill once he was old enough to realize that Billy sounded like a character from a preschooler's cartoon show.

But the guy was hot, so she was willing to cut him some slack. Besides, when it came to names, who was *she* to talk?

"I'm Pep—Penny," she said, shaking his hand.

"It's very nice to meet you, Penny." He cocked his head. "So? What do you say? Will you have dinner with me Friday night?"

"Hmmm." She pretended to mull it over. "I guess I could do that, seeing as how you did me a solid and ripped up my ticket."

His smile widened. "Good answer."

Five minutes later, they'd exchanged numbers, set a time and place to meet, and then Pepper was driving off

40

in the direction of her brother's office. She hadn't expected to land a date today, but she honestly wasn't complaining.

Truth was, trying to rile Jack up all week had succeeded in getting *her* hot, and what better way to release all that pent-up sexual energy than with the cute cop who'd let her off with a slap on the wrist?

Even if his name *was* Billy.

Jack stared at the papers in front of him without seeing a single word. He was so tired he couldn't think straight.

That's what happened when a woman moved into his apartment and insisted on traipsing around in bits of nothing. And they weren't even deliberately attractive bits of nothing. They were just...mostly not there, and Jack was getting tired of having to take matters in hand every fucking night and still waking up with morning wood that could help a Scot win the championship at caber toss.

Thank God Pepper had finally healed enough that makeup would cover the last tinges of her facial bruises. Not only because he was happy she'd healed, but it meant this morning had been the last time he'd have to watch her ass move under her loose sleep shirt—*his* T-shirt that she'd stolen and never given back.

He never wanted her to leave, but he couldn't wait for the torment to end.

"It's a sad, sad case." Dean's smooth drawl finally broke through Jack's haze, and he glanced up to discover his friend standing only inches away. More like squatting, his head in line with Jack's. The smartass had pulled an old-fashioned detective's microscope from somewhere, and was peering through it, one eye squinting at Jack, a forlorn expression on his face.

"What the hell are you doing?" Jack demanded.

"Elementary, my good man. I'm looking for your motivation." Dean dodged out of the way as Jack swung at him. "Also, your sense of humor. Both seem to have vanished recently."

"Fuck off."

Parker's brows rose. "Well, I thought Dean was kidding, but you are being an ass. I agree with him—what's up with you?"

"Nothing." As if he was going to admit to Parker that his issue was a certain redhead who used to follow them around. Back then one of her worst sins was dropping her licked lollipops on his jeans. No way would he admit he'd been getting an entirely new type of sticky over Parker's little sis.

Thankfully, Parker stopped the inquisition. "All right, let's get to work. We've got that end-of-summer gala we need to get moving on." He gave Jack another concerned glance. "This isn't something to do with you and Charlene, is it? You're not having any trouble working with her, are you?"

Hell, discussing the anniversary party planning was a welcome distraction. "I'm not dating her anymore—I already told you that—and things are okay between us. Talking with her about the details isn't a problem."

"Good, because she asked to have you as point man. You've got a Skype meeting with her and her parents next week." Parker rifled through some papers Didi had arranged for him. "We've already secured the venue—good job on that one, Dean."

"Easy enough when you've got contacts." The other man shrugged and offered a grin. "The coordinator of bookings and I go way back."

Maybe it was because Jack wasn't getting any these days, but for once Dean's hound-dog ways weren't so amusing. "Is there anyone in all of San Francisco you haven't slept with?"

"Nope. I thought we already established that the other day," Dean said cheerfully, and his smug face had both Jack and Parker looking for something to throw at him.

Dean's phone went off, and he grabbed it, glancing at the screen. "Sorry, guys, I need to take this." He gave Jack a serious glare. "Michael Frederick, the *bookings coordinator* at the hotel, is finally able to give me the tour." He got to his feet and grabbed his jacket. "Catch me up when I get back. If I go now, I'll beat rush hour."

Parker handed over the sheaf of papers. "I'm confused. You mean you actually organized an event *without* sleeping with someone?"

"It's a rare change to my modus operandi, I admit it. Don't expect it to happen too often. I was trying it out for variety."

Jack closed his eyes for a moment while Dean and Parker bantered a bit more. Only when the room went silent did he look up to see what was going on.

"You really okay?" Dean had vanished and Parker had settled on the edge of his desk, and his expression as he stared down was full-out concern. "Maybe it's not my business, but I haven't seen you like this for a long time. Not since you went through the hell of your dad dying."

This was an entirely different type of torture than that had been. Part of his exhaustion came from being teased with what he still couldn't take, *Pepper*, and the rest from the guilt of keeping a secret from Parker.

"I'll be fine. Just a lot on my mind."

"As long as you know you can talk to me about anything," Parker offered.

If Jack had his way, they'd be putting that one to the test soon enough. "Let's get back to work. What else is on the master timeline? I'll make sure I cover as much as possible when I meet with Charlene and her parents online, since the rest of the time it will just be Charlene dealing with us."

Not even fifteen minutes later, a firm knock rattled the door. An all too familiar dark head popped through the opening, makeup concealing the fading marks around Pepper's right eye. Her bright gaze shot straight to meet his, even as she spoke to both of them. "I suppose it's not kosher but I evaded you guys' secretary. I figured you kind of already knew who I was, so I didn't need an introduction."

Did she realize she licked her lips before changing her focus to her brother?

Parker left the paperwork to open his arms wide, obvious pleasure on his face. "Finally. Good to have you home, sis."

He wrapped her in an enormous bear hug that Pepper returned wholeheartedly. She squeezed him tight, her head barely poking up high enough to be seen. Yet the minx still had the audacity to make an "oh my God, ouch" face at Jack over her brother's shoulder.

Since the whole point of her staying at his place had been to avoid causing bloodshed, Jack let the moment go.

But he added her current mischief to the list he was making. The one for which he was going to extract revenge for every single moment of suffering.

He intended to get payment in full.

"Welcome home," Jack offered, rising to his feet.

She had to have a death wish. The exasperating woman let go of Parker and danced across the room, damn near diving at Jack so he was forced to catch her. Her body slammed into his, leaving no opportunity to hide the instantaneous response she pulled from him every single time.

"So good to see you again, Jack." She clung on tight like a monkey, and he debated which of his two first responses would get him in less trouble. Peel her off immediately and make Parker wonder why he was acting like she had cooties. Or he could let her remain Velcro'd against him and let her discover that the longer she wiggled, the harder his cock got.

The thick length was no longer a subtle thing between them.

Surprisingly, it was Pepper who gave the solution to his dilemma, dropping her feet to the ground and easing her body away. And strangely, there was a hint of something in her eyes that was more than just the mischief he'd become accustomed to seeing far too often.

"I'm glad you made it home safe. Mom and Dad sent word that we're having a family barbecue next weekend to celebrate." Parker returned to his chair, his grin still wide.

Pepper twisted in his direction but stayed close by Jack's side. Close enough he caught a whiff of the scent of the body wash she'd used in the shower that morning, and he shifted to a different position and willed his cock to ease the hell off.

"I told them I thought it was a great idea. Not just as a welcome home, but because I still need to meet Lynn."

Parker's grin got even wider. "You're going to love her."

"You love her, big bro, and that's good enough for me." Pepper hauled a chair over and swung it around, throwing her leg over to straddle the seat. She rested her arms on the chair back, the long black strands of her hair hanging over one shoulder. "So, what's the news? I've got a ton of things to do, and I only have wheels for a short while."

"I can help you find a—"

She waved a hand. "Talk, talk, talk. We'll discuss that at the barbecue, or is that why you called me over?" Pepper tilted her chin down, suddenly serious. "You didn't buy me a car already, did you?"

"Of course not." Parker looked indignant. He slid some papers across the desk. "Here's what we need your help with for the next month."

Her relaxed body language vanished, and she sat up straighter, as if a pole had sprouted through her spine. "What do you mean, 'need my help with'? Is this like, 'hey, sis, good to have you home and can you help with some things around the house?' Or are we talking something a little more formal?"

She stood up and grabbed the papers, a crease deepening on her forehead as she shuffled through them.

"It's for DreamMakers." Parker didn't seem to be aware of the warning signs Pepper was giving off. Or maybe after a week of living with her, Jack had clued in

46

to spotting when her pressure points began to build up steam. "Those are your first assignments."

Pepper didn't say anything, and that was scarier than anything that had happened to this point.

Parker carried on, unaware he was adding fuel to the fire. "The most immediate priorities are the promotional materials, then we will definitely need your expertise when it comes to the end-of-summer gala. We've never organized anything of that magnitude before, so having you on board is perfect timing."

"Isn't it just?" Pepper purred, her voice going sickly sweet.

Jack backed up slightly, wondering if it would be too obvious if he crossed his arms over his groin and covered his balls.

But even as the imminent shit-storm gathered power, there was another emotion itching up his spine. The fighting between these two—that part Jack had not missed. Not one fucking bit.

In the land of the clueless, Parker was living high and mighty. Jack's best friend frowned. "Isn't it?"

"I'm busy." Pepper threw the papers back on the desk.

Parker opened and closed his mouth a few times before tossing her a glare of doom. "You don't want to start right away? I thought you wasted enough time on your road trip that by now you'd be happy to have some money coming in, or were you planning on sponging off Mom and Dad for the next—"

"Fuck you, too, brother." Pepper folded her arms over her chest and glared laser beams at him.

Utter disbelief crossed Parker's face, as he'd obviously missed exactly where he'd gone wrong.

Actually, Jack's sympathies were with Pepper on this one. "I don't think she intends to sponge off anyone." He stepped forward so she had to look at him. Time to be a peacemaker between the siblings before they really got going. "Isn't this what you thought you'd be doing when you accepted the job?"

"What job? What job offer?" Pepper snapped back. "I never got asked anything about shit-all, and you know that's usually part of getting a job. At least that's what I've always heard."

"But you knew that I was going to hire you," Parker insisted. "It makes no sense for me to need a photographer and digital programmer and then hire someone other than you. Not when you've got all the training."

"Doesn't change the fact that you're supposed to *ask* me."

Parker rolled his eyes. "Pepper. I have a job for you. Would you like to come work for me?"

She shot to her feet. "See? You do know how to be a civilized human being when you try. And the answer is no."

She headed for the door.

"Hold on." Parker stepped in front of her, and Jack waited for the violence to begin. Fortunately, his friend was smart enough to realize when he'd pushed too far. "Okay, maybe I went about it the wrong way. But we really do need you. I thought this is what you wanted."

"I don't know if it's what I want, okay? I need some time to think about it."

"But it's a job."

"Working for you. My big brother."

Parker frowned. "What does that have to do with *anything*?"

She sighed, a huge, soul-sucking sound like she'd lost the will to live. "That right there is part of the problem. That you don't have the slightest idea that working for you could be anything other than peaches and sunshine."

"What are you talking about?"

"And that's why I need to think about it. That, and I have a job interview—" she glanced at her watch, "—in thirty minutes. I'll have to get back to you."

She was out the door before Parker could say another word.

Jack stifled a groan. The old bickering like cats and dogs had set his nerves on edge, but this time an entirely new emotion colored his usual wish that they can the fighting.

"What the hell were you thinking?" The words exploded out before he could stop them.

His friend spun around. "Not you too."

"Yes, me too." Jack thought through everything he had just witnessed. Pepper might have been driving him mad, and she still had some growing up to do. And the two of them needed to chill the fuck out instead of resorting to snapping at each other. But still, Parker had made one enormous mistake. "Did you really assume she would start working for you?"

"Working for *us*, and yes, why not? That's what family does—they take care of each other."

Jack stared at Parker in shock. "That wasn't taking care of her. That was telling her what to do and expecting she'd do it. Whether or not it's what she wanted."

"Of course it's what she wants. She went to school for media and digital promotion, and that's exactly what is on this list." Parker shook the papers in the air.

Clueless in San Francisco. "Are you sure you're actually living with Lynn?"

"What the hell kind of question is that?" Parker folded his arms over his chest, a tower of absolute frustration as he squared off against Jack.

"Because I assume that you're not typically a dick to Lynn, which is why she puts up with you when you are one. But ordering someone around isn't the way to get them to do what you want."

"I *asked* her if she wanted the job."

"Only once she pushed you."

"She's my sister. She's done with school, needs a job, and we need—"

"She's a *woman*," Jack snapped. "A skilled, intelligent woman who can get a job without your help, but who *might* work for DreamMakers if her brother isn't the jackass of the century to her every time he turns around."

The longer Jack spoke, the colder Parker's expression grew. And the longer Jack spoke, the more he wondered what the hell he was doing, because he certainly hadn't planned any of this.

But one fact was crystal clear. Parker was sure to pick up on—

"She's a woman?" Parker demanded.

Jack narrowed his gaze. "Hell, Parker. I know the concept is foreign to you, but that's what little girls grow up into. And the breasts were kind of a dead giveaway."

"Why the *hell* are you looking at my sister's *breasts?*" Parker roared.

50

"Oh, chill out. I was just making a point."

Parker looked ready to say more, but Jack had had enough of the conversation, especially since he didn't really know what he wanted to discuss. Not yet.

Was he planning on dealing with his revelation of Pepper as a woman? Fuck, yes. But he knew better than to count on anything with her before he actually *talked* to her. He was smarter than the average bear, especially after the lovely example he'd just witnessed. And while it wasn't up to Parker who Pepper dated, Jack knew damn well he'd still have to offer his friend some fast reassurances regarding his usual love-them-and-leave-them habits.

But right now, he took the high road. "We have prep to do. And I noticed Didi had a list of paperwork for you to deal with."

Parker hesitated then nodded. "This conversation isn't over."

They'd been friends for too long to not be able to read each other like open books. Jack nodded, his smile returning as Parker relaxed out of high alert. "It's just a new adventure, really. We'll get through this one same as always."

Parker tossed the paperwork on his desk with a sigh. "Some days I wish for something easy, like blowing up shit or sneaking through booby-trapped ruins."

"It can't always be C-4 and lengths of trigger wire." Jack patted his friend on the shoulder and headed out to grab some fresh air to clear his brain.

Chapter Four

PEPPER STIRRED her margarita with her baby finger, pausing to lick off the sweet, salty flavor. The family welcome-home barbeque had grown beyond family to include most of the neighbors—she figured her parents were killing two birds with one stone by having all their friends over at the same time. There had to be a dozen men her dad's age tooling around the place, discussing golf and the coming fishing season. And her mom had some kind of crafty thing with bonsai plants made out of papier-mâché set up in the kitchen for the ladies to try that screamed Martha Stewart high on glue fumes.

In self defense, Pepper had made a couple of blenders full of margaritas, and then she and the girls had retreated off the deck where there were too many masculine bodies getting in the way. Instead they'd hauled their lawn chairs into a circle so they could eat appetizers, drink, and chat.

This was the second time she'd met Lynn. They'd already shared a coffee break midweek, and she couldn't be more pleased for her jackass of a brother. He'd found an amazing partner who seemed to have that gentle patience Pepper definitely lacked. It meant Lynn could probably survive a relationship without wanting to kill the man. Didn't mean she was spineless.

In fact, Lynn was just finishing up a mini-rant. Pepper had decided to take the job with DreamMakers, at least for now, but after hearing the details, Lynn agreed the hiring process hadn't been the smartest move she'd ever heard of.

"Seriously. If Parker ever tries to pull another brainless trick like that, you let me know. I have no problem helping him learn his lesson." She held her margarita glass in the air and Pepper leaned over, holding out her own glass to clink them together.

"I know he doesn't do it maliciously," Pepper grudgingly admitted.

The curvy blonde Lynn had introduced as her best friend, Suz, adjusted her miniskirt evenly over her long legs as she clicked her tongue. "Honey, guys rarely do things maliciously. Or at least the halfway decent ones don't. But being fed stupid on a cracker sucks just as badly when it's intended as when it's accidental."

She wiggled her fingers towards the guys.

Pepper, Lynn, and Kendra all turned toward the house. Parker, Jack, and the new hire, Colby, with his enormous arms and close-shaved black hair, were large and in charge beside Pepper's dad, all of them seeming intensely interested in the barbecue. Except it was obvious they were all listening as hard as possible to see what else the girls said.

"Look at them, acting all innocent and everything." Pepper made a face. "Life is a lot easier when we don't have to deal with guys."

"But they're handy at so many things," Kendra offered.

"A few," Suz agreed, "but there's a whole lot of things that a good set of batteries can deal with just as efficiently."

Lynn laid a hand on her chest and looked shocked. "Do my ears deceive me, or did Miss 'I love to love them' make a disparaging comment about the male species?"

"I don't want to stick them all in a box and mail them to the moon, but in the interest of educating our younger girlfriends here, I was pointing out we don't have to put up with bullshit to get the good parts of the deal."

Pepper had to agree with Suz. "I'm really getting tired of putting up with the bullshit."

Kendra looked concerned. "Are you still getting harassed by a certain someone?"

Both Suz and Lynn shot to full alert. "Is there something we need to help you with?" Lynn asked. "I thought you were seeing that cop. Don't tell me he's giving you trouble."

Suz made a rude noise but didn't say anything, instead sipping her margarita and trying to look innocent.

"Billy? He and I have gone out a few times, but no, he's not the issue." Pepper wasn't quite sure what to think of the guy. She might have intended on jumping his hot bod in the beginning, but something had held her back that first date. And the longer they saw each other, the less interested she was in crawling into the sack with him. "Decent kisser, though."

"Decent?" Kendra wrinkled her nose. Pepper's friend was far too cute in a polka-dot sundress. With her hair up in pigtails she looked like one of those perky models for a high-fashion magazine. "That doesn't sound very thrilling."

"We're just getting to know each other. Maybe it'll get better with time." If Pepper didn't give up completely in the next week or so.

Lynn wouldn't let it drop. "So if it's not Billy the decent kisser, which guy's been bothering you?"

It seemed like whining, but Lynn was so easy to talk to, Pepper found herself confessing. "Old problem. One of the guys Kendra and I drove cross-country with is having a hard time taking no for an answer. He's not doing anything dangerous. He's just a pain in my butt."

"Really?" Kendra said in concern. "That rat bastard. I told him to leave you alone."

"Don't make a big deal over it," Pepper insisted. There was one thing though. She lowered her voice. "I have the strangest feeling he went through my suitcases before you gave them back to me."

"Ick." Lynn made a gagging noise. "Okay, that's officially creepy."

"I'm not one hundred percent sure, but I think I'm missing a few things. You know, like a T-shirt, and...underwear." She didn't want to outright accuse Adam, but it did make her feel uneasy.

Suz patted her on the knee. "Maybe he's into cross-dressing."

Kendra nearly spat out her mouthful of drink, choking momentarily before she managed to swallow. "You're nasty."

"Why, thank you," Suz replied, lifting her drink in the air. "As long as the creeper is out of the picture, I'd much prefer to talk about how to get Pepper someone better than a *decent* kisser."

"Oh, no, I don't need anyone's help matchmaking." Pepper raised a hand in protest.

"If you want to do any matchmaking—" Kendra twisted toward them and leaned forward conspiratorially, "—I'd love a formal introduction to Jack."

A shot of something dark and not very friendly tingled over Pepper's nerves. She glanced back toward the deck and caught Jack staring at them, his gaze drifting over the ladies in the group. The instant his eyes met hers, though, he jerked away, deliberately turning his back.

Oh my God, had he been checking out Kendra?

Pepper took another sip of her margarita, but it wasn't nearly as refreshing as she remembered. Or maybe that was the bitter taste in her mouth as she admitted to herself that the thought of Jack and Kendra together made her uneasy.

And *that* was a load of crap. How low of her to not want the guy but not want anybody else to have him either.

Lynn and Suz had spent the last ten seconds since Kendra's announcement exchanging glances. "Jack might be a little too much of a flirt for you, hon," Suz said earnestly.

"I don't want to keep him," Kendra insisted. "Just to take him for a test drive. Because holy moly, Jack Hunter is one fine man." Coughing and hastily stifled laughter broke out from the deck area, and Kendra pressed her hands against her cheeks. "Crap. How loud did I say that?"

Suz stretched her neck to look around Kendra. "I think loud enough that the people on the deck next door heard as well."

"I'm going to die." Kendra twisted her chair so her back was towards the deck, her cheeks flaming red.

Pepper snuck another glance at the guys. They seemed to have settled down, but it was obvious Jack was still stealing furtive glances at them. Perhaps now that he knew for sure Kendra was interested, he was planning to do something about it?

Dammit anyway. Pepper reached for the pitcher of margaritas and topped up her glass. Maybe her homecoming barbecue wasn't the right place to get absolutely pissed, but this was no longer drinking—it was therapy.

IT WAS a damn good thing the creep who was "decently" kissing Pepper wasn't in attendance today, because Jack would have cheerfully murdered him. Barehanded, too.

And wasn't that peachy—he was suffering from a serious case of jealousy, and that wasn't an emotion he experienced often. Envy he knew all about, like how he'd always envied Parker and Pepper for their idyllic childhood, which was epitomized at the moment by this fun family BBQ. There'd been nothing fun about Jack's childhood, just years and years of futilely wishing his mom would come back so he wouldn't have to stare into his dad's vacant eyes anymore. So, yeah, he knew all about envy.

But this fiery urge to hunt down Pepper's kissing partner and beat him so badly he'd never be able to lock lips with her again? That one was harder to figure out.

His raging hard-on for the woman hadn't ceased once she'd left his apartment. It only meant that now he had a lot more privacy to jerk off to fantasies of her. And she was definitely fantasy material today. Faded denim cutoffs revealed her long, tanned legs, and her teeny yellow T-shirt hugged the full breasts he'd had the privilege of seeing in all their bare glory. She'd tied her black hair into a ponytail, green eyes sparkling as she chatted with the other women.

He wondered if her eyes sparkled when she kissed that creep she was dating.

Actually, screw that. Didn't matter what expression she wore when she had some other guy's tongue in her mouth. From this point on, the only man she'd be locking lips with was *him*.

He was going to fuck Pepper Wilson.

Yep, it was *so* gonna happen. He'd fought the attraction when she'd stayed with him. Hell, he'd fought it for years, if he was being honest. He wasn't sure when it happened, but one day he'd simply stopped viewing her as the pesky brat who trailed after him and Parker, and started to see her as a beautiful woman he wanted to get naked with.

Now he just needed to find a way to make that happen without it all blowing up in his face.

"Jack? You in there?"

He blinked when he noticed Parker's hand rapidly moving up and down in front of his face. "Sorry, I spaced," he muttered. "What?"

His best friend rolled his eyes. "I asked if you'd be able to stop off at the banquet hall later to help Dean and Gillian with the Petersen engagement party. Half the cleaning staff came down with the flu, and it was too short notice for the company to bring in reinforcements, so we have to help out. I'd go myself, but I promised my folks that Lynn and I would stick around after the barbecue to play board games."

Board games. God. The Wilsons were the only family he knew who actually did stuff like that. Cue another rush of envy, which was all sorts of fucked up, because normally he found board games excruciatingly boring.

"Sure, I can do it," he answered, all the while keeping half his attention on the ladies. They'd lowered their voices, and he could no longer hear even a snippet of conversation.

"Me too," Colby spoke up, uncrossing his massive arms. "I'm pretty good with a mop."

"Awesome. Dean'll be happy. He was so pissed he drew the short straw and had to handle the event today."

Jack snorted. "Yeah, and then Gillian volunteered to help and suddenly he was all sunshine and rainbows."

"Do you think he knows he has zero chance of getting into her pants?" Parker said with a grin.

"*Parker!*" Pamela Wilson scolded, appearing in the sliding door that opened onto the deck. "That is not proper barbecue conversation."

Parker was instantly shamefaced. "Sorry, Mom. We were just...well, you know...it's a Dean thing."

Pamela's lips twitched. "A Dean thing..." The smile broke free, her dark green eyes taking on that resigned glint Dean usually inspired in people. "Fine. I'll bite. Whose pants is that rascal trying to get into this time?"

The three men snickered. "One of our new employees," Parker explained. "But don't worry, she's too smart to fall for his charms."

"Let's hope so. Now, can one of you give this to Pepper and tell her that it's been ringing off the hook for the past hour?" Pamela held out a sleek black iPhone. "She left it in the kitchen and it's driving all of us nuts. Her ringtone sounds like a bunch of cats meowing." Pepper's mom sighed. "I swear, if I hadn't given birth to her, I'd really think that girl was adopted. I'm pretty sure she's made it her mission in life to be difficult. I have no idea where she gets it from."

"Really? You have *no* idea?" Parker flashed his mom an indulgent smile. "Because I'm pretty sure Dad accuses *you* of being difficult on a daily basis."

"Ha. If anything, your sister learned her headstrong ways from *him*," Pamela said primly. Then she reached up, ruffled her son's hair, and disappeared back into the kitchen.

Jack fought a wave of longing as he watched the exchange between mother and son. It was obvious to anyone who saw the Wilsons together that they all loved each other deeply. Even when Pepper was driving everyone nuts with her pig-headedness, or when Parker was acting like a know-it-all asshole, their parents adored them. And Pamela and Patrick were the coolest people on the planet. They were both comic book illustrators, for Chrissake—how could they *not* be cool?

"I'll give this to Pepper," Jack said, snatching the cell phone out of Parker's hand.

Before his friend could question him, he took the deck steps two at a time and headed for the circle of chairs where Pepper and the girls had stationed themselves.

"Ladies," he drawled when he reached them. "You all having a good time?"

"We're having a great time, Jackjack," Pepper responded, then held up her glass and waved it around. "Margaritas always equal a good time, don'tcha know?"

Pepper's blonde friend twisted around to smile at him. Her name was Kendall. Or was it Kendra? He couldn't lie—he hadn't paid much attention when Parker told him her name because he was too busy checking out Pepper's legs on the sly.

"What about you?" Kendra asked coyly. "Are you enjoying yourself?"

He shrugged. "Sure."

Lynn glanced over at him. "This is Kendra—I'm not sure you two were formally introduced."

"We weren't. Nice to meet you, honey," he said absently.

Kendra's smile widened. "It's *very* nice to meet you."

61

Jack didn't miss the flash of irritation in Pepper's eyes. "Is there a reason you crashed our private party?" she asked.

It took him a second to remember he was holding her phone—his gaze had snagged on her bare feet and the cute toenails that she'd painted bright red with little black dots, making them look like teeny ladybugs. "Oh, uh, yeah. Here. Your mom says it won't stop ringing." Unable to help himself, he glanced at the screen before handing the phone over. "Huh. Six missed calls from Billy. Someone's pretty eager to talk to you." He cocked a brow. "Who's Billy?"

Her lips tightened. "Just a guy I'm seeing."

Jealousy once again burned a path straight up his chest. "Yeah? Anyone I'd know?"

"Doubt it."

"He's a cop," Kendra piped up.

Jack's eyes narrowed. "A cop, eh? Some big-shot detective, I guess?"

"Traffic cop," Pepper said tersely. "Well, parking enforcement."

A snort slipped out before he could stop it, which instantly put Pepper on the defensive.

"What?" she demanded as she set her glass on the plastic table next to her chair.

"Nothing." He swallowed the rising wave of laughter. "It's just...parking cops aren't *cops*. In ocean talk, they're like the bottom-feeders of the police force."

A strangled laugh came from Suz's direction, prompting Pepper to aim her next scowl at Lynn's curvaceous best friend.

"I'm sorry," Suz blurted out, her eyes dancing with humor. "But he's right. Trust me, I'd know. Everyone in

62

my family is in law enforcement. If you want to date a real cop, I'll give you my brother Jake's number. Or my brother Chase. Or my brother Mike. Or my brother—"

"Sweet Lord, how many brothers do you have?" Kendra exclaimed.

Suz pouted glumly. "A lot."

Pepper, who didn't seem the slightest bit amused by the conversation, abruptly shot out of her chair, clutching her phone in one hand. "'Scuse me. I'm going to listen to these voice mails."

"Aw, hell, I think I offended her," Suz said, looking genuinely remorseful.

"Naah," Jack said lightly. "Pepper's not easily offended." He edged away. "But to be safe, I'll go and apologize on both our behalves."

He hurried after Pepper before any of the women could get another word in, catching up to her just as she reached the wooden gazebo on the other side of the spacious backyard.

"Oh, for fuck's sake, Jackjack. What do you want?"

He slid his hands into the pockets of his faded jeans. "Jeez, you're so damn snippy today." A smirk formed on his lips. "Let me guess, it's because your boy Billy isn't lighting your fire, huh? His kissing skills are—what did you call them? *Decent.*"

Green eyes glared daggers at him. "I *knew* you were eavesdropping on us. Congratulations. I now have another item to add to my *Why Jack is Mega-Annoying* list."

Then she spun around and climbed the steps into the gazebo, effectively dismissing him.

Jack followed her right inside.

"Seriously, would you just go away?" Pepper grumbled. "I want to check my messages."

He leaned against one of the wooden posts of the covered structure. "Then check your messages. I'll wait. I have something I wanted to run by you."

Rather than look intrigued, she scowled at him again. "Why don't you go run something by Kendra instead?"

His brows instantly furrowed. "Why would I do that?"

Pepper's jaw went tight. "We've already verified that you were listening to us talk, which means you know she thinks you're hot, and I saw you checking her out, so..." She shrugged, an action that was incongruous with her impossibly stiff shoulders. "So go make a love connection with her and give me some privacy."

Several seconds ticked by as Jack made a startling, wonderful, *delightful* realization.

Pepper was jealous.

Hell yeah. Clearly he wasn't the only one who'd been affected by her calculated teasing during her stay at his place. Unless he was misinterpreting...but finding out wouldn't be too difficult.

He took a step closer, deciding to test the waters. "You know me, Candy Cane, I'm not too interested in love connections. *Sex* connections, on the other hand..."

Jack let the comment hang, hiding a smile when he saw the unmistakable gleam of heat in her eyes.

Oh hell *yeah*.

But of course, Pepper remained stubborn to the core. "Then have sex with her," she said flippantly. "I'm sure she'd enjoy it."

"Trust me, she would." He very deliberately licked his bottom lip, and enjoyed the way her breath hitched. "Man, there are so many ways I could make Kendal—*Kendra* feel good, you don't even know."

He expected Pepper to respond with a biting remark. Or maybe change the subject altogether.

What he *didn't* expect was the note of challenge in her voice.

"Yeah? Like what, Jackjack?"

He erased a few more inches of distance, pausing when they were two feet apart. To anyone at the barbecue who glanced over at them, they looked like two people having a conversation. But Jack knew better. The electric bolts of heat moving back and forth from her body to his could have burned the gazebo to the ground.

"Hmmm. Not sure where I'd even start." He slanted his head. "Do you think she'd like it if I went down on her?"

Pepper's soft gasp echoed between them. "W-what?"

He played dumb. "Going down on her...you know...licking her pussy. Eating her out."

The flush that bloomed on Pepper's cheeks was so sexy his cock thickened behind his zipper. Holy fuck. Would her skin blush as deliciously pink when he ran his tongue over every tantalizing inch of it?

"I know what you meant," she ground out. "There's no need to be so crude."

"Crude?" A dark laugh escaped. "You think *that's* crude? You have no idea what a filthy mouth I have, do you, Pepper? No, of course you wouldn't." He met her eyes, trying hard not to laugh again when he saw passion, anger, and jealousy warring in her expression.

65

"What about dirty talk? I'd hate to scare anyone off by coming on too strong."

Pepper's jaw opened and closed, closed and opened. She seemed to be at a loss for words, which was goddamn unheard of.

"Come on, help a guy out," Jack said mockingly. "I don't like going into situations blind. It's the soldier in me, you know?"

She finally voiced a reply. "Yes, I think dirty talk is fine."

"You sure?"

Her head jerked in a nod.

"So there's no issue when I tell her how sweet her pussy tastes?"

Another abrupt nod, accompanied by another intake of breath.

"What about if I say I want to shove my tongue in her cunt and fuck it until she screams?"

A tortured sound left Pepper's lips and drove a spike of desire right through his cock. Christ, she looked as if she were in the middle of a very naughty dream. Cheeks flushed, lips parted, her breathing erratic.

Satisfaction swiftly surged through him. He hadn't imagined it, then. She was feeling the same lust he was. The same lust he'd denied for years.

Now that it had been unleashed, he knew there was no going back.

"Yes, Jack," she damn near moaned. "She'll probably love it."

"Good." He licked his lips again. "That's all I wanted to know."

The sudden chime of a phone cut through the haze of sexual excitement suspended in the air. It was his cell, and he only slipped the phone out of his pocket in case it was an SOS about the Petersen job. But the incoming text message hadn't come from Dean, and when Pepper murmured "Who is it?", Jack replied without thinking.

"Just Charlene. She wants—"

He didn't get to finish that sentence, because Pepper set free a string of curses that made him gape.

"You are *unbelievable*," she blurted out. "Oh my God, I don't believe you! You're standing around talking about all the dirty things you want to do to m—my best friend, but you're still seeing your bimbo on the side? Do you honestly think that...*Kendra*...would be cool with you screwing around with another woman at the same time you're seeing her? Because she *won't*. And you're a total jackass for thinking it's okay to do that."

With that, Pepper squared her shoulders, shot him a death glare, and stalked from the gazebo.

Goddamn it.

Jack stared at her retreating back, feeling like breaking his phone into a million pieces. If Pepper had let him finish, she'd know that Charlene had been texting about her parents' engagement party and nothing more. The woman had easily accepted it when he'd told her they wouldn't be seeing each other anymore, a fact he could have made clear to Pepper if she hadn't stormed off as per usual.

Wonderful. All the groundwork he'd just laid had been crushed into dust.

Back to fuckin' square one.

Dean

"WE HAVE a client in the boardroom in five." Gillian stood outside Dean's office, feet braced apart, arms folded over her chest. Despite the professional stance, she somehow still managed to exude a dangerous sexual vibe that turned him on. Her gaze snapped from side to side, taking in everything, including the pile of crap on his desk—he had no idea what most of it even was anymore.

Dean liked the woman. *Really* liked the woman, especially when he'd hit on her before their first assignment together, and instead of caving instantly or giving him the *sexual harassment* glare, she'd simply informed him he couldn't handle a woman like her, and proceeded to move her things into the lockers they'd set up for the new recruits in the staff area.

He hauled himself out of his La-Z-Boy, tossing aside the resort magazine he'd been poking through for ideas. "You're eager."

She shrugged. "I'm on the payroll. I may as well work."

"God, don't let Parker hear you say that. He's going to expect all of us to follow suit if you set the example."

Her lips twitched. "Bullshit, sir. I've only been here for a couple of weeks, but I'm already aware *you* work very hard at not working."

"Hilarious." Her smartass comment only made him smile harder. It was nice to have another person around who he didn't have to walk on eggshells with. He gestured to the shoulder harness peeking from under her jacket. "You want to lose the pistol while we're in the building? Or at least while we're grilling clientele? My desk has a lock, and I'll get you a key."

Gillian stiffened. "You don't think I should be armed while on the job?"

"Of course not." Dean made a rude noise. "I'm not talking about cutting off your hands, but there's a metal detector at the front door, and we screen all clients regarding their firepower—we have a no-Uzis-until-the-third-date rule—so, while you're in the building, stow them."

She paused a beat before nodding and stepping forward into the room. "Yes, sir."

"Just Dean is fine," he reminded her again, looking around for the best spot to offer her. He pulled open the top drawer on the left side of his desk. Fished out the condom packages lying scattered inside and dropped all but two into another drawer. He tucked those into his pocket, glancing back to see she had one brow raised in a perfect Spock imitation.

If he ever felt guilt, this would be a perfect time. Fortunately, he and guilt weren't on speaking terms. "And now you know where the emergency stash is kept. Feel free to help yourself."

"Thanks." Gillian moved closer, crowding him until he had to step back or get pushed over. "You might need to get me another drawer, though. Don't know if this skinny thing will do the job."

Dean snorted. She'd kept her gaze leveled squarely at his crotch while she spoke. Yeah, he liked her a lot. Comrade in arms and all that.

Then she took out her pistols, and he got a hard-on— one that was way bigger than *skinny* anything.

The 9 mm in the shoulder harness he'd known about. She unloaded and slipped the cartridge into the top section of his desk, separating the ammo and body. But then she pulled another pistol from a back harness. Then one from her ankle. And when she revealed two switchblades and a final fixed knife in a sheath on her thigh, he fell in love.

"Sweet Jesus. Are you always this heavily armed?" He admired the arsenal as she expertly disarmed the lot and stored them.

Her dark eyes twinkled mischievously. "You've heard of my former unit, right? When you play with the big boys, you master the big toys."

The remark was accompanied with another pithy glance at his crotch, which brought a burst of laughter. "Marry me?" he asked.

"Sorry, you're not my type," Gillian said flippantly.

"What is your type? Because I need to be out of range the day you two fight."

"Still looking for Mr. Right, but I'll keep you informed." She tilted her head toward the door. "Shall we?"

Dean locked the desk and passed her the key, opening the boardroom door a moment later and letting her enter ahead of him. It wasn't just old-fashioned politeness anymore—he'd found it was always good to mind his manners around women who were deadly with long-range projectile weapons.

And less than twenty minutes later he knew she was smart as well.

"You haven't known your date for long," she reassured the client sitting across from them who'd made a dismal job of filling out the standard DreamMakers "everything about your partner" information form. "It's to be expected you don't know a lot about the girl yet."

"But I want to know more about her," Billy Taylor insisted. "That's what I thought you helped with."

Dean jumped in to back up Gillian. "Maybe instead of hiring us you should simply date her a little longer. You might be able to figure it out on your own."

Billy shook his head. "I'd like to fast-track the relationship, and I'm willing to pay. Are you saying you don't want my money?"

Frankly, no. Dean wasn't that desperate, and DreamMakers had grown successful enough working the big gigs that they didn't need to take on all the nickel-and-dime jobs. Especially the ones that had that sensation of edging into sleazy.

Before he could find a way to gracefully bow out, Gillian beat him to the punch, holding out the set of papers they'd been going over. "As long as you understand that even with us helping set up the date, there're no guarantees that this will fast-track *anything*, you can take these up front. Didi will help you sign them and take your deposit."

Billy shot to his feet. "Awesome. That's what I'm talking about."

He all but glared at Dean then hoofed it from the room.

Dean leaned back his chair and gave Gillian a sharp look. "You didn't seem too concerned there. Jumping in without my go-ahead."

Gillian returned his gaze evenly. "He's a creep under that glossy surface. Not a dangerous one, but the type who would blame us if things don't go well. Any woman can see it after a few times, which is probably why he's not getting anywhere with—" she glanced at the forms, "—Penny. So, we set up the date in a public place to ensure she's got room to run, and he can't blame us for either turning down coordination or ruining things."

Very smart woman. "You sure you won't marry me?"

She flashed a cocky smile. "You couldn't handle me...*Dean.*"

Dean figured she just might be right.

Chapter Five

IT WAS Friday night and Jack was at the office. Jeez. He remembered a time when Friday nights meant hitting the bars with Parker, getting loaded, and going home with a hot chick who wouldn't care if he didn't remember her name the next morning. Now here he was, finishing *paperwork* before he went home alone and probably jerked it to thoughts of Pepper.

Pepper, who'd been giving him the cold shoulder all week long. He'd bumped into her at the DreamMakers office a couple of times when she'd popped in to discuss the project they'd hired her for. The first time, Parker was in the room, so Jack hadn't been able to talk to her alone. The second time only increased the tension between them, because Charlene had stopped by to go over the details for the digital presentation Pepper was creating which would be simultaneously displayed on multiple screens in the hotel ballroom where the party was being held.

Pepper had taken one look at the big-breasted redhead and glared at Jack so hard he was surprised her face hadn't frozen in that murderous mask.

But enough was enough. He needed to clear the air with her, make sure she knew he hadn't been dicking her around in the gazebo last weekend. He didn't want Kendra or Charlene or any other woman—he wanted *her.* And it was time she knew it.

Setting aside the questionnaire he'd been reading, Jack grabbed his phone and dialed Pepper's number. She took so long to answer that he was about to hang up, but then her breathless—and heavily annoyed voice—slid into his ear.

"What do you want, Jackjack? I'm literally walking out the door."

"Hot date?" he couldn't help but crack.

"Actually, yes."

Just like that, his heart plummeted to the pit of his stomach, joining the knot of jealousy rapidly twisting his insides. "I won't keep you, then," he said coolly.

"For Pete's sake, I already picked up the phone. You might as well tell me what you want."

Her aggravated tone sparked his own irritation. "Don't worry about it. It was a work thing. We can deal with it on Monday."

"Fine. Great. Later, Jack."

She'd hung up on him.

She'd *hung up* on *him*. Because she was on her way out to spend the evening with another man.

Jack shot off the couch, anger and frustration warring inside him. Screw it. Maybe she had the right idea. Maybe he needed to go out with someone else and forget about this stupid attraction to Pepper. All they ever did was argue, anyway, and he hated arguing. Even if they did wind up in bed, the insufferable woman would probably just yell at him the entire time.

Setting his jaw, he gathered up the papers strewn all over the couch and marched out of the office toward the file room at the end of the hall. He wasn't going to spend his night reading about other people's love lives. Nope, it was time to jump-start his own.

"You're still here?"

He jerked at the sound of Dean's voice, turning to find his partner coming up behind him. Dean had a frazzled look in his gray eyes, which were focused on the cell phone in his hand.

"Just taking off now," Jack answered. "I didn't realize you were here, too."

"Yeah, I was cleaning up the mountain of shit on my desk." Dean sighed. "Gillian keeps ragging me about how messy I am, and don't you ever fucking repeat this—but she's right. My phone got buried under the pile and it took me ten minutes to find it." A curse slipped out when the phone beeped. "God. I should've left it buried. This creep is driving me crazy. You won't believe the texts he's been sending."

Jack cocked a brow. "You got yourself a stalker, bro? And it's a *he?*"

Dean made a disparaging noise. "It's a client. One we will never, ever work with again, I might add. He's turned out to be a slimy, demanding loser who needs to be removed from the dating pool because no woman should ever have to touch him. Check this out—" Dean recited from his phone. "'This date better get me laid, dude. Tired of yanking it every night.'"

Jack blanched. "Gross."

"I know, right? And listen to this one—'Glad you set us up at a place with a fancy dress code. Hope whatever she's wearing is tight and low-cut.'"

"Grosser."

"I feel like I arranged a date for one of those fuckers on *To Catch A Predator*. But this last message— 'I'll text you tomorrow with all the dirty deets. Definitely gonna get some tonight.'" Dean gagged. "Um, how about you *don't* text me tomorrow, asshole? I'd rather wax off all my body hair than hear about this creep's sex life."

Jack shook his head in amazement, unable to believe guys that sleazy actually existed. He and the boys were known to joke around about sex, even have serious convos about it every now and then, but to brag about bagging a chick to a total stranger? That was just wrong.

"Who is this guy?" he asked Dean. "Is he one of the clients you and I interviewed last week?"

His partner shook his head. "Gillian and I met with him. Name's Billy something-or-other. Billy Taylor. Yeah, Taylor."

Jack froze. "Billy?"

"Yup." Dean held up the stack of papers in his free hand. "His file is in here somewhere."

An uneasy feeling trickled down Jack's spine as he grabbed the files from Dean's outstretched hand. He was probably being paranoid. There were tons of Billys and Bills and Williams in the world, thousands in San

76

Francisco alone. No way was this the same Billy who Pepper had been talking about at the barbecue.

With an impressive feat of speed, Jack shuffled through the files. Names, dates, and data flashed in front of his eyes until he finally found what he was looking for.

There. Billy Taylor.

Place of employment?

SFPD.

"Shit," Jack mumbled, before his gaze snagged on something even more disturbing. The name of Billy Taylor's date—Penny Wilson.

Jack stared at those eleven letters for what felt like an eternity.

And then he exploded.

"What the *fuck* were you thinking?"

The tornado of fury inside him homed in on Dean, who blinked in confusion. "What?"

"You set up a date for Parker's *sister?*" Jack shouted. "With *this* asshole? Jesus Christ, Dean! Parker's going to kill you for letting this creep get anywhere near Pepper—"

"What the hell are you talking about?" Dean cut in, genuinely flabbergasted. He leaned in and tapped the top of the page. "Her name is Penny. P-E-N-N-Y. *Penny.*"

"That's Pepper's goddamn alias! I can't believe—"

"Why the fuckity-fuck does Parker's sister have an alias?!"

"—you didn't vet his date before you took the job!"

"It wasn't necessary!" Dean yelled back. "Because he obviously doesn't want to get to know her! He just wanted us to set up a romantic date so he could *bang* her—"

"Gonna be hard for him to do that after I *murder* him!"

"Who has an *alias*, for fuck's sake? How was I supposed to know it was Pepper?"

The two of them abruptly stopped shouting, breathing hard as they stared each other down. Dean still looked confused, so much so that Jack's anger dissolved. He couldn't blame his friend for not knowing about Pepper's ridiculous habit of using another name when she met new people. Jack had grown up with the Wilsons, but Dean had only joined the fold a few years ago. Pepper had gone off to school by then, which meant that Dean had never even met her.

"Shit. I'm sorry for flipping out on you," Jack said, guilt and disgust at having lost his temper warring with fury that *Billy* was out with Pepper. "You couldn't have known."

Dean shook his head in bewilderment. "I had no clue he was trying to get with Parker's sister. I mean—she's a redhead, isn't she? The file said Penny had black hair, and…oh, *fuck*. You're right. Parker is gonna kill me."

Another wave of blind rage obstructed Jack's vision, except this time it had nothing to do with Dean's inadvertent screw-up and everything to do with Pepper's sleazy date.

Definitely gonna get some tonight.

Jack's hands curled into fists, crumpling the files he was still holding.

That slimebag fake-cop loser actually thought he stood a chance of getting Pepper into bed?

Not if Jack had anything to do with it.

PEPPER'S TEMPER was still raging by the time she crawled out of her cab at the restaurant, carefully adjusting the skirt of her little black dress over her knees as she exited. She did up another button on her jacket, breathing out slowly in an attempt to blow out the rest of her frustrations. Her smile had to look forced, but Billy didn't seem to mind, his admiring gaze taking in every inch as she approached the door of the restaurant.

Unfortunately, his admiration lingered a little too long on her chest, and that after she'd deliberately made sure to wear something that covered most of her assets.

Talk about awkward situations. Pepper had been within thirty seconds of calling the big evening off. Then *Jack* had to go and screw things up.

She didn't really want to be here tonight. She'd had her phone in her hand to call and cancel, when *he* called instead. At that point there was no way she could back down, and now she felt like a creeper for being at one of the most expensive places in town when she totally planned on telling Billy she never wanted to see him again.

Damn Jack Hunter. Damn him to hell.

"You're gorgeous." Billy managed to pull his eyes above her neck level briefly, flashing his pearly white smile that now made her think of cannibals preparing for a feast.

It wasn't his fault that she'd gotten cold feet. Or shoes of ice. He hadn't done anything specific to make her leery, but after the debacle at the end of her road trip, maybe her spidey senses were tingling. A little too hard, and not in the way of good tingles.

Still, time to make the best of it. "You look pretty good yourself."

And he did. The man cleaned up nice, in a sharply cut suit she wondered how he could afford. Even that was a thought she had to thank Jack for putting in her brain, along with Suz, if she were honest, because cops were notoriously underpaid. Pepper would hate to know what a parking jockey pulled an hour.

"If you'll follow me to your table, please."

Small talk was cut off as she wove between small tables in pursuit of the maître d'. Billy snapped to attention and pulled out her chair, his hands lingering a little too long on her shoulders before he made his way to his own seat.

A flurry of attention hit their table as water was poured and silverware rearranged, their napkins laid in their laps. By the time the waiter returned with menus in his hand, Pepper was ready for something to hold onto to stop herself from fidgeting.

Only Billy beat her to the punch, waving the menus off as he caught her hand in midair and laid it on the table under his. "We won't need those. I've already decided what we're going to have."

Oh really? echoed very loudly in her head, but Pepper managed to cling to a smile. She wasn't sure what kind of a smile though, because her teeth were locked together and the muscles in her neck had all turned to iron.

"I'd like a bottle of the Asti Spumante, and we'll have bacon-wrapped scallops for an appetizer. Followed by the chef's special."

Their waiter hesitated. "One order or two?"

"Two, of course," Billy snapped before turning his attention back on Pepper.

At this point Pepper hoped the special was steak and lobster that had been hand raised by royalty in the Caribbean Islands then paddled all the way to San Francisco in long boats. She didn't give a damn how much it cost, because Billy had stepped over a line that he never should have approached.

She'd worked restaurants while going to school. It was hard, often thankless work, and the jackasses had always made themselves known. She glanced around the room, seriously considering excusing herself to the washroom then outright leaving.

Billy still had her fingers locked in his grasp. "You look amazing. And are you wearing contacts? I don't remember your eyes being that vivid emerald green before. It's so unusual with your black hair."

Pepper grimaced before she caught herself. She did have colored contacts. Pale green ones she used to *hide* her real eye color. Jack had gotten her so riled up she'd forgotten to pop them in. "Good catch. They are different tonight."

"I look forward to staring into them," he said, stroking his thumb over her hand. "All night long."

The noise she made must have been close enough to a sneeze he let her go, and she scrambled in her purse for a tissue. Pretending to have to blow her nose was better than gagging.

This was ridiculous. While he hadn't been nearly this skeezy on their previous dates, tonight his true colors were flying too high to ignore. She was ashamed of herself for having let things go on as long as she had. It was one thing to tell him that she didn't want to see him anymore, but now she was getting spiteful, and she'd always detested that in people.

Except when it came to tormenting Jack. There it was all systems go, because *some* things were sacred.

As for her current dilemma, maybe if she said something quickly their order could be canceled. Or she could offer to pay for half the damages and just take a taxi home.

"Billy..."

He turned back with a jerk and a guilty expression. Confused, she glanced to the side where he'd been looking. A beautiful woman wearing a long gown had bent over to get something from her purse. The woman *and* her gown were both fantastic, the bodice clinging to breasts that had to be held in place with two-sided tape. But even while Pepper went through a mental scroll of which A-list model could be seated next to them, it registered that Billy had been ogling the woman's boobs.

His phone buzzed, and though he looked apologetic he pulled it out and checked the screen. "Never know when work will call," he said importantly.

"Of course." Although she didn't think parking attendants were on the emergency response list.

He tapped something in response, his confusion clear.

"Something wrong?" Pepper asked.

"Nothing to worry—" The phone went off again, and this time his eyes widened and his face grew completely white. "Excuse me."

Before she could ask anything else, he got up from the table and left, headed for the washrooms.

Pepper collapsed back in her chair, the inelegant pose not doing anything for her figure, but she was done pretending. It was the perfect moment to escape. She reached for her wallet and pulled out a number of twenties, eyeing them sadly.

She was about to dash a quick note to go with the money when someone sat opposite her. She killed the curse before it could escape her lips and worked up the courage to explain in person that it was time for her to go.

Only it wasn't Billy sitting across from her.

"Jack?"

"Pepper," he responded, his gaze fixed on hers as if he didn't give a damn who else was in the restaurant, or that he was sitting in some other man's chair.

"Jack." Firmly this time, because she did not need his bullshit right now.

"Pepper." The bastard signaled to the waiter who rushed over as if his ass were on fire. "Cancel whatever was ordered for this table. Something has come up, and I'm afraid they won't be able to stay."

Her jaw hit the ground, and she suddenly understood the whole concept of *sputtering mad*. Even as Jack passed over a wad of bills to the suddenly willing waiter, Pepper prepared for battle.

Gentle piano music playing in the background. The low murmur of polite dinner conversation and utensils clinking against fine bone china. The ambience was one of peaceful luxury, but she was ready to salt the earth and burn it all down.

She leaned forward. "I hope you're wearing a cup."

Jack's expression didn't change. He just kept smiling. "You look more as if you hope I'm not wearing one."

"Well, since I'm never *ever* finding out what comes between you and your Levi's, why don't you get your bossy ass out of here before my date gets back?"

"He's not coming back."

"He's not—" Oh God. What had Jack done?

She shot to her feet, gave him one last dirty look, and raced for the washrooms.

She wasn't sure what she would find. If Billy's sudden absence involved decapitation or blood, she wasn't dressed to hide the evidence. Though considering *Jack* was on her tail, two steps behind her as she stomped from the table, maybe she'd be the one to pull a citizen's arrest and get him locked up for a night or two. Damned bastard.

There were no dead bodies in the hallway, which she figured was a good sign. The men's room door was closed, and she hesitated for all of two seconds before pushing it open and walking in.

No dead bodies there either.

She whirled to face Jack. "What the hell did you do to him?"

Masculine cursing broke out at her back from the man at the urinal.

"Why don't we discuss this outside?" Jack suggested. "Give the poor man some privacy, for God's sake."

Her cheeks were flaming hot, but a little bit of seclusion for when she skived him would be a good thing. She darted down the hall, slipping past the front desk even while the waiter gave an enthusiastic farewell to Jack.

"How much money did you give him?" Pepper demanded over her shoulder as she hurried into the parking lot.

He caught her by the arm and tugged her to the side into a small garden area with fountains. "More than Billy would've given him, I can almost guarantee."

The death grip on her arm meant it was easier to follow him instead of protesting again in front of the group of elegantly dressed women making their way to the front entrance.

They were tucked all the way into a back corner of the garden before Jack finally stopped. He pointed at the ornate granite bench. "Sit."

"You sit. Or play dead—that would be even better."

Jack shrugged. "Have it your way."

He planted his butt on the bench, all without letting go of her. She had a position of authority over him, staring down with her arms firmly crossed. Or at least it seemed authoritative until she realized his legs were wide open and she was standing between them, and the position of her arms lifted her breasts in line to his direct gaze.

Fine. If he wanted to stare at her tits they could have this conversation while the girls were in the way.

"What did you do to Billy?" she demanded.

"Read this." Jack held out his cell phone.

She grabbed it from his hand and checked the screenshot. "What is this? Some of your bathroom humor?"

"Messages forwarded from Dean's phone."

"Ha! Why am I not surprised?" She thrust the phone back at him.

He caught her by the hips and held her immobile, the position too damn intimate, especially when the images he'd raised the other day in the gazebo flashed back.

If she stepped on the bench, feet on either side of him, he'd be able to do all those things he'd taunted her about—and she wasn't stupid. He *hadn't* been talking about Kendra at all. She was the one he wanted to go down on, and when he moistened his lips, all she could think about was his tongue slipping into intimate places.

A whole lot quieter now, Jack locked his eyes with hers and refused to let her look away. ""Read the damn messages. All of them."

She had no choice but to obey. The rising sense of *ick* rolled to outright nausea as the text messages got dirtier, and when the fourth one mentioned *Penny*, she froze.

Oh my God. "That fucker."

"Keep reading," Jack insisted, but his grip on her hips had loosened. No longer trapping her in place, his fingers rubbing lightly as if he couldn't resist touching her.

The dirty messages stopped, switching to messages from Jack to Billy.

Touch her, and you die.

Who is this? How did you get my number?

Jack Hunter. I'm Penny's boyfriend, and I'll be there in five minutes. Run.

Good grief. Pepper's mood flipped between exasperation and relief. "I didn't ask you to rescue me," she pointed out.

"The guy was bragging to Dean about fucking you. And I didn't rescue you, I just kind of hurried along what would've happened before too long anyway. Because he's not the guy for you."

He had that right. Her frustration and bluster faded. "Okay, I'll say it. Your methods are unorthodox, but this time, thank you." And again she became ultra aware of his hands holding her, and that wasn't good, because he and she were just…

Were just…

Oh God, she had to get out of there. She shifted her weight from side to side. "I'll see you at the office."

"What's your rush?" The tension in his body changed, as if he was aware that his earlier actions were no longer the most important item on her agenda. Now the relentless tingles spreading from where his open fingers had slipped back to cradle her butt had her in danger of setting off a power outage over the entire city quadrant.

He kept touching her, but his gaze stayed locked on hers. She couldn't even get mad at him for being a hound dog and staring at her body. "Stop looking at me like that," she ordered.

Or, she *meant* to order—the words slipped out more like she was pleading with him to never stop.

"Looking at you like what?" he asked.

"Like you're hungry."

Full pause. Utter silence. Then…

"You're right, I should stop. Because I'm not hungry." He shifted his hips to the front of the bench, pulling her toward him until the fronts of their bodies made contact. "I'm starving," he confessed.

It was the perfect moment for a smartass response, but her vocal cords seemed to be frozen. Every heartbeat intense enough to shake her body.

It took forever to get a single word out. "Jack."

His lips twitched. "Pepper."

She was desperate to get some moisture back to her mouth, and his gaze finally slipped to her lips as she licked them, the heat in his dark brown eyes flashing like the first moment of flint against steel. "*Jack...*"

"Pepper. Are you going to let me take a bite?" His words were a husky growl that made goose bumps rise.

He was making her decide? Right now she had the brain capacity of a gnat. Good thing it seemed to be a rhetorical question because he rose to his feet, magically taking her with him. She clung to him, her legs instinctively closing around his body as her skirt rode up. He adjusted her, supporting her weight with one arm.

The other arm moved higher until his strong fingers wrapped around the back of her neck. Her breasts were crushed against his powerful chest, their lips only inches apart.

Her fingernails dug into his shoulders, although it was unlikely she could move him in any direction. Those beautiful eyes burned her with their intensity.

She waited. Wanted.

But like usual, Jack seemed determined to push her every last button. So close, and yet he refused to move, waiting until she couldn't stand it anymore.

"Are you going to—"

He swallowed the words, his mouth moving over hers decisively. No room for escape, no retreat. Pepper responded enthusiastically, letting him take control because, oh *God*, the man could kiss. His lips were firm for just the right amount of time before demanding that she open to him, their tongues connecting briefly before she was no longer analyzing every move, but clutching him even harder to stop from floating away.

His hand at the nape of her neck slid into her hair, knocking out the couple of pins she'd used to hold the loose knot in place. Her hair fell over his hand and her shoulders, suddenly cool against her heated skin.

Jack turned on the spot, cradling her closer, and for one instant she had thoughts of him laying her on the cold granite bench and stripping her. Straight-out fucking her right there in the shadows not fifty feet from one of the premier restaurants in the city.

The idea didn't make her nearly as uncomfortable as it should have.

But instead of readying her for a wild ride, he sat, rearranging her so her legs were together as her butt rested in his lap. The very solid evidence of his arousal was rock hard against her hip.

The entire time he kept kissing her. As if to prove he hadn't been exaggerating about being starving.

Pepper twisted until she could run her hands over his shoulders to his back, wishing the material between them was gone. The evening might have started as a dud, but this was better than anything she could ever have hoped for.

When they finally separated, neither of them was breathing very steadily. Jack slid his hand forward to cup her cheek, gently running his thumb over her swollen bottom lip. "I'd apologize, but I didn't do a damn thing that I haven't wanted to forever."

"If you apologized I'd have to hurt you," Pepper whispered. What came next? That was pretty obvious as far as she was concerned. "Take me home."

Only the bastard did exactly what she asked.

Ten minutes later, she stared up at her parents' house in shocked dismay before turning back to him. "What kind of joke is this?"

He had the wheel clenched hard enough to turn his knuckles white. "You didn't think I was going to take you to my place, did you?"

"Ummm, yes."

He took an enormous breath as if gathering his strength. "If I took you home, about five seconds after we got through the door you'd be naked. And about five seconds after that I'd have my cock in you."

A shiver shook her from top to bottom as images flooded her mind and heat pooled between her legs. "Good by me."

He shook his head. "That's not going to happen."

"You're not serious." He couldn't be serious. She peered at him closer, dismayed to discover he looked damn serious. "I have no problems going home with you and getting jiggy. And you just said you want that, too."

He groaned in frustration. "You have no idea."

"Then I don't get it," she complained. "Why?"

"I need to talk to—"

Pepper snapped up a hand. "If you dare say the words 'I need to talk to Parker before I fuck you' I will rip your spleen out."

"Trust me, I'm not doing it out of any misguided sense that he's in any way in charge of you or your sex life."

Holy mother of pearl. He really was going to talk to Parker. "I can't believe you're going to do this. And I can't believe you're making us wait. And I can't believe I just had my tongue down your throat, and you're not hauling me home with you so you can fuck me blind."

The utter pain in Jack's expression echoed her own. "The man saved my life more times than I can count. He's walked beside me through hell, but none of that is why I'm going to talk to him before you and I get official."

If she were a flouncer she would've flounced by now. "Please explain the logic before I go insane."

"Because he's a damn good shot, and he knows how many women I've been with before, and I don't want him gunning for me because he thinks I'm just dicking around with you."

She wasn't sure which part of that comment to respond to first. "How many women?"

His serious expression broke, those lips curving into the familiar grin that had exasperated her and taunted her for so many years. "I've forgotten. There's only one woman I want."

Good answer. "And you're not just dicking around?"

He shook his head.

Sudden warmth rushed through her at his absolute attention. Fine. It was obvious she wasn't going to be able to change his mind. "Then here's my counteroffer. You talk to Parker, and I get to be in charge."

A snort of disbelief escaped him. "Right. Like that's ever going to happen. Sorry, Candy Cane, but I'm not the type to jump if you start issuing orders."

Stubborn ass. He wasn't lying, but then, she already knew ways to make him burn. "You expect to call all the shots? Like that's ever going to happen," she echoed his words. "Or, *maybe* in the bedroom. *If* you're any good."

That intense heat was back in his eyes. Nuclear destruction in three, two, one...

"Am I any good in the bedroom? I don't know, Pepper. You tell me. Am I a *decent* kisser?" He paused, just long enough for her to remember the devastation his lips had caused. "Now imagine my mouth all over your body. On the curve of your neck, on your breasts. Dropping over the smooth slope of your belly until I'm between your legs, kissing you until you can't breathe without gasping my name."

A whimper snuck out before she could stop it.

He cupped her face again, stroking his thumb over her cheek. "Stop driving us both mad and get in the house. I'll give you a call tomorrow."

Pepper didn't tease for another kiss because she didn't think she could take it, not without changing her mind and begging him to change his. She got out of the car and headed to the house.

All the time intensely aware that Jack was watching her.

Chapter Six

BETWEEN THE Wilson house and the stop sign at the end of the street, Jack almost pulled a screeching U-turn five times to hightail it back to Pepper. He'd never been more primed for sex, so hard his cock felt like it was going to explode. He was actually afraid to work the clutch with his foot because even the slightest friction might trigger a spontaneous orgasm.

Holy hell, kissing Pepper had been sheer heaven. Her eager tongue dueling with his, her delicate fingers clutching his collar. He shuddered, trying valiantly to ignore the tingling at the tip of his cock. Sweet Jesus. He really was at risk of coming in his pants.

But despite his aching groin, he still couldn't stop the parade of wicked images that blasted through his head.

Pepper naked.

Pepper moaning.

Pepper screaming his name after he'd made her come.

Christ, she'd responded so eagerly to his kiss. Didn't surprise him, either. Pepper always dived headfirst into any situation, and that attitude apparently included hot make-out sessions.

He couldn't wait to get her in bed.

Couldn't. Frickin'. Wait.

But not until he spoke to Parker. There was no turning back—Jack would have her no matter what Parker said—but he respected his friend enough to give him the heads-up and a few reassurances.

And seeing as how the only thing waiting for him at home was an empty bed, he figured he might as well get The Talk over with.

Decision made, Jack sped out of the Wilsons' residential neighborhood and headed for Parker and Lynn's apartment in North Beach. Parker wouldn't be thrilled with Jack showing up unannounced on a Friday night, but screw it. Jack was nothing if not impulsive, and when he set his mind on something, he didn't like waiting around for things to happen. He *made* them happen.

There wasn't a single parking space on Parker's street, so he was forced to park two blocks away, and the short jog to his friend's apartment didn't ease the discomfort in his body's southern region. The humid night air slid over him like a seductive caress, reminding him of Pepper's hot, sexy mouth moving over his.

Once he'd punched the intercom button on the stoop of Parker's building and waited for a response, he mentally recited the names of every American president in an attempt to rid himself of his massive erection. He'd just reached Ulysses S. Grant when the intercom finally crackled to life.

"Who the hell is it?" Parker's voice was thick with annoyance.

Jack hit the button. "It's me. Let me up."

"Jack? What the fuck, man? I'm busy."

"Five minutes, bro. I just need five minutes."

After an impossibly long silence, the front door buzzed loudly. Jack dashed through it and rode the elevator up to the fourth floor.

When the door to Parker and Lynn's apartment swung open, it was easy to figure out what Jack's buddy had been "busy" doing. Bare-chested and scowling, Parker raked a hand through his mussed-up hair and cursed in disbelief.

"This better be important," he said in a warning tone.

"It is." Jack brushed past his friend, then halted when he poked his head in the living room and spotted Lynn.

She looked equally rumpled, long dark hair tousled as she straightened the hem of her oversized T-shirt. Parker's shirt, clearly. And it was inside out.

"Hey, Jack." She greeted him with a sheepish smile and a rosy blush on her cheeks.

As usual, he got lost for a second in her mesmerizing eyes. They were the palest blue he'd ever seen, like the sun hitting ice deep inside a glacier. But there was nothing icy cold about the woman. Every time he saw her, he felt like patting his buddy on the back for a job well done. Plus, Lynn wasn't only gorgeous. She was also smart and compassionate.

And incredibly intuitive. She took one look at Jack's face and headed for the doorway leading to the corridor. "I'll give you boys some privacy so you can talk."

The second she was gone, Parker advanced on Jack like a predator stalking its prey.

Or like a man who'd just been royally cock-blocked.

"Seriously?" Parker demanded. "You show up on a Friday night without calling first? When you *know* that Fridays are reserved for Lynn—"

"I like Pepper," Jack blurted out.

Silence.

Followed by more silence.

Then Parker narrowed his eyes. "Jack. I sincerely hope you're talking about food. As in, you like pepper in your eggs, or on your steak, or maybe in a salad. I mean, I'll still kick your ass for interrupting me just to talk about something that inane." His face turned to stone. "But not as hard as I'd kick your ass if you're talking about my *sister.*"

Jack met his friend's heated gaze. "You knew we'd have this talk eventually. We already started it the other day." He sighed. "We're finishing it now."

Parker's stiff body language didn't bode well for their impending discussion. He marched to the couch but didn't lower his rigid frame onto it. Instead, he pointed at the cushions and snapped, "Sit."

Jack arched a brow. "You've got to be kidding me."

"Sit the fuck down."

He decided to humor his friend. Flopping down on the plush cushions, he rested both hands on his thighs and loosely crossed his ankles. Parker stood in front of

96

him. No, he *loomed*. Arms folded, jaw tight, mouth twisted. Like an overprotective father interrogating his daughter's prom date. Only thing missing was the shotgun.

Another sigh slipped out of Jack's throat. "I swear to God, if you ask me what my intentions are, I'll kick you."

"No need. I already know what your intentions are." Parker's frown deepened. "I'm not stupid enough to try to talk you out of it, either, because we both know what a stubborn son of a bitch you are."

Jack's lips twitched.

"And my sister's a hundred times more mule-headed. Which means I won't bother talking her out of it, either. You wouldn't be here if she wasn't on board, and I'm not in the mood to have Pepper rip my throat out." Parker paused, shooting Jack that terrifying *look* he'd seen the guy direct at enemy soldiers. "I need to know two things. One—that this isn't one of your love-'em-and-leave-'em hookups. You won't be sneaking out the window the morning after you..." Parker blanched. "You know."

Talk about awkward.

Jack shifted in discomfort, but when he spoke, his tone rang with assurance. "It's not, and I won't."

His friend nodded. "Two—tell me you won't break her heart."

"I don't plan on it," Jack said quietly. "But I also can't be certain where this will go. It might not lead to forever. But I promise, whatever happens, I won't hurt her, at least not deliberately."

"Good." Parker pursed his lips, then slanted his head. "Face, ribs, or balls?"

Jack blinked. "Huh?"

"Where would you like my fist to go if you don't keep your promise?" Parker asked pleasantly.

"Wait—*what?*" a feminine voice exclaimed.

Lynn suddenly appeared in the doorway, clad in black yoga pants and a blue tank top, and displeasure flashed across her face as she caught the tail end of the conversation. She turned to her boyfriend in suspicion. "Why is your fist going anywhere near Jack?"

Parker held up a hand. "One sec, sweetheart. We're in the middle of something." He glanced back at the couch. "Well?"

Jack thought it over for a moment. "Face."

That earned him a nod from Parker, and a gasp from Lynn. "Jack, no. You have such a pretty face. You picked wrong."

He flashed her a grin. "Don't worry. It won't ever reach that point. I always keep my promises."

A knowing smile lifted her lips as she came up beside Parker. "So. You and Pepper, huh?"

Parker swiveled his head to glower at her. "You *knew?*"

"No. I just had a feeling." She rolled her eyes at Jack. "You weren't being very subtle at the barbecue, you know. Stomping around like a caveman, staring at her when you thought no one was looking." Lynn clapped her hands in delight. "Oh gosh, this is so exciting. I've gotta tell Suz."

She dashed off before either man could respond, causing both of them to stare at the empty doorway. Parker's expression became bemused. "Christ, women are weird. I swear, she calls Suz about the most trivial shit, and then they talk about it for a good hour, picking apart every last detail."

"Don't try to make sense of it, P. You'll break your brain."

Parker sighed. "I know, right?"

Then again... Jack snickered. "Maybe it's not just women. I seem to remember you and I having detailed conversations about the stupidest shit, too."

His friend looked shocked. "Us? Never. We're always about the important stuff."

"Like which brand of canned beans causes the least internal combustion?"

That pulled a reluctant smile from Parker.

Lynn wasn't gone a minute before she barreled back into the room. Disappointment flashed on her face as she wandered over to the couch and plopped down next to Jack. "Suz is out. Hot date." She sighed. "I guess I'll just have to gossip with you, Jack."

In the center of the living room, Parker gawked at his girlfriend. "Um? Sweetheart?"

She spared him a glance. "Don't be rude, babe. We have a guest. Go get Jack a beer."

Parker's jaw went even wider, all amusement Jack had teased from him gone. The death stare he sent Jack's way was even scarier than the one he gave to soldiers. It was the one reserved for *terrorists*.

Too bad Jack was as helpless as his buddy. Settling into a cross-legged position, Lynn had grabbed one of his hands and was firmly looking into his eyes. "Okay. Tell me everything. When did you realize you liked her?"

A groan sounded from Parker's vicinity. "Lynn, I love you to death, but there is no fucking way I'm going to stand around and listen to this. She's my *sister*."

"No one asked you to stay," his girlfriend said primly, before looking over expectantly. "Jack's beer?"

99

After a beat, Parker stomped out of the room in a damn good imitation of a five-year-old in the middle of a tantrum.

Jack had to grin. Man, it was ridiculously fun seeing his best friend get ordered around by this sweet woman. Though a part of him did feel for Parker. His Friday night sexfest had been shot to hell, all thanks to Jack. On the other hand, *Jack's* sexfest had been ruined thanks to *Parker*, so he supposed it was fitting.

Parker returned a minute later and thrust a bottle of Bud at Jack. "I'll be in the bedroom." He gave Lynn a pointed look. "Alone."

She absently waved a hand. "I'll be in eventually." Her attention was wholly focused on Jack. "Now tell me *everything*."

Jack couldn't help but shoot his friend a please-help-me look, which only got him a smug smirk in return. Parker shrugged as if to say, *good luck arguing with that,* and then he waltzed out of the room, leaving Jack at Lynn's mercy.

THE NEXT morning, Jack strode into Starbucks after a sleepless night that had involved constantly rolling over onto a throbbing erection, waking up thanks to said throbbing erection, then taking care of that throbbing erection so he could try to get some frickin' sleep. Hadn't worked, and now his right hand hurt and his dick was just mad at him. Because his dick wanted Pepper, and Jack had given it his *hand*.

To make matters worse, he'd gotten a text from Charlene at nine o'clock reminding him about their ten o'clock meeting to discuss her parents' party. It was a good thing she'd contacted him, otherwise he would have completely forgotten all about it, and being a no-show for a meeting wouldn't have reflected well on the company.

His former flame was already in the coffeehouse when he walked in, taking up residence at a table near the window. A stack of papers sat next to her tall coffee cup, and she was flipping through it, her dark red hair streaming over one shoulder.

Catching her eye, Jack smiled and gestured to the counter, then headed to place an order. A couple minutes later, he pulled out a chair and joined her, setting his steaming cup on the table.

"Morning." Her eyes sparkled as she looked him up and down. "You look like shit. Late night?"

"Not really. I actually went to bed at ten thirty," he admitted. "Couldn't sleep, though. It sucked."

She laughed. "Ten thirty? I'm disappointed in you, sugar. What happened to the wild Jack I knew and fucked?"

He shifted in his chair, uncomfortable with where the conversation had gone. He had fond memories of sleeping with Charlene, but being reminded of it now felt...wrong. And it did absolutely nothing for him. His mind was consumed by dirty thoughts of Pepper, and his body tightened with anticipation. Now that he'd gotten the talk with Parker out of the way, he could take Pepper to bed and make all those dirty fantasies come true.

Without responding to Charlene's flirty remark, Jack pointed to the papers. "Is that the final guest list?"

"Among other things." She popped the lid of her cup and took a quick sip. "I also brought a list of allergies— pretty much the only thing my grandmother can eat is lettuce. Okay, that's a joke, but she is allergic to a bunch of things." She grinned. "And yesterday I did some sleuthing and got my folks to talk about the songs that played on their first date and at their wedding. You said you have a list of bands that play covers, right?"

Jack nodded. "We can audition a bunch of them if you want, and you can pick whichever one you think is the best fit. Or we know some great DJs—you've got options."

"That sounds wonderful." Dimples appeared as she smiled again. "Why don't we arrange to see some of them tonight?"

He hesitated. "Uh...you know, I think I'd prefer we do it during business hours."

Charlene rolled her eyes. "Right. Because it's unprofessional for you to fraternize with clients."

He offered another nod.

"Jack..." She set down her cup and reached for his hand, snatching it before he could pull away. "I get that you don't want to get in trouble with your partners at DreamMakers, but..." her eyebrows waggled, "...what they don't know can't hurt them—or us. There's no reason why we can't see each other on the sly."

Jack gulped. Crap. And here he'd thought she'd been cool with the end of their fling.

"We had fun together, didn't we?" Her voice lowered to a seductive pitch. "I mean, I know *I* had fun."

"So did I," he said awkwardly. "But...um...yeah. The thing is..." A breath flew out. "I'm seeing someone."

Charlene's hand left his abruptly, unhappiness clouding her expression. "Oh. You are? Since when?"

"It's pretty recent. Like, really recent," he confessed. "But it's an exclusive thing, you know?"

Her head jerked in a nod. "I get it."

She avoided his gaze, and he stifled a sigh as a fresh wave of awkwardness swept over their table. Hell. This was what he got for being such a damn player. Flings and one-night stands were all fun and games—until they ended.

"I'm sorry if this is awkward for you," he said quietly. "If you want, I can ask Dean to be your point man from now on."

Charlene finally met his eyes. "No, that's fine," she said, her tone terser than he liked. "We're both grown-ups. I'm sure we can plan a memorable celebration for my parents without our brief history getting in the way." As if to punctuate her not-so-convincing conviction, she picked up another piece of paper and slid it across the table. "This is a list of the out-of-town guests who are flying in. They'll need hotel rooms and transportation from the airport."

"We can handle that."

"Good. Okay. Let's talk flowers."

Jack swallowed another sigh. Shit. It was going to be a long morning.

PEPPER STOOD at the railing of the fifth-story apartment balcony, supposedly to examine the view

Kendra had informed her was killer, but really she wasn't concentrating nearly as hard as she should.

She'd forgotten she and Kendra were scheduled to go apartment hunting that Saturday. Heck, she could have had anything on the calendar for that day, and it would have been forgotten in the mental blur of wondering when Jack was going to call.

She refused to be the one to chase him. All it would have taken were two moves on her phone, and she could have a text message flying his way. But *no way.*

No way would she let herself appear that needy.

Except if he didn't call by this evening she might have to reconsider. Maybe go back to his place and knock some sense into him, but hopefully it wouldn't come to that.

She pulled out her phone again to double-check if she still had battery power, and catching herself in the act just pissed her off even more.

"I like this place best of all we've seen so far," Kendra said, resting her elbows on the railing next to where Pepper stood. "The kitchen is a little small, but the bedrooms are a good size, and I really like that there's two bathrooms—we wouldn't have to share."

Pepper pulled herself back to attention. If she wanted out of her parents' house stat, she needed to focus. "Two bathrooms? Really?"

Kendra nodded. "Didn't you see there's one off the bigger bedroom? Come on, I'll show you." She exited the small balcony and headed back into the living space. "There's enough room in here we could put a couple of work desks, or do you think it would be better to put them in our bedrooms?"

A rude noise escaped before Pepper could stop it. "I know we had desks set up like that in our dorm room, but I really don't want my office in my bedroom. Bedrooms are for other things."

She swallowed hard, thinking exactly what kind of bedroom things she could be enjoying before the day was out.

"You're right," Kendra agreed, leading the way down the tiny hallway, past the main bathroom to the master bedroom. She opened what Pepper had originally thought was a closet door, and pointed inside. "See? Just a shower, sink, and toilet. But it's got a window, although the view doesn't look like much."

Pepper snuck into the miniscule room, checked out the view, and laughed. "That right there is some of the best graffiti in town. Do they charge extra for that?"

There was barely enough room for the two of them when Kendra joined her, peering outside. "Fire escape. That's good."

The door swung shut behind them. "We won't be holding any dances in here," Pepper joked. "You don't get claustrophobic, do you?"

Kendra laughed as she reached for the doorknob. "Maybe it's like a circus act. One of those cars where the clowns keep coming out and out and out." She turned the knob and pulled, but nothing happened. "What the hell?"

She tried again, jiggling the doorknob. Still nothing.

"Great. How come we couldn't get locked in a room that had a refrigerator?" Pepper asked.

Kendra banged her knuckles on the door. "Hello. Hello, we're stuck."

Fortunately, the woman who had been showing them around noticed they were missing pretty quickly. She knocked lightly on the wood paneling. "Are you girls nearly done in there?"

Pepper snickered. "What the heck does she think we're doing?" she whispered to Kendra.

Kendra grinned at her, but answered the landlady. "We're fine, if you can just help us get the door open."

In the end, though, it took the building attendant with a set of tools to get the door off the hinges to let the girls out.

The maintenance man shook his head in confusion. "I swear I fixed this door only last month. Don't you worry. I'll get it done up again, and this time, hopefully it'll hold."

Thirty minutes of paperwork later, Pepper and Kendra were the proud owners of a three-month trial lease.

"I'm so excited." Kendra lifted her cup of coffee in the air in a toast. They'd marched out of their new apartment building into a small coffee shop right next door where Pepper could see herself spending far too much money in the near future. "To independence and a place of our own."

Pepper clinked her coffee cup against Kendra's, before glancing at her phone for the millionth time that morning.

Kendra laughed. "Are you still waiting to hear back on that interview? I thought you'd decided working for DreamMakers would be enough for now."

It wasn't that she was trying to keep anything secret, more that the whole idea of her change in relationship status was still so shiny and new that she didn't want to share. But at the same time, this wasn't a secret she could keep for long, not with Kendra having expressed interest in Jack.

It was like walking a tightrope carrying lemon meringue pies in either hand. No way this could go without getting at least a little messy.

"I'm waiting for a call," she admitted.

"Oh, right, the big date last night with Billy." Kendra rested her elbows on the table and leaned forward, eyes bright with interest. "Confession—maybe this is a little creepy, but I wanted to see where he was taking you. I Googled the restaurant. Bizarre."

Which fit Pepper's assessment of the evening perfectly, since her date had been pretty bizarre as well. Her curiosity got the better of her. "What do you mean?"

"The chef's specials? Oh. My. God."

Not that Pepper could tell her anything about them, since Jack had ix-nayed that bit of the evening. "Spectacular?"

Her friend's nose crinkled. "Spectacularly disgusting. Last night it was tripe and haggis."

Pepper choked on her coffee. It appeared Jack had saved her from more than she'd expected. "You're not serious."

Kendra nodded enthusiastically. "So, tell me, how did things go?"

It was one of those situations where Pepper wasn't sure she could really describe everything without writing an essay. Or a short story. Or at least a really bad pun. "They didn't. But they did. But not with Billy, and actually nothing really happened, but it looks as if it might in the future."

Which was a whole lot of nothing.

Kendra looked suitably baffled. "What?"

There was no direction to go but straightforward. "My date got interrupted. Turns out Billy wasn't as much of a catch as he wanted me to believe."

"You're kidding. Oh, that's too bad. He seemed like such a nice guy." Kendra sat back in her chair, playing with the swizzle stick from her drink. She shrugged. "So that means you and I are back on the market."

"Umm, not completely. And I'm not quite sure how to tell you this, but then, I don't want to *not* tell you because that would be worse. Jack and I are seeing each other."

Kendra's jaw hung open. "You and..." A crease appeared between her friend's brows as she puzzled that out.

Pepper shifted awkwardly in her chair. "I guess there's always been something there between us, and last night he showed up to kind of rescue me, and..."

"Well, of course." Kendra bumped the palm of her hand against her forehead. "All that time you were complaining about Jack it was because you secretly had the hots for him."

Pepper didn't think so, but it was as good an excuse as any. "I didn't want you to think I did anything to get in your way."

"You stole him right out from under my nose." Kendra glared for a second before her expression broke, lips folded to blow a long raspberry. "I don't think so. I mean, yeah, he's cute, but he's too old for me." She glanced over her shoulder at the guy working the coffee bar. "Now he, on the other hand, is both cute and closer to my age."

"Well, nice surprise, ladies. Can I join you?"

A familiar voice interrupted their conversation, and Pepper couldn't help but smile as Lynn's friend Suz slid onto the chair next to them. "Hey, you. What are you doing down in this neck of the woods?"

"I just finished an interview at the precinct around the corner. Something for my job with the special events page at the Bay City Press. And then I had to say hi to everyone—one of my brothers is stationed there, so the whole department is like family." Suz turned toward the drink counter and waved a perfectly manicured hand. The young man Kendra had been admiring waved back.

"Do you know him?" Kendra asked.

"I have a feeling Suz knows most of San Francisco's population, especially if they're male," Pepper teased.

"Guilty as charged." The gorgeous blonde flashed her brilliant smile. "Why live in the City of Love if you don't believe in sharing the message?"

Pepper could see more and more why everyone down at DreamMakers enjoyed having the woman around. "What do you think of this area? Kendra and I are going to be living here."

Suz paused and considered. "It's not as safe as some, but it's not as bad as others. If you keep your eyes open, you should be okay. Which apartment? And it better have security at the door, or I will harp on your ass."

Kendra pointed next door. "The Towers. And yes, they have security at the front door, and we have both a deadbolt and peephole."

"Make sure you use them," Suz warned again. "Drives me crazy when I see people propping the front door open with a box, or letting somebody in who casually stood in line behind them, waiting until the security code gets entered."

Pepper pretended to cover a yawn.

"Trust me, you don't need to continue the lecture. If Parker lives up to his usual standard, I will not only get briefed for longer than you could talk about the dangers for a woman in public places, he'll provide me a report in triplicate and expect me to memorize it and initial the bottom of each page after I finish reading it." She sighed. "I thought he'd outgrown it, but in the past couple weeks he's gotten even worse than before I went to college. I wonder at what point he's going to actually realize that I'm no longer twelve."

"That's what family does, hon. They worry about you. I've got the five brothers, plus my mom and dad—all of whom are cops. Either I could let it make me crazy, or I could learn to live with it." Suz turned to face the eager young man who had brought her drink to the table. "Well, aren't you a darling? Thanks, Timothy."

She slipped him some money, and he smiled at them, his gaze darting over Kendra as he backed away without a word.

"Maybe since I'll be living close by, you should introduce me to Timothy," Kendra suggested. "He's cute."

"He's a baby," Suz admonished her. "A cute baby, I give you that, but it's hard to find them attractive when they still look like they might be surprised they have pubes." She ignored the sputtering, taking a sip of her coffee before looking far more serious as she addressed Kendra. "I thought you were interested in Jack Hunter?"

Kendra rolled her eyes. "Fat lot of good that did me. Pepper snapped him up."

"It wasn't like that," Pepper protested.

Suz looked very interested in this new development. "Oh, so that's what had Lynn attempting to interrupt my date last night. Hmmm, this *is* juicy. And so is Jack, if I might say so."

"I thought you said he was too big of a flirt for me," Kendra complained.

"He was. He is." Suz rested an elbow on the table, leaning closer to Kendra. "Look, the man has been setting the world on fire, but I think it's because he couldn't have what he wanted. And what he wanted..."

She tilted her finger across the table at Pepper.

An electric pulse raced through her belly in response. "Oh, stop it. He has not been longing for me forever."

Suz shrugged. "I call them as I see them, and I think that boy is smitten. But you can go on denying it if it makes you feel better."

"I'm going to pout," Kendra announced. "I don't think this is very fair. Why do some girls always get the guy?"

Pepper opened her mouth to protest, but Suz beat her to it, patting Kendra sympathetically on the hand. "I know it seems one-sided when someone like me has *all* the boys following her like bees beaconed to a flower patch. Like wasps to an open bottle of beer. Like ants to a picnic."

"You're making me want to break out a can of Raid. Just saying," Kendra warned.

Pepper agreed, but from everything she'd heard, Suz *was* that desirable. "Maybe you have the right pheromones."

"You know I was talking about you," Kendra grumbled, "but that's fine. I can be the poor, spinster sister, sitting at home and polishing the silver."

If she didn't know how much Kendra had dated in college, Pepper would have felt more guilt. "I thought you said you needed about a year to recover from that debacle

111

of 'accidentally' dating three guys at one time? On the same night?"

Across the table from her, Kendra's and Suz's expressions were opposites in extremes. Suz looked impressed, Kendra resigned.

"You had to go and remind me of that?"

Pepper grinned. "That's what friends are for."

"I think I need to hear all the details," Suz said, "but I have to run pretty quick. Do you two want to get together with Lynn and me for girls' night out? We were planning one pretty soon, and we'd love to have you join in."

"I'd like that," Pepper agreed quickly.

"Ditto." Kendra dug in her purse and pulled out a card, handing it over to Suz. "Cell phone numbers, Facebook, the usual."

"Fab." The curvy blonde tucked it away, finishing the last of her drink and putting the cup back on the table. "And now I really have to run, but Pepper, have fun and remember, no glove, no love. Kendra? You let those babies grow up. Cowboys are far more exciting once they've had a little time in the saddle. If you know what I mean."

She left in a flurry of golden hair, a swinging bright blue purse, and killer heels that really shouldn't be out on the street.

Pepper locked eyes with her friend, and the two of them managed to keep a straight face for all of ten seconds before bursting out in laughter. By the time Pepper caught her breath she felt a whole lot better. "I really do like her."

"Oh, me too. I wasn't laughing *at* her or anything." Kendra wiped her eyes. "But how does she come up with those things on the spur of the moment?"

"I don't know, but she's fun to be around." And the brief respite had been desperately needed. It was with a lighter heart that Pepper laid a hand on Kendra's arm. "You're fun to be around, too, and I hope you know that. I'm glad we're going to share the apartment, and I really hope you're okay with the Jack thing."

"Of course I am." Kendra pushed her empty coffee cup forward. "It was a bit of a shock, but I couldn't be happier for you. Really."

Pepper smiled, and suddenly the butterflies were back. Strange butterflies of nervousness that she rarely had when it came to fooling around. Suz's comment about *experienced men* had hit home. Pepper had never worried about holding back in sexual experimentation, but no way would she be able to match the things Jack had seen and done.

The good part? She was pretty sure he wouldn't mind helping her take the training wheels off.

Suz

SUZ SETTLED behind the wheel of her fire-engine red convertible, sliding back the roof before she pulled out her phone. Better get this conversation out of the way before she got into traffic.

"Returning your call, doll face."

Her best friend Lynn all but squealed with excitement. "Oh my God, do I ever have the best gossip."

It was cruel, but these things had to be done. Suz cleared her throat then dove in.

"Jack and Pepper are going to do the nasty. Parker knows about it, and now he's giving you the evil eye for grinning while thinking about how hot those two are together, but he's also happy because thinking about how hot those two are together totally got your engine going, and you did the freaky-deaky all night long."

Dead silence greeted her from the other end of the line.

Suz chuckled.

Lynn finally caught up. "Number one, you are such a shit. Number two, how the *hell* do you do that?"

"Ah, now, if I told you my methods, I'd have to kill you."

"You're amazing, that's all I can say."

"I know."

Lynn laughed. "Bitch. I love you. And if you say *I know* again, I will serve liver and onions the next time you come over."

That would be a fate worse than death. "Hey, I just chatted with Pepper and her bud. They're going to join us for our next girls' night out. You got a date that works for you yet?"

"One sec." Rustling noises in the background. "How about next Thursday?"

"Perfect by me. I'll email them and see if it's good, and book us spots at the spa." She thought of something else. "You want to chip in to help cover their costs? I think things may be a little tight for a while, with them just getting out of school."

"Okay by me. I've got to run, though. Parker's still in bed."

She checked her watch. "Wow. You did wear him out. You go girl."

Lynn signed off, and Suz tucked her phone away, turning to grab her seat belt right in time to see a familiar face appear beside her driver's door.

"I'm afraid I have to write you a ticket for loitering."

They were never going to grow up, but Suz hadn't been lying when she'd told Pepper she'd learned to appreciate her family. "You put my name down on your little pad, Chase, and I will tell Mom about the time you opened *all* the Christmas presents early to see what was inside before wrapping them back up."

Chase frowned. "Stop holding that over me. I was twelve."

"Never. You know you'd never get another Christmas present from her again if she found out, and if anybody is a Christmas junkie, it's you."

It was a standing joke, and Chase accepted her teasing with a smile. "I heard you stopped in at the shop. Everything okay?"

"Peachy keen and twice as sweet." She jerked a thumb over her shoulder. "Got a couple of friends who are moving into The Towers. I'll introduce you to them sometime. Good kids."

"Oh, so *friends* isn't code for something more explicit."

Suddenly Suz had an inkling of what Parker was going to feel like having people talk sex and Pepper in the same sentence. "I'll just pretend you didn't bring that up."

All six foot four of annoying sibling stood back from her car, putting his sunglasses back in place. "Introduce us sometime. And take care of yourself, little sis."

"I always do."

She made sure she was buckled up before pulling into the traffic, because no matter how close they were, her siblings would have no problem slapping a fine on her and laughing while doing it.

Family. Couldn't live without them, but sometimes it would be nice to try.

Chapter Seven

JACK LET Pepper in later that evening, surprised to find her outside his door at seven o'clock sharp. Punctuality had never been her strong suit, so the fact that she was actually on time startled him.

Though not as much as the flicker of unease in her eyes.

"Hey." He furrowed his brow. "You okay?"

She brushed past him and dropped her purse on the hall table. "I'm great. Kendra and I signed a lease today, which means I'll be out of my folks' house in less than two weeks. Halle-frickin'-lujah."

118

Now he frowned, trailing after her as she headed for the living room like she owned the place. "I'm sure it hasn't been *that* bad living with them again."

She sighed, tossing her hair over one shoulder as she flopped onto the couch. She was wearing tiny denim shorts that revealed a helluva lot of firm, golden thigh, and a tank top that was so low cut he was momentarily distracted by the creamy swell of her cleavage.

"It hasn't been happy fun time central, either," she answered. "Dad is being his usual overprotective self, and Mom has been bugging me for weeks to consider working at DreamMakers permanently."

Didn't sound at all bad to Jack, but he kept his mouth shut. He didn't want to antagonize Pepper right off the bat. But still, he often thought her attitude toward her very loving, very supportive family was a tad...ungrateful, maybe? Insensitive? But she was also young, and she'd never had to experience the *other* side of the spectrum—a family that didn't support or protect you at all. A family in which you were totally and utterly invisible.

Pushing aside the bleak memories, Jack joined her on the sofa, sitting right next to her and slinging an arm over her shoulder. When she tensed, the frown returned, deeper than before.

"What's wrong?" he demanded.

Pepper shifted, her teeth digging into her perfect pink bottom lip. "Nothing."

"Bullshit. I've known you forever. I can tell when something's up with you."

Other women might have voiced another denial, flashed a cheerful smile, and pretended he was imagining things, but Pepper Wilson wasn't other

119

women. She was notorious for speaking her mind, and after only a brief moment of hesitation, she opened her mouth and did just that.

"I feel weird about this," she said frankly.

Jack arched a brow. "This?" he echoed.

"Like you said, I've known you my whole life. You've seen me throwing temper tantrums when my parents wouldn't let me watch an hour more of TV. I watched you go through your horrible zit-face phase. God, I was hiding under Parker's *bed* the day you told him about losing your virginity to that airhead Elaine Tomilson—"

He blinked. "Wait, *what?*"

"—and now we're sitting on your couch, and your arm is around me, and we're probably going to have sex any second." She blew out a breath. "I feel awkward and nervous and totally unprepared for any of this."

Jack stroked her bare shoulder before bringing his hand to her face to grasp her chin. "First, our past history has nothing to do with this moment, Candy Cane. We're adults now, light years away from the immature kids we used to be." His thumb swept over her jaw. "Second, it's okay to be nervous. I promise, I won't push you to do anything you're not ready for." He captured her bottom lip between his fingers and pinched it in reprimand. "And third, what the *hell* do you mean you were hiding under Parker's bed? How much did you hear, damn it?"

Her mouth twitched, then stretched into the sassy grin he knew and loved. "Everything. I heard everything."

Jack couldn't stop a groan. "You're such a sneaky little brat. We had no idea you were listening."

"Duh. Otherwise I'm sure you wouldn't have told Parker about how you were worried Elaine didn't have an orgasm because you shot off your rocket too fast."

He stiffened. "It was my first time. I had no clue what I was doing."

She batted her eyelashes at him. "Don't worry, Jackjack. A lot of people don't knock it out of the park on their first try. I mean, the boy *I* had sex with my first time managed to make me come, and he was a virgin, too, but I'm sure that doesn't mean *your* experience was uncommon or anything."

He all but growled, his lips crashing down on hers in a hard kiss before he pulled back to glare at her. "Who was he and where does he live now so I can kill him?"

She flashed another grin. "Brandon Hill, and I'm pretty sure he still lives in the old neighborhood." She gasped. "Oooh, I should look him up. I wonder if he still knows how to do that incredible thing with his tongue—"

Another animalistic noise ripped from deep inside him. "Say one more word about some other man's tongue and I'll spank that naughty ass of yours."

"Promises, promises." She stuck out her tongue. "You've threatened to spank me before, but I'm starting to suspect you're all talk and no action, Jackjack."

She was goading him. He knew that. But he didn't care. He didn't need to be goaded into taking what he wanted—that had been his intention when he'd invited her over. Besides, seeing the defiant gleam in her eyes told him that her nerves had ebbed, which was exactly what he'd wanted.

"You want action, Pepper?" He slanted his head.

"I'm here, aren't I?"

"Then you have five seconds to get naked and spread your legs for me. Spread them wide, too. I want to see every inch of your pussy."

Her breath hitched, her expression burning with heated anticipation. "And if I don't?"

"Then I'll rip your clothes off myself. And I mean *rip*. They'll be in shreds when I'm done with them." He met her eyes, then counted in warning. "One."

He supposed she must've had a deep attachment to the outfit, because her hands found the button of her shorts in lightning speed. With a smirk, Jack watched as pieces of clothing flew off in a blur and hit the laminate floor. In a heartbeat Pepper was naked, leaning back against the cushion as her legs parted seductively.

Jack slid off the couch and stood in front of her, his mouth flooding with saliva as his gaze fixed on the sweet paradise she was so brazenly offering to him. She was goddamn perfection. Utter temptation.

"Are you still feeling awkward?" he said roughly.

Very slowly, she shook her head.

"You sure? Because I want you totally relaxed before I get started."

He saw her swallow. "I *was* relaxed, you jerk, until you made it sound so formal! 'Get started'," she grumbled. "What is this, a medical procedure? I thought we were going to get it on."

Jack chuckled. "Not just yet."

Pepper narrowed her eyes. "Is there another reason I'm buck-ass naked on your couch, then?"

"Of course." He tipped his head to the side. "Would you feel more comfortable if I talk you through the procedure?"

"Sweet baby Jesus—are we seriously playing *doctor* right now?"

He dragged his tongue over his bottom lip and ignored the incredulous question. "It's a two-step process, baby. Step one, I'm going to get on my knees in front of you. Step two, I'm going to lick your pussy until you can't move, see, or breathe and the only words you're capable of saying are *Jack, Oh God,* and *I'm coming again.*"

Her eyes glittered. "You sound very confident of that."

"I *am* confident." He stepped closer, and enjoyed the way her breath caught again. "I'm good, Pepper. I'm very, very good. So now sit back and hold on for the ride."

"God, you are so arroga—"

He was on his knees with his mouth on her pussy before she could finish her sentence. Pepper jerked as if he'd struck her, then practically melted into the cushions as a throaty moan slipped out.

Jack circled her clit with his tongue before drawing it between his lips. The gentle sucking was for him, not her, because the fleeting contact with that sensitive bundle of nerves was all he'd be giving her right now. He'd be licking and kissing and suckling that little bud again...but not until she begged for it.

Rumbling in contentment, he licked down her slit and headed south, the tip of his tongue lapping at the moisture clinging to her delicate folds. She tasted as sweet as he'd known she would. God, he didn't even need food anymore—the taste of her could sustain him for the rest of his life.

"Jack..." His name shuddered out of her mouth. "Stop going so damn slow."

He lifted his head and smiled. "No."

123

Then he resumed the lazy exploration, planting tiny kisses on her inner thighs before kissing his way back to her core and rubbing his lips against it. She shivered, and he smiled again. Oh yeah, this was going to be fun. She was so damn sensitive to his touch, each shiver telling him exactly what she liked, each anguished noise telling him exactly what she needed.

He didn't give her the latter, though. No, he'd waited too long for this. He planned on dragging out every last second until he'd had his fill.

Groaning, he pushed his tongue inside her and stroked her hot channel with it. Pepper's hips shot off the couch, frantic hands tangling in his short hair to keep him in place. He fucked her with his tongue until he couldn't breathe anymore, coming up for air just as her hand slid down her flat belly and over the reddish heart-shaped hair on her mound so she could touch her clit.

He promptly swatted her hand away. "Keep your palms flat on either side of you, Candy Cane."

"No," she burst out. "I need…I…" Raw need filled her expression as her head lolled to the side.

"You'll get what you need when I decide to give it to you," he rasped in warning.

She glared at him. "I want to come!"

"You will." His lips tugged up in an evil smile. "When I decide to let you."

"I hate you so much right now."

"Uh-huh. I'm sure you do." Then he parted her labia with his fingers and licked her hot, swollen flesh, making her cry out again.

He continued to avoid her clit, teasing her with languid swipes of the tongue everywhere but that hypersensitive center of nerves. His cock strained against his fly, so hard it was liable to rip a hole in his jeans.

"I can't wait to fuck you," he muttered as he brought a finger to her opening. He plunged it inside, groaning when her inner muscles rippled around him. He couldn't wait to feel her squeezing his dick like that. Couldn't fucking wait.

But not yet. Not until he showed Pepper Wilson all the wicked things his tongue and fingers were capable of.

He licked up and down her slit, stopping each time right before he reached her clit, while his finger pumped inside her, nice and slow. Sweat broke out on his forehead, his restraint downright miraculous.

"*Jack*," she wailed when his tongue did another pass that neglected her clit. "Please."

He slipped a second finger into the mix, pumping harder. "Beg for it," he ordered, looking up to meet her eyes. "Beg and I'll let you have it."

Her emerald-green eyes flashed with both lust and resentment. Pepper Wilson didn't ask for things, she *took* them. He knew that, knew she would never show an iota of vulnerability if she could help it, but he needed her surrender. Needed to know that she was as desperate as he was, that she wanted it as badly as he did.

"Touch my clit," she choked out. "Touch it, lick it, suck it, just do *something* to it. Please, Jack. Please, please, please, *please*."

A dark laugh slid out, his cock thickening even more as her pleas echoed in the air. As they unleashed something hot and primal and *male* inside him. He lowered his head and wrapped his lips around her clit, sucking hard as he fingered her.

"Oh *God.*"

125

He felt it the moment she came. Her swollen bud pulsed against his tongue, her pussy tightened around his fingers, and her lower body rocked into his face.

"Oh God...Jack..."

Satisfaction coursed through him as she moaned out the words he'd known she would, as she convulsed on the couch from an orgasm so powerful it nearly triggered one from him. Jack clenched his ass cheeks to ward off impending release, ordering his cock to behave. He focused on Pepper, on riding out the orgasm with her, flicking his tongue over her clit in fast, thorough strokes.

When she finally grew still, sighing in pleasure, he kept going. Eased the pressure, slowed the tempo of his fingers. But his tongue stayed on her clit. Slow, fleeting licks and feather-light teases, until he felt her beginning to squirm again.

He snuck a peek at her face, floored by the flush on her cheeks, the hazy passion in her eyes. She lightly stroked his hair, bringing a shiver that scurried down his spine and tickled his balls. This was heaven. This was where he belonged, between Pepper Wilson's thighs, with his lips on her pussy and her fingers in his hair.

"Goddamn it, I'm addicted to you," he mumbled. A sense of urgency overtook him, spurring him to act, to plunge his fingers inside her again and lap at her clit like a man starved.

Pepper's moans heated the room and vibrated in his body, and then she was clawing at his hair and moving her hips again, her voice bursting out in a desperate pant. "Oh God, Jack. I'm coming again."

His laughter rumbled against her pussy as she trembled from another release. He licked until she went limp, her head falling back against the couch, eyes closing, arms dropping to her sides in a useless heap.

Rising to his feet, Jack reached for his belt buckle. "Open your eyes, baby. You're not gonna want to miss this."

Those eyelids cranked open, her glazed expression summoning another wave of pure satisfaction. Pepper's gaze followed the movement of his fingers as he released the belt from the buckle. As he undid his pants, dragged his zipper down. Jack eased the denim down his hips, then reached inside his boxers and slowly withdrew his aching cock.

He arched a brow at her, fingers wrapping around his erection to give it a firm stroke. "Pepper, I'd like you to meet Big Jack. He's real happy to see you."

What he got in response was a...*noise*. Kind of like a snicker. It seemed to start at her toes, traveling all the way up until her lips curled into a full-out smile. She lay relaxed on the couch, and in spite of him standing there with his dick in his hand he had to smile in return.

She curled upward, and one hundred percent mischief flashed at him.

And then? She lost it.

<hr>

OH. MY. God.

While it was impossible to control the first burst of amusement, she was damn proud that she managed to stifle all of the other things she wanted to say. Had to be the endorphins flooding through her system that were leaving her giddy and foolish and far too reckless.

The man's tongue was magic. But...he'd named his penis.

Pepper snickered again.

Jack's cocky stance adjusted slightly. "What?"

She pressed her lips together in an attempt to keep control, but it was impossible. "Big Ja—"

The word disintegrated into a jumble of noises as she pressed a hand over her mouth and looked away.

Beside her, the couch moved as the heavy weight of his body joined her.

"Pepper." There was disapproval in his tone.

She would've given anything to be able to simply say his name. To taunt him back with that little repetition thing they seemed to have going, but all she could think was *he'd named his penis*. "Big Jaa-aa-ack."

It was no use. Peals of laughter escaped. One after another. She finally wrapped her arms around her waist to try to get back under control. Her stomach hurt, and there were tears running down her cheeks. She chanced a glance to her left. Jack was staring at the ceiling, a look of infinite patience on his face, the rest of his...*anticipation*...muted.

Pepper felt guilty, or she would have, if she could stop laughing.

He leaned over her, one arm on either side of the back of the couch. "You're pissing me off."

"Sorry," she squeaked, gasping for air. "And I apologize to Big Jack as well—"

She slapped her hands over her mouth again, desperate to stop. A moment of panic snuck in. She'd worried about being less experienced when maybe what she should have been worrying about was being considered too childish for Jack's taste.

Laughing at his equipment certainly wasn't a good way to make an impression, but *God*—

There was no way to stop.

"You're impossible." Strong arms snuck around her body, and Pepper found herself moving through the air as Jack carried her down the hall. She grabbed ahold of his shoulders gratefully, burying her face against his chest and letting her laughter fly in the hopes she could stop sometime before he got *too* annoyed.

She wasn't sure where he was taking her. Bedroom, probably. Sure enough, when he pushed open a door, her quick peek revealed his king-sized bed, a deep burgundy quilt pulled military neat over its surface. The familiar sight helped dull her amusement. She drew another couple of gasping breaths to calm herself, careful to keep her gaze lowered to the floor in case meeting his eyes set her off again.

Jack lowered her to a cushioned surface—not the bed. She glanced down to find herself seated on the edge of an exercise bench. "Workout time?" she joked.

"I think so." Two steps later he was straddling her, his muscular legs trapping her in position on the padded surface of the bench. "It seems you've gotten over your *hesitation*."

"If you'd just told me you'd named your penis right off the bat..." Pepper squeezed her eyes shut and clenched her teeth to stop laughing all over again.

He clicked his tongue. "Pepper, Pepper, Pepper. You are one hell of a woman."

She took a final deep breath and looked up to see him hovering over her, no annoyance in his expression, just a contented grin and a whole lot of full-fledged one hundred percent American hero. Stark naked.

And carrying a fully engaged and loaded cock, and at that moment she didn't care what he'd called it. She wanted it. Any way she could get it.

"You're very talented."

"I told you I was," Jack gloated.

She made a rude noise. "I was talking about how fast you stripped."

One of Jack's brows went skyward as he leaned over, his abdomen tightening, emphasizing the to-die-for ridges of muscles she couldn't wait to examine with her tongue. "You were laughing for quite a while. Trust me, I had time to do a lot of things."

Her gaze dropped. "There are a few things left undone."

"My cock?"

"Big *Ja*—" She swallowed hard. "Nope. Can't say it."

"Dammit, Pepper. I was just trying to make you feel more comfortable."

She wrapped her hands around his naked hips, smoothing her fingertips over his rock-solid buttocks. His cock was right there between them, and she was all too aware of it. "I don't need childish reassurances. I need you."

Before he could speak, she slipped one hand forward and wrapped it around the base of the shaft, sliding her hand upward carefully as her eyes locked with his.

A couple of strokes later his jaw had tightened. She was getting to him in a whole new way. Or in an old way they could finally satisfy.

His hand cupped her cheek, his thumb brushing lightly over her lower lip. "I need you, too."

She didn't need a roadmap to know where they should go. She stuck out her tongue and licked his thumb, stealing the opportunity to wrap her lips around it and suck lightly.

The heat in his eyes flared, and he moved his hand, as if fucking his thumb into her mouth. "Oh yeah, that's what I like to see. Gorgeous."

He pulled back, escaping with a soft *plop*. He adjusted his stance, and Pepper leaned over, extending her tongue to greet the tip of his cock. The tortured moan of satisfaction that escaped his lips was all the reward she'd been looking for. She played, twirling her tongue over the smooth head for a second before closing her lips.

"Hell. It feels so good when you do that." Jack tunneled his fingers into her hair, pulling it back into a ponytail and holding it with his hand. His gaze locked on her lips as she rocked over him, sucking and swirling and having a damn good time. "Stop, Pepper. This isn't how we're going to end things today."

She pulled her head back, smacking her lips. "That's right, you're so old if I get you off now, you'll never ever get it up again tonight."

"Brat," Jack snapped, but he was smiling. "It's not a case of not being able, it's that I'm dying to get inside you."

Pepper shrugged, leaning back slightly on the workout bench. "You're the one who put me here."

"Just until you settled down." His strong fingers crept past her cheek. "Get on the bed."

"Assume the position?"

His eyes flashed. "You have no idea."

Oh, really? "Well now, Jack. You have secrets I don't know about? Should I check the bed frame for buckle straps and chains?"

She rose to her feet, and his gaze swept over her body. Lingered on her chest, where her breasts moved erratically as her breathing grew unsteady. That expression in his eyes—she'd taunted him for days in this same apartment, and she'd seen lust on his face before.

The man drawing her into his arms was just a wee bit more intense than she'd expected. She scrambled to find some kind of joke to make, but it was impossible. As he laid her on the bed and trapped her there with his body, it was as if all the laughter had escaped moments earlier. All that was left was dark, intense passion.

Jack wrapped his fingers around her wrists and pulled her arms over her head. He stared at her for one brief moment, just long enough to scald her with his eyes.

"Keep your arms there," he commanded.

Pepper didn't even *think* of disobeying. Her fingers moved as if triggered, fisting the sheets.

He slipped down her body, hands moving in a slow, mesmerizing caress. When he lowered his head to her breasts to tease and torment, Pepper let out a sigh of satisfaction, then focused on all the happy endorphins that were dancing all over again.

"I'm ready," she muttered softly.

He ignored her, continuing to bring her back up. His hands far more gentle on her clit this time, which she was thankful for, but his touch was relentless until she was squirming under the dual contact to her breasts and sex. It was as if he had more than two hands—and another dirty thought spun wildly through her brain as she momentarily imagined having four hands and two mouths working her over.

That had been a fantasy she'd dreamed of for a long time, even tried to reach for—with disastrous results—

but maybe it wasn't necessary. Maybe she just needed someone as talented as Jack because *whoa, Nelly*, the man was everywhere.

Everywhere, except where she needed him most.

"Fuck me," she begged.

Jack lifted his head from her breasts, examining her face for a brief second before making as if to roll away.

Shit. She'd forgotten to mention this before. "You don't need a condom."

He swore, every muscle in his body going taut as he hesitated. "Dammit, Pepper—"

She tugged on his shoulders, wiggling underneath him until the heated length of his shaft nestled once more against her pussy. "Birth control, and I'm clean. I swear."

He ignored her, except for the stream of curses escaping his lips. He was gone for a moment, rolling a condom onto his shaft. Crawling between her legs and holding himself over her torso as his hips settled over hers. "I'm clean too but we'll talk later. Put your hands over your head *now*."

Pepper snapped her arms upward. "Don't stop," she ordered.

He rocked back and forth a couple of times, sliding his cock over her clit before finally pressing the thick head to her opening. She held her breath, pulling her legs open and waiting. He was right there, the broad length just inside her passage, and still the damn man didn't move.

Until he did. All in one motion, his hips riding forward until she was completely filled with his cock. "Holy jiminy, *yes*."

Jack lowered himself to his elbows, their torsos touching as he stared into her eyes and thrust again. "Jesus. So. Damn. Good. Your pussy feels like heaven around me."

The temptation to move her arms was strong. "Jack. I want to hold you."

He thrust harder, the bed rocking under him, and a moan of satisfaction escaped her lips. Fine. If she couldn't touch him, she'd just have to deal. She tightened her grip on the sheets and focused on the parts of him she could feel. It was more than enough, especially when he tilted his hips, grinding his pelvis over her mound and hitting her clit on every rock.

Wet heat enveloped her nipple a split second before his teeth nipped hard, and an electric jolt shot through her. She gazed down happily, no energy to do anything as his strokes grew quicker, the tingling in her core rising toward the moment when—

She broke. Her orgasm rolled into her not like a wave but like being slammed into the sand then shoved down the side of a dune. She couldn't breathe, it was that damn intense. Her body tightened around him and she let out a low cry.

"Oh, hell, *yes.*" Jack stopped with his hips locked with hers, his cock stretching her passage. His hips jerked helplessly, the slick of sweat on his skin red hot under her fingers.

Somewhere in the past moments she'd let go of the sheets and grabbed him, and she smiled.

Holy shit.

He vanished briefly while her head was still spinning. Then two hundred or whatever pounds of sweaty, satisfied man lowered himself onto her as Jack pressed his face to her neck and nuzzled affectionately. She dragged her fingers through his hair, amazed that she could breathe.

She went willingly when he rolled them over and placed her on his chest. Sprawled on top of Jack was her new favorite position in the entire world. "I'm going to have a nap now," she announced.

"Fine by me."

A tiny whisper of amusement snuck in. Sated from sex, she might not be thinking as straight as she should, but she couldn't resist.

"Hey, Jack?"

"Yeah?"

"I'm going to name your cock—something more appropriate to its fine and upstanding abilities."

He sighed. A long, exasperated, oh-so-patient sound. "Give it a rest, Pepper."

She giggled for a second. "No, this is obviously very important to you. You just need something a little snappier. I'd love to give it some thought."

"You're so generous."

"Ain't I just?"

He was stroking his fingers through her hair, a relaxing, intimate move. Pepper dropped the topic, but she'd bring it up again sometime.

Right now she was too contented to keep teasing.

Chapter Eight

JACK ROCKED his chair as he looked around the boardroom at DreamMakers. There was a warm spot of satisfaction in his gut, not only from being the first into the room for their weekly planning meeting and getting to pick his favorite chair. Nope. His happiness went a lot deeper than scoring the best seat in the room.

"You'd better get rid of that expression before Parker walks into the room if you know what's good for you," Dean said, plopping into the chair next to him.

"What expression?" Jack asked innocently.

Dean leaned forward, his eyes lighting up with amusement. "You look well fucked."

He didn't need to answer. Dean's jealousy was obvious.

Especially when his friend double-checked to make sure they were still alone, then lowered his voice. "She's a wildcat in the sack, isn't she?"

"I'm far too much of a gentleman to kiss and tell."

Dean made a rude noise. "Come on, just one little breadcrumb."

Jack shook his head. "Why are you asking me for dirty details? I thought you had a hot date last night. Did something go wrong?"

His friend leaned back in his chair. "It was a little too clingy. She didn't only ask about the next date, she wanted to know what my plans were for the fall."

Kiss of death in a relationship with Dean. "I take it you told her you were liable to be going wheels-up at any time?"

"You know it. Bullshit on long-term planning." Dean patted the leather boardroom table in front of him. "Only girl I'm interested in that far into the future is DreamMakers."

"Married to your job?" Gillian strode into the office, her perfect posture carrying her to settle in the seat next to Dean. "Why, that doesn't sound at all like you."

"I'm very dedicated to DreamMakers," Dean insisted vigorously.

"Uh-huh, I'm sure you are. As evidenced by your attention to detail and the sacrifices you make. Like going undercover into..." She glanced down at a card in her hand. "Enticing Massages by Merrill." She grinned at Jack, ignoring the sputtering noises coming from Dean. "Good to see you again, sir."

"Hey. How come he still gets a *sir*, and I don't anymore?" Dean complained.

"Because you asked me not to call you that!" Gillian said in exasperation. She rested her elbows on the table as the DreamMakers staff slipped in one after the other. "Besides, I could never go back to calling you *sir* now that I've seen you naked."

Didi jerked to a halt. The older woman was dressed entirely in neon, rainbow colors alternating from her bright orange sneakers all the way up to the garish pink bow in her hair. "Do I even want to hear this?"

"Do *any* of us want to hear this?" Parker asked with a frown. "Right now, I mean. I want to hear all the details *later*, but this is supposed to be a staff meeting."

Dean shuffled uncomfortably in his seat. "It wasn't anything important. The last recon we did had some complications."

Jack's curiosity was at an all-time high. "Are you blushing? My God, you are." He glanced over at Gillian. "Okay, now you have to tell us. In the interest of staff well-being I need to know what happened."

She seemed to be fighting laughter, and a part of him wished she'd let it loose. He suspected Gillian Reyes was a firecracker under her professional surface, which had been more or less confirmed by their other new hire Colby, who knew one of the men in Gillian's former unit. Her old teammate claimed that Gillian had fit right in among the all-male crew, shooting the shit with the boys and drinking more than one of them under the table when the unit was on leave.

"It was a simple misunderstanding," Gillian began with a barely restrained smirk.

"I really don't think anyone needs to hear this." Dean folded his arms and pouted.

VIVIAN AREND & ELLE KENNEDY

"If I find out you've violated any DreamMakers rules and regulations, I will be very disappointed with you, young man." Didi focused on Dean, her glasses perched on the tip of her nose as she glared down forbiddingly. "That's why I gave you the easy pocket version of our most important commandments."

The rest of the team had settled around the table, Pepper joining them. Jack couldn't help but smile even harder. Her expression showed complete contentment, and he was the one who'd put it there.

The new guy, Colby, observed the interplay at the end of the table like he was watching a tennis match, his dark eyes bouncing back and forth, his shaved military haircut a mere buzz of black over his head. The tattoo covering one muscular arm stood out against his mocha skin, and he would've made a seriously deadly picture if not for the one line of ink at the bottom of the tat—the one that read *Mom*.

Jack liked the guy, whose charming smiles came fast and easy.

"I don't know what I'm more curious about," Colby said with a dimpled grin. "The pocket version of the rules, or how you ended up naked when you were supposed to be gathering recon on a *librarian*?"

"Ooh, Colby!" Didi turned with a smile. "What a good boy you are. I'll make sure I get you a set. I was at a scrapbooking party and decided it would be a fun way to help everyone remember the rules. I even found the cutest little sticker to go with 'no recording devices'."

Dean groaned. "Is that why I have cut-out flowers and sparkles all over the damn thing?"

"Language, Mr. Colter. How many times do I have to remind you?"

"With Dean? At least a million more," Parker offered. "Spill the details, or let's get on with it. We've got work to do."

"I don't know what you're all making such a fuss about. The mark went into a massage center. I followed her. End of story."

"Nearly end," Gillian teased. "For some reason Dean decided he needed to actually get a full-body massage, which meant when the fire alarm went off and the building was evacuated, he ended up outside wearing nothing but a towel." Her dark eyes twinkled at Jack before she went back to complete seriousness. "It wasn't his fault that woman tripped and ended up pulling his towel off."

"And on today's agenda...?" Dean lifted his head from where he'd rested it in his hands while Gillian spoke. "Parker, do you mind?"

Jack's best friend had grown soft, his recent love life mellowing him—Parker took pity on Dean and changed the topic.

"Three major projects we're working on." Parker nodded in his direction. "Jack, Charlene is supposed to be in the office this afternoon with more information about the end-of-summer gala. Pepper, if you can take some time from your other assignments to sit in with them that would be great. Charlene has more ideas for that slideshow, and I'd love to get your opinion of how we can best execute them."

"Okeydokey with me." Pepper held up a file folder in the air. "I'm working on the brochures and flyers you requested. I need to know, does anybody need new business cards?"

Gillian and Colby held up their hands, as well as Didi.

Pepper turned to Jack. "You already have something?"

"The three of us got cards made up the first year. I'm good."

"What about for Big—?"

Shit.

"No problems with the gala birthday," Jack interrupted, the feigned look of innocence on Pepper's face all too clearly showing what she had planned on asking. *Minx.*

While the rest of the meeting was fairly standard, Jack was very cognizant of two things. One, he was glad Colby and Gillian had joined the crew as the workload before him dwindled to manageable amounts. Especially considering the second thing—he had nowhere near gotten Pepper out of his system. He swore he could smell her skin even though she sat down the table from him. Every time the woman spoke it was like she was running her fingers up the back of his neck. Or over his cock.

In fact, walking down the hallway after the meeting into his office, his mind was full of pretty much nothing except ways to get her to join him for a quickie. Desk sex sounded damn good right about then.

He hadn't had nearly enough time to work up a good plan when Parker stuck his head around the doorframe. Jack shoved all the dirty fantasies aside and focused on conveying a "do not let it show on my face that I'm thinking about rocking your sister's world" look to his best friend. "Can I help you?"

"If you have some time before you meet with Charlene, could you help me do something about the smell outside the back door?"

"Smell?" Jack strode to the door and joined Parker as they headed to the back. "Are you talking about in the parking area? I parked out front today."

"I think we all did. I only noticed when I went to grab some stuff for Pepper from the storage shed."

"Don't blame me." Pepper looked up with interest from where she'd set up her computers in the staff area near the back door. She rose to her feet and followed them. "I didn't do it."

Her brother sighed. "I didn't accuse you of anything."

"But you *looked* at me funny."

"For fuck's sake, don't start that again, Pepper."

Pepper grinned. "I'm telling Mom you swore."

Even though it was lighthearted, Jack still felt an edge of unease along his spine as the two siblings bantered. It was like walking into a time machine, the good and the horrific. He ignored the worst memories and tried to focus on the childishness of what he was hearing. "If one of you tries the 'he started it' spiel, I'm telling your mom myself."

Parker pushed open the back door, and a dose of fragrance hit Jack like a two-by-four. He must have grunted, or made some kind of noise, because Parker pulled him forward rapidly, Pepper joining them. She shoved the door shut and they didn't stop moving until they were standing in the middle of the parking lot behind the building.

"It's rather overwhelming, isn't it?" Parker asked.

Jack's eyes were watering. "What is it?"

"Lilacs. Definitely lilacs." Pepper fanned a hand in front of her nose. "You do have a higher standard of garbage in this area, don't you?"

It made no sense. Jack glanced around, but there was nothing there that explained the smell. The dumpster was down at the end of the alleyway, and he couldn't imagine what would possibly make it smell like an explosion in a perfume factory. "Someone throw a perfume bottle at the side of the building?"

Parker took a deep breath before moving forward, rapidly examining the area at the base of the brick wall before sprinting back to their side, a shard of purple glass held gingerly between two fingers. "You're brilliant."

"Oh God. Get rid of it." Pepper caught hold of her nose, pinching it tight. "I love that scent, but this is way too much even for me."

Parker hightailed it toward the dumpster, while Jack examined the wall more carefully. "That's the answer. Someone threw a bottle against the wall."

Beside him, Pepper stiffened slightly. "Oh, shit." She turned to Jack, catching hold of the front of his shirt. "I wonder...if this was my fault."

Behind them, Parker was back. He cleared his throat. "You want to explain that a little more clearly?"

Pepper's usual devil-may-care attitude cooled slightly. "I'm sure it's nothing. But..."

Jack slipped his arms around her. He ignored the fact that Parker was glaring just over her shoulder. "If you've got something that sheds light on this, say it now."

She had her stubborn face on. "I don't want to say anything and get someone in trouble for no reason. What if we check the security tapes first?"

He caught her chin in his hand and tilted her head up until she had to meet his gaze. "Pepper. Who do you think did this?"

"One of the guys I traveled with seems to have some issues. I didn't think he knew how to get ahold of me, but when Kendra returned my suitcases the other day there were some things missing. Including a makeup bag that might have had perfume in it. Lilacs."

Parker was no longer standing quietly behind him. "You're telling us someone is stalking you? That's unacceptable."

"No shit, Einstein." Pepper twirled on her brother. "I don't like the idea, either. But it's pretty childish, throwing my stuff at your building, and I'm still not about to accuse *anyone* until we have some proof. So let's go look at the security tapes."

Only when they cued them up, the tapes showed nothing but static for the previous twelve hours.

"How the hell is that possible?" Jack demanded. He had no idea what was going on, but the idea that someone could have it in for Pepper made his blood freeze.

Pepper pointed to the time signature. "You've got a digital security system that's a dinosaur. The scans are easy to corrupt if you've got enough interference in the area. Somebody shut down your system before they did this."

"Seems like a hell of a lot of work just to throw some perfume at our back door," Dean commented, having joined them in the staff room.

"Unfortunately, it's not really that difficult." Pepper poked the recording device they were examining. "Since your system is so ancient, it wouldn't take too much knowledge to knock this out even from a distance."

"It's still a lot more work than simply walking up and spraying graffiti. Somebody planned." Parker turned on Pepper. "That's it. I'm escorting you to work every day until we figure this out."

"No way," Pepper snapped. "I mean, fine that you're worried, even though I think it's just some stupid one-off event, if it is Adam. I still don't understand how it could be him in the first place—he didn't know my real name, so I don't know how he could've tracked me down to my new job. But if it *is* him, I don't need you babysitting me."

"Of course you don't need Parker looking after you," Jack interrupted. "You get me instead."

It was Parker's turn to stiffen in dismay briefly before nodding. "Surveillance is yours. Ask for backup if you need a hand."

No way was anyone going to touch Pepper, not with Jack on the job. "I'll take it from here."

Parker left abruptly, Dean hard on his heels as they headed toward the front of the building.

Pepper leaped in front of Jack, catching hold of the front of his shirt and jerking his head down toward her level. Her bright green eyes flashed with furious frustration. "I don't like it when you talk about me like I'm not right. Fucking. Here."

"I don't like it that someone out there might have it in for you."

She rolled her eyes. "They threw a bottle of perfume. I'm in danger of asphyxiation, not of being kidnapped and sold as a sex slave. And I don't mind being more careful for a while, but you really need to stop trying this alpha-hole business on me. I will cut off your balls, and you can take that literally or not, however you prefer."

He inched closer, his lips brushing her ear. "You're unbelievably sexy when you're pissed off."

Disbelief dripped from her tone. "Seriously? You're hitting on me? In the staff break room?"

Slowly and methodically, he backed her up against the wall as his arms came down on her waist to tug her closer. "Ha. Like you haven't thought about it too all frickin' morning."

To his relief, the anger in her expression dissipated. Darkened with heat. "I'm not going to deny it. But there's a reason I haven't jumped your bones today."

He arched a brow. "Yeah? Why's that?"

"Because it's *unprofessional.*"

Jack blinked before barking out a laugh. Now *there* was a word he hadn't thought existed in Pepper Wilson's vocabulary. The woman was all about whims, act first and think later—since when did she care about showing any restraint?

"Don't laugh at me," she grumbled. "I may not particularly want to work here, but as long as I am, I'm not going to give my brother any ammunition against me. He already thinks I'm an impulsive airhead."

"He doesn't think that." Jack came to his friend's defense, as he always did.

And Pepper frowned, as *she* always did when he defended Parker. "Yes, he does." She gave his chest a tiny shove, sidestepping away from him. "So keep those pants zipped, Jackjack. There won't be any office shenanigans, capiche?"

He knew better than to argue with that steely look in her eyes. "Capiche," he said with a sigh.

She brightened. "Good. Now let's go meet with your ex-lover, *sugar.*"

Jack stifled a groan as he remembered the meeting with Charlene. Shit. The last thing he wanted was for Pepper and his former fling to be in the same room together. But since he didn't exactly have much of a choice, he sighed again and followed Pepper to the conference room.

JACK LIKED redheads. Redheads with big boobs, Pepper amended as she examined Charlene Halliwell from head to toe. She supposed she ought to be flattered that she too fell under the category of *Jack Hunter's Type*, but it was impossible to stop the rush of jealousy that seized her.

Especially since the visible evidence of Jack's preferences raised the old chicken-and-egg conundrum. Had Jack hooked up with the redheaded Charlene because she reminded him of Pepper?

Or was it the other way around?

The thought that it could be the latter boiled Pepper's blood, prompting her to greet their client in a much sharper tone than intended. "I'm Pepper," she said tightly, thrusting out her hand. "I'm the one handling all the media displays for your parents' party, including digitizing any older photos and memorabilia."

Charlene seemed to be fighting a smirk as she leaned in to shake Pepper's hand. "Pleasure to meet you, sweetie. I've seen what you've done so far, and I'm very pleased."

Sweetie?

Oh *hell* no. The word *sweetie* was reserved only for Pepper's mother and grandparents. When other women called you that, it was an outright sign that you were being patronized.

"Well, bless your heart, *hon*, I'm so glad you like it," Pepper responded.

The two women stared at each other for a moment, until Jack cleared his throat and gestured to the table. "Why don't we have a seat and go over everything?"

They settled in their chairs, Pepper flopping directly next to Jack, leaving no question as to who belonged at his side. It was a childish move, she knew that, but it got the desired result—Charlene's eyes gleamed with displeasure as she was forced to sit across from them.

"All right, so why don't you tell Pepper about the slideshow additions you had in mind," Jack told Charlene.

Looking as if she'd rather talk to Hannibal Lecter, Charlene turned to Pepper and began in a curt voice, quickly explaining everything she needed done. Pepper dutifully scribbled notes on a yellow legal pad, nodding and cutting in with ideas and suggestions every so often. It was all very aboveboard and professional, but the catty undercurrent continued to run beneath the surface as the two women interacted.

Pepper hated Charlene. The woman was smart and articulate and gorgeous and she *clearly* still had a thing for Jack. She smiled at him way too much. And at one point, she even reached across the table and squeezed his hand when he offered a brilliant solution to getting extra pictures from family and friends delivered in a timely manner.

Pepper had to stop herself from slapping the woman's hand with her ballpoint pen. Jealousy simmered through her veins, more powerful than she'd ever experienced in her life, mingled in with a peculiar, soul-crushing sense of inferiority that made her throat close up. Charlene was Jack's age. She was experienced and sophisticated, and not a single word she said seemed to come out without careful thought beforehand.

Just being around the woman made Pepper feel like...like... A child? Like she might not be good enough for Jack?

But that was ridiculous. They *were* good together. So what if she was younger than him? So what if she didn't have Charlene's elegance and perfectly manicured talons?

Still, by the time the meeting wrapped up, Pepper was overcome with relief. The three of them headed for the door, where Charlene stopped to shoot Pepper a sweet—no, a *dangerous*—smile.

"So you just finished college, huh? You must be excited to be done with school."

Pepper nodded warily. "Yeah, I am."

"And now you're joining the workforce," the woman said brightly, all too eager to remind Pepper of her inexperienced place in the world. "That must be exciting for you, too."

Condescending much?

Pepper had to grit her teeth to avoid making a blatantly nasty remark. "It is." The smirk, she couldn't fight. "Especially since I'm working *so* closely with Jack."

A flare of anger lit Charlene's eyes. "Yes, I imagine that's an added bonus." She checked the delicate silver watch strapped to her wrist. "I should get going. Jack, always a pleasure." She practically purred the word *pleasure*, before her voice sharpened. "And we'll schedule another meeting in a few days, sweetie. If you're done by then you can show me the first draft of the presentation."

"Sure thing, ma'am," Pepper chirped.

With a look of irritation, Charlene disappeared down the hallway, perfect ass swaying seductively as her high heels clicked on the floor.

There was a beat of silence, and then Jack glanced over with an incredulous look. "What...was *that?*"

Pepper feigned innocence. "What was what?"

"You. Scowling at her the whole time. Calling her 'hon' and 'ma'am'. Implying you like working here because it gives you the opportunity to bone me." He shot her a dark look. "When twenty minutes ago, you laid down the no-boning law."

She shrugged. "I have no idea what you're talking about. I was very polite to your precious Charlene."

Pepper took off, crossing her fingers he would leave it at that, but it was too much to hope that Jack Hunter would shy away from a confrontation. She was halfway down the hall when he tugged on her arm and shoved her through the open doorway of his office. He closed the door and turned to her with folded arms.

"You were not polite," he said flatly. "You were being—pardon my French—a total dick."

She bristled. "Gee, excuse me for not rolling out the red carpet for the woman you were sleeping with before me."

Jack's brown eyes narrowed, and then understanding dawned. "Shit. You're jealous." A husky laugh slipped from his mouth, laced with pure satisfaction. "Your little claws came out, eh, Candy

150

Cane? Drove you nuts to think about me and her getting it on, didn't it?"

The green-eyed monster reared its ugly head again, this time slashing forward with razor sharp nails. Pepper took a breath, trying to quell the images of Jack and Charlene in bed together, but a few had already flashed to mind, and she found her hands curling into fists.

"I swear to God, Jackjack," she ground out, "if you don't kiss me in the next two seconds, I'm going to fly into a rage."

He was laughing as he closed the distance between them, stopping when his mouth was inches from hers. "You need some validation, is that it? You need me to prove you're the only woman I'm interested in?"

"Yes," she said through clenched teeth. Maybe it was juvenile and needy of her, but damn it, seeing the splendor that was Charlene Halliwell had done a number on her confidence.

"Well, tough." Jack's lips hovered over hers briefly before he took a firm step back. "You're not getting off that easy."

Her jaw fell open. "You're really not going to kiss me?"

"Why would I? It goes against your rules of professionalism," he said mockingly.

"I changed my mind."

"Even so, I'm not about to reward you for being rude to our client." His eyes gleamed. "You were a bad girl, Pepper. Bad girls need to be punished, not rewarded."

Her pulse kicked up a notch. The wicked look on his face was both terrifying and promising.

"So if I accept my punishment like a good girl, will I be rewarded then?" She tipped her head, locking her gaze with his.

Jack's tongue slid out to sweep across his bottom lip. "Maybe."

"Fine. Then let's get started. Punish me, Jack." She licked her lips, too, knowing how hot it got him to see her do that.

Sure enough, a glance at his groin revealed the thickening bulge beneath his fly. His eyes burned hotter, heavy-lidded and intense as he pointed to the sofa. "Take your pants off and bend over the back of the couch. Now."

As her heart pounded furiously, she took a deep breath and did exactly what he asked.

Chapter Nine

JACK WASN'T sure if he was more pissed off or entertained by the whole situation. He really should be a lot firmer with Pepper. No way should she treat a client like—and then he couldn't think straight because her pants had already hit the floor.

Pepper twisted her butt toward him, her barely there panties covering a miniscule amount of the smooth curves, especially when she put her stomach against the back of the couch exactly as ordered. She bent forward, wiggling until her toes were off the ground. He was mesmerized by the thin line of blue fabric curling in on itself and disappearing between her cheeks. Fuck, he might even be able to see a glimpse of pussy lips.

She glanced over her shoulder, absolutely no contriteness in her expression whatsoever. He didn't give a single solitary fuck. He'd wanted to do this for days.

"Bad girls need to be punished," he repeated, closing in so he could grab hold of her hips. The thin side straps of her thong lay under his fingers, delicate enough he could snap them without any effort whatsoever.

"So you say." Pepper stretched upward, letting loose an exaggerated yawn as she covered her mouth with one hand. "Go ahead. Get on with it. I can't imagine—"

He brought his hand down sharply, the sound of his palm meeting the soft surface echoing sharply off the office walls, mingling with her sudden gasp. She slammed her fingers over her mouth to stifle a scream.

Jack moved his hand slowly. Her skin heated up as he tugged the scrap of fabric aside, rubbing gently where he'd hit. "There are a few things you've been naughty about."

"I let you smack my ass," Pepper complained, squirming under him. "That's the only thing I've done wrong."

"Really? That's all? Hmm." He hoisted her hips even higher, and she rumbled in surprise as her torso slipped entirely over the couch back. She was now held precariously in position with only Jack's grip to keep her from tumbling all the way onto the seat cushions. "I'll have to remind you so you can learn your lessons like a good girl."

He brought his hand down sharply three times in a row, in a slightly different spot every time. The creamy surface of her skin went a pretty pink color, tiny noises escaping her lips on each strike. When he paused, she wiggled against him as if looking for more.

The urge to fuck her was a driving need throughout his entire body, but first they had some unfinished business, and this was as good a moment as any.

"You were very bad last night. Telling me out of the blue we didn't need a condom," Jack scolded.

"Really?" Pepper sighed mightily. "My naked ass in your face, and this is the topic—?"

He landed another sharp smack, and another, not giving her time to snark any further. "And as excited as I am at the news, you *never* simply take someone's word. Not about something as important as safe sex."

She stiffened. "I wouldn't. Not with just anyone. But this is you."

The idea of another guy getting his cock anywhere near Pepper was enough to send a flash of red-hot anger through Jack. Still, he shoved the jealousy aside—he had no idea where this thing between them would end up, so in spite of wanting to go all caveman on her and start issuing ownership papers regarding her pussy, the lesson had to sink in so she'd never ever be so stupid again.

"I'm glad you trust me, but don't take chances. Not with something that could mean your life. Get proof, or use a condom."

"Yes, Jack." It was the most apologetic and sincere statement he'd heard from her in a long time. Their eyes met for a brief second, and it was clear she'd gotten the message.

The heat of the past minutes had been temporarily banked, but she was right. With her nearly naked ass right there before him, it was time to play. He knew exactly how to get the fire roaring again. He bent over and pressed a kiss to one smooth butt cheek.

Pepper snorted. "So eager to kiss my ass, Jack?"

"Fucking right, I am." But the next time he put his teeth to her, biting lightly as she sucked in a quick breath. He used his tongue as he moved to the opposite side, giving it the same treatment. A kiss. A quick nip. A lave of his tongue to cool the spot.

Every time he moved to a new location she twisted in reaction, the hand he'd placed against her lower back barely containing her squirming as he paid attention to the crease where her leg met ass.

He avoided her pussy, but it was damn obvious she was wet, the rich scent of her arousal taunting him. Jack shot to his feet and cracked a hand down again, the strike a sharp contrast to the sensual tease of a moment earlier.

Pepper moaned, and his groin responded instantly to the throaty noise, his cock attempting to burst free from his jeans.

"Good girls don't deliberately taunt their coworkers," Jack muttered softly.

"I promise to stop flirting with Gillian."

Jack laughed then ignored everything else to focus on driving her mad. He didn't think she'd done this before, not from her comments, but was she ever responsive. His palm connected with her ass again and again. With each spank Pepper's breath escaped with a tiny puff, low and throaty and utterly wicked. As if she were stroking his cock on every single exhale.

He lowered his aim and landed a strike over her pussy, and this time her gasp rolled into a moan that nearly undid him.

"*Jack*. What...? Oh, *God*..."

She opened her thighs slightly, tilting her pelvis upward like an offering, and he couldn't hold back any longer. He caught hold of her thong, peeling the soaking scrap of fabric off between her legs. The lips of her labia were puffy and wet as he dropped behind her and buried his face in the paradise between her thighs. He lapped over every delectable inch, fucking his tongue into her pussy as deep as it would go.

He could stay there all day and be a happy man. Licking and teasing and soaking in the taste of her. Listening to the sounds of pleasure she fought desperately to keep at a low volume.

Except his cock was compressed behind a far too unyielding fabric, and the longer Pepper made those damn noises, the less chance there was he'd be able to hold back from ripping open his jeans and shoving his cock into her welcoming heat.

And *that* wasn't any kind of deterrent, thinking about being surrounded by the tight heaven of her body.

Distraction. He needed a distraction really badly. He tore himself away from her, moving to the side so he could lean over the back of the couch beside her.

She turned her head toward him, cheeks flushed, eyes wide and bright. So open and honest and fucking beautiful his heart skipped a beat.

He was so damn turned on his cock attempted another impossible escape. She licked her lips, and the sheen of moisture on them drew him in. He pressed their mouths together and kissed her briefly. Hard and intense, before he jerked away, their eyes still locked.

"Count," he demanded.

A little furrow appeared on her forehead. "Count...?"

He stepped behind her again, his hand skimming her ass in a smooth circle. "Count to ten. Once every time I spank you, and *then*, if you're good, I'll give you my cock."

Pepper swallowed hard. Nodded, just the briefest of motions.

He paused, slipping his fingers over her pussy. Sliding through the wetness to graze his fingertips over her clit ever so slowly. And when he slipped a finger into her, moisture coating him as she moaned loudly, he wasn't sure which of them he was punishing more by prolonging the playtime.

"Jack," she begged, twisting around to look at him. "For God's sake, hurry up and spank me. I need you inside me."

"That's not counting."

"Fuck." She took a deep breath, her muscles clamping down on his finger in a far too enticing move. For a second Jack wondered if he could survive the game he'd set before them. Then, thank God, she relaxed and faced the other way again. "I can't count until you start."

Jack adjusted his stance to keep his left hand on her pussy, circling his fingers over her clit while slipping his thumb inside her wetness. A second after he had finished the adjustment, his right hand made contact with her ass again.

"One." The word came out low and husky, her sex-soaked voice rushing over his nerves like the first hit for a drug addict who'd been deprived for months.

Jack paused for long enough to dance his fingertips over her clit, not so much rubbing as pushing down on the sensitive nub, while Pepper wiggled her ass towards him, attempting to spear herself harder on the single digit inside her passage.

This was so damn hot he was going to lose control sooner rather than later. He hurriedly applied another slap against her left cheek, two in succession following it.

Pepper gasped out the countdown, purring in satisfaction as he followed up and used his hand to tease her clit and rub the tender entrance to her pussy.

Their entire world narrowed down to there and then. Jack didn't give a shit that they were standing in his office with his coworkers, including his best friend, somewhere just outside the four walls. He'd said it before—they were adults, him and Pepper, and if what they chose to do was fuck each other's brains out in the privacy of his office, that's what they were going to damn well do.

"FIVE." PEPPER got the word out with great difficulty. It was as if all the mental processes required for speaking had melted away because of the inexplicable volume of pleasure rolling through her. And it wasn't just the physical part, although, holy macaroni, she'd had no idea what a turn-on spanking was. The first time Jack had put his hand to her ass she'd already been one second away from coming.

With every strike since she'd had to make a conscious effort to hold off the mother of all orgasms that was hovering, ready to knock her feet out from under her and leave her in a whimpering pile on the floor.

Or worse than that would be her screaming his name loud enough that everyone in the office would know they weren't just having a "quote unquote" business discussion.

Damn Jack Hunter to hell for being a sex god. Damn him, yet at this moment she was more than happy to worship the man's skills in rocking her world.

She only had five more spanks to go, and as the next landed, Pepper found herself gasping *six*, immediately followed by *seven* and *eight* as Jack managed to not only hit all the erogenous zones in her ass, but the talented man kept using his fingers at the same time. Fucking her, and tearing apart everything she was using to stabilize herself.

How had she reached the age of twenty-three without knowing she had erogenous zones back there? Who cared, they were there, and he was...

Jack paused. Again. The *bastard*.

"Don't stop," she croaked, throat tight from containing the screams of pleasure that wanted to burst free.

But he held off the final two blows. Anticipation hung over them like a tangible thing. Her skin tingled as he pumped his fingers deep inside her, rubbing the front of her passage and making stars appear before her eyes. She knew better than to put her tongue between her teeth for fear she would bite it straight off, so instead she locked her jaw and stared hard at the closet door and prayed he'd get frustrated enough to forget the rest of his threats and instead blow her mind.

She was ready to be fucked. She was oh so ready.

Jack took his hand from between her legs, gripping her ass and massaging the tender cheeks. A low growl escaped him as he slid both thumbs over her labia then teased the entrance to her pussy.

One hand slipped higher. "You ever have anal sex?" he demanded in a harsh whisper.

Oh, Lordy, surely he wouldn't? "Yeah. I like it. It's hot..."

For a second he tightened his grip on her hip, obviously on the verge of losing it. Thank goodness, because so was she. Still, he teased the sensitive nerves between her butt cheeks for just long enough she was ready to flip around and lock her legs around his waist so she could stab herself down on his cock.

"I'm going to fuck your ass sometime. Not here, not now, but someday I want to see my cock sliding into you. You'll take every frickin' bit of me and I'll fuck you so hard you won't be able to sit down for days."

His hand connected with bare skin.

"Nine!" Pepper all but shouted before remembering where they were. She was so turned on the room seemed to waver, the walls moving, the door she was staring at no longer closed, but partially opened.

But as Jack thrust his fingers into her to fuck her rapidly, Pepper realized it was no closet door she was gazing at, but a connection between Jack's office and the one next door.

She tensed, ready to call out a warning when the final slap against her ass hit at the same moment her eyes met Dean's.

"Ten," Pepper moaned.

That wasn't what she'd intended to say. It wasn't *stop* or *wait* or *get the hell out of here*, because finishing the countdown was the only thing that mattered even as she stared into the shocked gray eyes of her boyfriend's partner while he stood motionless behind the narrow gap as if unable to turn away.

And then there was no other chance to protest because Jack had the hard head of his cock pressed to her opening. He gripped her hips tightly and with one thrust buried himself deep.

"God, *yes...*" she hissed, hands clutching the leather seat. Trapped by her need for completion as Jack slammed his hips forward, fucking her as if he were possessed. Nothing around them now but the sounds of their heavy breathing and the wet moisture where their bodies joined.

And Dean observing from the doorway.

She was all kinds of twisted, because it should have felt like a creeper was watching them, but the expression in Dean's eyes as he gazed hungrily into the room—she couldn't stop an enormous shudder of intense desire from rocking through her body.

Between all that had come before, and the relentless pounding from Jack's oh-so-skilled thrusts, and the fiery approval with which Dean soaked in their raunchy scene...

Pepper clamped her lips together to stop a scream from escaping as her orgasm took her out, her vision blurring as endorphins slammed into her system so hard she couldn't breathe. She couldn't do anything but accept the pleasure winging through her.

Behind her, Jack groaned, his hips pulsing helplessly as he came as well. Heat flashed hotter inside her, wetter than usual. His strong arms wrapped around and lifted her. Her back glued to his chest as his lips found hers, heads twisted to the side as they gasped for air through the kiss. Bodies held tight together as the room spun.

Pepper kissed him back, reaching up to lock a hand around his neck as he held her vertical. She could have been floating in midair for all she knew.

162

Somehow they ended up on the couch, Jack under her, her naked ass resting in his lap as he held her against his chest and they found their equilibrium. Under her ear his heart pounded, his hands stroking her shoulders gently.

"Wow." Once she could finally take a full breath again, Pepper let out a contented sigh. "That was...freaking *awesome*."

"Dirty girl," Jack teased. "I should have known you'd like the kinky stuff."

Oh hell. His words reminded her of the *other* unforeseen part of the adventure. Pepper's gaze darted to the still-open door, but no one stood there anymore—the hairline crack between rooms revealed nothing but a dark, empty space on the opposite side.

Had she imagined Dean? Not likely.

But she was honest enough to admit it wasn't her imagination exactly how hot it had gotten her to have someone watch.

Jack pressed a kiss to her temple and she smiled. She'd tell him what had happened once they had their clothes straightened out. Meeting up with Dean the next time—maybe she should feel worried or weird, but somehow she thought even that would work out fine.

It was *alllll* fine.

She snickered.

"What?" Jack asked lazily.

"I'm so mellow right now I don't think anything could get me riled up," Pepper confessed.

"Good to know." He caught her by the chin and twisted her face to his so he could give her another kiss, this one languid and thorough, exactly like two people who'd just fucked themselves into a sated post-sex coma.

Issues would be dealt with later. Right now Pepper wasn't worried about anything but relaxing in Jack's embrace.

Lynn

"TOMORROW NIGHT'S a go. I've booked massages for us at seven o'clock." Suz's cheerful voice chirped over the extension before Lynn even had a chance to say hello.

Rolling her eyes, Lynn balanced her cell phone on her shoulder as she peeled off the tinfoil covering last night's lasagna. "Hi, Suz. I'm great. How are you?"

"We've known each other for more than a decade, hon. I think we're past the whole pleasantry bullshit."

"Good point." Lynn pursed her lips and stared at the casserole dish. There were only two decent-sized servings of lasagna left, not nearly enough to satisfy Parker's voracious appetite. Even if she threw together a salad, it wouldn't stop him from grumbling afterward about how hungry he still was.

165

She headed for the freezer, poking her head inside to see if she could scrounge up some chicken breast or steak. Or both. Lord, that man could eat.

"Anyway, I'll text Pepper the details," Suz was saying. "I swear, girls' night is *absolutely* happening. Nobody is allowed to cancel this time."

"We've all been busy," Lynn answered.

"Uh-huh. If by busy, you're referring to you and Pepper forgetting about us little people because you're getting your rocks off, then sure, you're *busy*."

"Ha. Says the woman who cancelled last week because Tony and Diego flew in."

"Lynn, when you have a standing arrangement with two bisexual pilots who only fly in once or twice a year, that's not considered cancelling. It's called common sense."

"Hey, I'm just saying. You can't begrudge me and Pepper our very active sex lives."

"Oh, Pepper's been *active*, all right." Suz's admiration echoed over the line, a hint of jealousy in her voice. "I always suspected Jack knew his way around the bedroom, but every time I get on the phone with the girl, the stories she tells blow me away. *Me*, the *inventor* of kinky sex. Did she tell you how a few weeks ago, Jack spanked her in the office without realizing Dean was watching them?"

Lynn grinned to herself as she grabbed a tray of chicken breast from the freezer. Maybe they hadn't gotten together very often, but she and Pepper were chatting on a regular basis. "Yup."

"And then when Jack found out Dean had stumbled on their spank fest, he got so worked up he did her right there in the apartment pool. Lordy, some girls have all the luck."

Lynn snorted. "Bisexual pilots, babe. That's all I have to say to that. But I do love hearing you all jealous. Pepper and Jack's escapades remind you of your glory days, huh?" She couldn't help but needle her friend a bit more. "Poor Susanna, growing slow and tame, while young'uns like Pepper get freaky action in offices and public spaces and—" At the sound of footsteps nearing the kitchen doorway, Lynn's mouth snapped closed.

Parker strode in a second later, his green eyes narrowing. "What?" he demanded.

"Suz, I've gotta go," she told her friend. "The boyfriend's home."

"Ugh. You are *so* cock whipped. I still love you, though. Later, hon."

Lynn hung up and set the cell phone on the counter, while Parker's suspicious gaze bore a hole into her face.

"Why'd you stop talking the second I walked in?" he said warily. "You keeping secrets from me, sweetheart?"

"Nope." She looped her arms around his neck, then leaned up to brush a kiss over his lips. "We're having lasagna and grilled chicken for dinner. And a salad. Are you cool with that?"

She should've known better than to think her big, stubborn man would drop the subject. "What were you and Suz talking about?"

Lynn stifled a sigh. "I'm not telling you."

Chiseled features hardened to stone. "Why not?"

"Because it's not something you want to hear."

His expression became downright petulant. "But I'm the *boyfriend*. You just said so. That's one of the perks a man has when he's in a relationship—he gets to hear all the latest gossip and not be judged for *wanting* to hear it."

Resting her palms on the center of his broad chest, Lynn arched a brow. "Fine. We were talking about Jack and Pepper and all the wild, kinky sex they've been—"

"Stop!" Parker shouted, his hands shooting up to cover his ears. "Don't you say another fucking word, Lynn."

Laughter tickled her throat, then spilled over when she glimpsed the sheer misery on his face. Although Parker seemed to be handling Jack and Pepper's budding relationship fairly well, and with surprising maturity, Lynn knew he still wasn't entirely comfortable that his best friend was dating his little sister.

"See, I was trying to spare you!" she protested between giggles. "I *told* you it wasn't something you wanted to know."

His arms slid down and crossed over his chest, a dark look clouding his eyes. "As far as I'm concerned, my sister is a virgin. And that's all I'm ever gonna say on the subject."

Swallowing a laugh, she gave him another kiss. "I'm glad you didn't say 'she wears a chastity belt', because from what I hear, I think Jack could open any lock, in the dark, while handcuffed—"

"Lynn!" Two seconds later her wrists were behind her back, Parker's fingers carefully but firmly trapping her in position. Her breasts were pressed to his rock-hard torso, and the rough contact sucked a little noise of pleasure from her lips.

His eyes flashed with heat. Suddenly all teasing and gossip and dinner plans were forgotten as her eager boyfriend dragged her to their living room and made her glad all over again that she was his.

Chapter Ten

JACK SHOWED up at Pepper's apartment earlier than planned. They'd arranged to go out for a late dinner so he could do some recon on the girlfriend of a new client beforehand, but it hadn't taken long to gather all the info he needed for DreamMakers to organize the perfect date. Some women were *that* easy to figure out, broadcasting their personalities like neon lights.

Other women—one Pepper Wilson, for example— were chock full of surprises. In the past three weeks, he'd discovered sides to Pepper he'd never expected. Like her penchant for kinky, kinky sex—which he didn't mind one damn bit. Or her surprising amount of bubbly energy first thing in the morning—which he *did* mind, because he preferred to stay curled up in bed for as long as

170

humanly possible. Plus there was her total obsession with trying new scented soaps and creams, which meant with how up close and personal they were getting, half the time he smelled like he'd been present when a bomb went off in a flower shop.

Of course, the one thing that didn't surprise him was her argumentative nature. It was exasperating and infuriating and goddamn sexy. He found himself looking forward to doing verbal combat with her, especially since their bickering always resulted in explosive sex that blew his mind.

The raunchy memories brought a grin to his lips as he rapped his knuckles on Pepper's door. He'd texted her to let her know he was heading over early. He hadn't heard back, but since Pepper was notoriously terrible at responding to texts, he'd come anyway, knowing she wouldn't care about the change of plans.

When the door swung open, he realized why she hadn't responded.

"Jack," Kendra greeted him in surprise. "Hey. Are you here to see Pepper? Because she's not back yet."

He couldn't mask his disappointment. "Oh. Where'd she go?"

"Out for a run." Kendra opened the door wider. "Come wait inside. She shouldn't be too much longer."

He followed the petite blonde into the apartment, smiling at the overflowing shoe rack braced against the wall in the front hall. A multitude of footwear was crammed into the small space, and when Kendra followed his gaze, she let out a laugh.

"Pepper and I have way too many shoes," she said, sighing. "The closet is jam-packed with them, too. I think we need a better system."

"Maybe I can build you guys something," he offered. "Some built-in shelves for the closet or something."

She looked impressed. "You can do that?"

"Sure. I'll take some measurements and see what I can come up with."

"I didn't know you knew how to build stuff."

He shrugged. "My dad did some construction on the weekends whenever we were strapped for cash. Sometimes I'd come along to his job sites."

Kendra nodded. "That's cool. I wish I was handier, but I can't even use a hammer without hurting myself."

Jack chuckled, sweeping his gaze over her tiny frame, which was clad in a short blue sundress with white polka dots. "Ah, don't worry. You're too cute for manual labor, anyway."

Her cheeks turned a rosy shade of pink as she twined a lock of hair around her finger. "Ha. So you're telling me to just sit there and look pretty?"

The two of them laughed as they headed into the living room. It had a lot more furniture than the last time he'd stopped by. The end tables on either side of the couch were new, and he noticed that Pepper had hung some photographs over the TV unit. He could tell they were hers—her love of bright colors and quirky subject matter were her trademark.

"Do you want something to drink?" Kendra asked as he settled on the couch. "We've got orange juice, water, and a couple of beers, I think."

"Naah, I'm good." He swiped the remote off the coffee table. "I'll just channel surf until she gets here."

"Cool." Kendra hesitated. "I was on the phone when you knocked. Do you mind if I leave you here so I can call my friend back?"

"No prob."

"Okay. I'll be in my room if you need me."

As Pepper's roommate hurried off, Jack switched on the television and scrolled through the list of channels until he located ESPN, then leaned back to watch the week's baseball highlights. The sound of Kendra's voice wafted in from the hallway, and he frowned at the distress in her tone. He was about to raise the TV volume when he heard Pepper's name.

"...how to tell Pepper. She's going to be *mortified!*"

Jack didn't make a habit of eavesdropping, but Kendra's agitated remark brought a rush of uneasiness. He warily rose from the sofa and crept down the narrow corridor toward the bedrooms, then paused near the door Kendra had left ajar.

"Maybe I shouldn't say anything," Pepper's friend was murmuring. "It's not like she's on Facebook, anyway, so she probably won't find out about it." A long pause. "I know, but she'll be furious." Another pause. "Ugh. You're right. I have...tell her."

Kendra was talking more softly now, so Jack took another step toward the door—and the floor beneath his feet creaked so loudly he froze.

In the bedroom, Kendra stopped abruptly, then spoke again. "Mags, I've gotta go. I'll call you back in a bit."

Jack swallowed a curse as hurried footsteps snapped toward the door. He had nowhere to hide and no time to sprint back to the living room, and when Kendra appeared in front of him, all he could do was offer a sheepish grin.

"Seriously?" she huffed. "You're eavesdropping?"

"I'm sorry. I shouldn't have listened in, but you sounded upset, and..." He shrugged in apology, then met her eyes. "What's going on, Kendra?"

Her hesitation was palpable. "Nothing."

"It didn't sound like nothing," he said firmly. "What happened, and why is Pepper going to be furious?"

Kendra's silence dragged on and on. And on and on. Her teeth dug into her bottom lip, hands fidgeting with the silky fabric of her dress.

Just when Jack was about to voice another demand, Kendra's mouth opened and a defeated breath flew out. "Fine. I'll tell you. Actually, maybe that's better. That way *you* can be the one to break it to Pepper. You know, as her boyfriend."

His chest tightened with alarm. "Break what to Pepper?"

Sighing, Kendra gestured for him to enter her bedroom. Jack stepped inside and followed her to the desk by the window, where a silver laptop sat, the browser open to what he recognized as a Facebook profile page.

"So I'm sure Pepper told you about that guy we were traveling with, right?" Kendra started awkwardly. "Adam? He started a fight with the other guys, the night Pepper got hurt?"

Just thinking about Pepper's cuts and bruises sent a jolt of anger through him. His jaw went so tense all he could offer was a jerky nod.

"Well, this is Adam's Facebook page." Kendra gestured to the screen. "And this is what he posted about an hour ago."

Jack leaned in to study the screen. As he read the paragraph on the page, his eyes widened, but the shock swiftly transformed into a hefty dose of anger. Cursing under his breath, he lifted his head to look at Kendra.

"People actually write shit like this for everyone to see?" he exclaimed.

"Yup," she said glumly. "Social media is the devil."

He shook his head, then reread the words on the screen. His gaze shifted to the profile picture on the corner of the page, which revealed a decent-looking guy with curly black hair, bright eyes, and a cleft chin. Rage bubbled in Jack's gut the longer he stared at the picture. As innocent as he looked, this was the creep who'd caused the fight that Pepper had tried to break up. The asshole who'd given her a black eye. Accident or not, the guy deserved an ass-kicking for putting Pepper in harm's way like that.

"Is any of this true?" he asked Kendra.

She paused before answering. "I'm not sure, but that's not the point. I mean, everyone we went to college with knows Pepper as Penny, so there's not much chance of any of her friends or family here reading this. And she's not on Facebook, so she probably won't care. But all our college friends will see the post, and I'm worried people will start calling her about it, or saying stuff behind her back." Kendra's face collapsed. "I don't know if I should tell her about it."

Kendra looked so upset that Jack couldn't help but reach out and squeeze her slender arm. "Hey, there's no need to freak out this hard. Clearly this guy is hung up on Pepper, he's pissed that she's not into him, and he decided to act like a petulant, spiteful brat and spread gossip about her on the Internet. We'll tell Pepper about it together, and she'll most likely laugh it off. You know her—she doesn't give a shit what people think about her. It's what her friends think that matters."

Concern still lingered in Kendra's eyes. "You're probably right. She's not the type to shoot the messenger."

Jack grinned. "Naah. But she might shoot *him*—" he pointed to the face on the computer screen, "—so it'll be up to you and me to talk her out of any craziness. Deal?"

A hint of a smile lifted Kendra's lips. "Deal."

"Good. Now stop stressing and come watch some baseball highlights with me. And when Pepper gets back—"

The sound of a door slamming, followed by Pepper's cheerful "Helloooooooo, roomie!" interrupted Jack midsentence. His grin widened as the entire mood in the apartment shifted. Pepper had that effect on every person, and every room she was in. Electrifying the air with her larger-than-life personality and mellow attitude.

"Come on," he told Kendra. "Let's go."

This time she squeezed *his* arm, her touch more friendly than intimate, but soft with concern. "What about you?" she said urgently. "Are you okay with this?"

He furrowed his brow. "With what?"

"What he wrote." Kendra lowered her voice. "I mean, if it's true, then…"

"Then nothing," he said easily. "Whatever Pepper did or didn't do before we started dating doesn't affect me."

Kendra paused, then nodded. "Good."

They left the bedroom, entering the living room just as Pepper strode in from the hall. She was wearing the tiniest shorts Jack had ever seen, and a tight tank top damp with sweat clung to her spectacular tits. Maybe it made him a hound dog, but even concerned about breaking the bad news to her, he got semi-hard the second he laid eyes on her.

Pepper arched a brow when she spotted him. "Whatcha doing, Jackjack? I thought we were going out at eight."

"I finished up early." He went over to give her a kiss, forcing himself to keep it brief because her roommate was standing two feet away. "I texted you saying I was coming by."

"Oh. I didn't have my phone on me. I was out for a run." She removed the earphones hanging over her neck, slid off the armband that had been holding her iPod, and tossed both items on the coffee table. Then she popped into the kitchen, returning a second later with her phone in hand. She glanced at the display, frowning in displeasure. "You've got to be kidding me. I have *nine* missed calls from Adam. What does that fucker want now?"

Jack and Kendra exchanged a look, which Pepper didn't miss.

"What?" she demanded. "Why do you two look all guilty?"

Kendra heaved out a sigh. "I'll be right back. Just grabbing my laptop."

After Pepper's friend dashed off, Pepper fixed Jack with a suspicious glare. "What the hell is going on?"

"Your friend Adam is causing trouble again," he admitted. "He wrote something about you on the Internet."

Alarm skittered across her face. "*What?* What did he write?"

Before Jack could fill her in, Kendra hurried back into the room and set her open laptop on the glass table. Pepper wasted no time rushing to the screen, her ponytail falling over her shoulder as she bent over to look at it. Jack saw her back stiffen as she read Adam's post. When she finished, she straightened up and released a string of curses that made him blanch. Lord, the woman could give a sailor a run for his money in the expletive department.

"What. The. *Fuck*." Pepper spun around in anger, her cheeks flushed, green eyes glittering. "How could he put that on the *Internet*? He's Facebook friends with everyone we went to college with!"

Kendra's expression conveyed serious misery. "I know," she moaned. "I couldn't believe it when I saw it."

Pepper looked ready to swear some more, but her phone rang before she could get another word out. She checked the screen, and damn near growled. "Adam again. Probably calling to make sure I know he's a total fucking *asshole*—"

Jack snatched the phone from her hand. "I've got this," he said, his lethal tone brooking no argument. He swiped to answer the call, then raised the cell to his ear. "Adam," he snapped.

There was a beat, followed by a surprised sputter. "Who is this? I'm trying to reach Penny—"

"This is Penny's boyfriend," Jack cut in. "The name's Jack. Jack Hunter. And fun fact—I was an army Ranger. You know what that is, right, Adam?" When the other man didn't respond, Jack went on, keeping his tone pleasant and cool. Maybe icy cold. "It means I can kick your ass three ways to Sunday. Which is precisely what I'm going to do if you ever spread another goddamn rumor about my girlfriend again. Do you understand me, Adam?"

He got a whole lot of stammering in response. "I'm s-sorry! I—I—I don't know why—"

"Shut up and listen," Jack interrupted. "First, you will erase that god-awful post you put up. Second, you're not allowed to call this number anymore. You're not allowed to call her, text her, *think* about her. From this point on, Penny doesn't exist to you. And if I find out you tried contacting her, I will hunt you down and beat you until every bone in your scrawny body is shattered into dust and you're nothing but a mass of blood and pain."

With that, he slammed the *end* button, then tossed the phone back to Pepper, who stood there staring at him with amusement.

Kendra, on the other hand, looked more stunned than amused. "Wow. Remind me never to piss *you* off," she breathed.

Jack shrugged. "It was time someone put that jerk in his place. Let's hope he got the message." A sigh slipped out. "I'm not exactly looking forward to another perfume incident. Took weeks for the stench to go away."

"That might not have been Adam," Pepper protested, but she didn't look convinced, and neither was Jack.

A sudden beeping noise went off, and Kendra jerked to attention, glancing at her watch in a near panic. "Damn, that's my alarm. I gotta run if I want to make it to my game on time." She flew to Pepper's side to give her a quick squeeze before rushing to the front door and digging into the chaos of the shoe pile. "You going to be okay?" she asked over her shoulder even as she slipped her feet into a pair of strappy things with big pink bows on the toes. "Because, I could—"

179

"Go, geek girl. You can't miss your weekly chance to chase dragons and take over the world," Pepper said. "I'm fine."

Kendra's eyes slipped over Jack, her hesitation clear.

"Get going," Jack affirmed, though he was glad Pepper had such a caring friend looking out for her. "I'm sticking around."

But once Kendra was gone, his concerns still had to be answered. He turned to Pepper and searched her face. "*Are* you okay? Adam posted that shit using your fake name, but it's still a crappy thing to have show up on the Internet."

"I'm fine." She let out a tired breath. "And even if I was online, it's not like I could deny it."

Jack blinked. The mental adjustment was too quick to register. "Wait. You mean that actually happened?"

"Well, I don't know that I'd call myself a 'sex-addicted whore', but the gist of what he wrote was the truth." Her gaze locked with his, almost as if she was daring him to disapprove. "The night I got bruised up and fell down the hill...it happened because Adam walked in on me, Ben, and Dirk—right before the three of us were about to have sex."

PEPPER BRACED herself, prepared to see the support Jack had shown change instantly to disappointment. It was great he'd been all tied up on her behalf, and hell to the yes regarding Adam getting yelled at. She figured the jerk had probably pissed his pants listening to Jack's threats—and after the physical pain she'd dealt with, she was vindictive enough to be just fine with that.

Only as wild as Jack liked her in the sack, she had a feeling he still thought of her as a little girl at times. Innocent, at least until he led her willingly into their next sexual escapade.

Well, maybe he didn't expect virginal white, but he probably never dreamed she had fantasies about experimenting with more than one guy in her bed.

Jack stood dead still in the middle of the living room, his face unreadable as he examined her carefully.

She waited for the hammer to fall.

Something went dark in his eyes, but it didn't look as if he was about to toss her aside. "Pepper."

"Jack?"

He closed the distance between them. Staring down at her intently. "I thought you fell down a hill."

"I did," she insisted, "right after Adam was a jackass and stormed in and demanded they get their grubby paws off me."

Even thinking back made her cheeks heat up. She'd worked for simply ages to convince the guys she really was interested in trying out the two-at-once thing. Thus her distracted march in the dark when Adam screwed things up so royally.

"Done a lot of threesomes, have you?" Jack asked. Every word carefully enunciated, his body utterly still as if he were waiting for the opportune moment to pounce on his prey.

It wasn't judgment in his tone, for which Pepper was very grateful, but there was something there that made her tread warily. She curled her arms around his waist so she could rest her forehead against his chest, speaking her confession toward the floor.

"I never have, but the idea intrigued me. And I thought I'd worked out all the angles. Made sure it was safe, even while I had a little fun. But I guess I wasn't as good a judge of character as I thought. And it was such a disaster that I want to forget the entire thing. Some fantasies aren't meant to be experienced, I guess."

Jack's fingers buried in her hair, his thumb stroking back and forth in a caress that seemed to envelop her entire body. "Sounds as if this Adam is a complete jackass. That type is sometimes hard to spot."

She nodded, suddenly aware she was sweaty and stinky and still wearing her running gear. Everything about the last fifteen minutes felt unclean. Everything, that was, except Jack and how he'd treated her. She lifted her gaze to meet his, smoothing a hand along his strong, chiseled jaw, the short bristles of his five o'clock shadow scratching the palm of her hand. "I'm glad you're not mad at me."

"Nothing to be mad about."

He stood at attention, though, every muscle braced as if ready for an attacker to strike at any moment. Pepper was okay with the bit of awkwardness. She got it—he'd had a shock. Hopefully he'd get over it quickly, but there wasn't much she could do at this point except wait and see.

She lifted up on her tiptoes to press a kiss to his neck. "I need a shower."

An unexpected hum of approval rumbled under her lips. "I'm good with soap, if you need a hand," Jack offered.

He didn't wait for an answer, simply lifted her into the air as if she weighed nothing. He carried her to the teeny bathroom off her bedroom, then proceeded to show her exactly how good he was with soap and bubbles.

Chapter Eleven

"OH MY God, he didn't."

Pepper whirled away from Suz, snatching up the fluffy robe she'd momentarily discarded to rinse off after their time in the sauna. "Hey, no touching the tushie."

The other woman simply snickered, slipping her own robe around her ample figure and knotting the belt at the front. "I doubt that's what you said to Jack yesterday. Not if that bite mark on your ass means anything."

"Someone bit Pepper on the butt?" Lynn asked. "Well, not *someone*. It's pretty obvious we know whose teeth have been where."

Borderline giggling ensued as Pepper drew herself up as regally as possible and ignored the raunchy comments that continued to fly as the four of them made their way back into the private spa room Suz had arranged.

It had been an incredible night. Especially on the heels of what could have been a complete disaster. Pepper had gone online and poked again at the Facebook page, pleased to discover the damning comments about her were gone. Still, it *was* the Internet. Somewhere out there she expected a screenshot or two were still floating around, but at least Jack was right about one thing. The people who mattered didn't give a damn.

Three of whom she'd just spent the past hour and a half with, getting massaged and mud-bathed and reveling in all kinds of decadence. Kendra and Pepper had been equally hesitant when they'd heard what was planned for the night, but Lynn and Suz had been so insistent and sincere about wanting to treat them it was impossible to not let the older women pick up the charges for the extravagant evening of luxury.

Pepper crawled into the cushiony easy chair and willingly obeyed the spa woman's command to stick her feet into the bucket of warm, sudsy water. She glanced in the massive mirror across from her, pleased beyond measure to finally see her natural hair color again. One of the women at the spa had magically stripped all the black dye away, leaving Pepper's hair unbelievably soft and sparkling with highlights. It had been a long time since she'd last let the red show, but after a couple very subtle comments from Jack, she'd realized it was time.

Enough hiding. Penny was retiring for good. Pepper was back.

Three minutes later, all of the spa workers abandoned the room, leaving the four of them to soak their feet.

A vibrating motion clicked on automatically underfoot, sending water swirling around Pepper's toes. "I can't decide if I like how this feels or if it's freaking me out."

Lynn had leaned back in her chair, eyes closed. "I can take or leave a manicure, but a pedicure is sheer heaven. Worth every penny, and every second, even if I have to push myself through the ticklish moments."

"Yes, because it's such a sacrifice to have people fawning over your feet," Suz teased. "Although I thought you'd be used to it by now, what with how much time Parker spends down there, kneeling between your legs."

No denial from Lynn. Just a mischievous smile.

Pepper snickered. "I don't need more details. I refuse to picture my brother as anything other than a royal pain in the butt."

"You don't want the conversation to go there, either." Suz laughed at her own joke. "You are just setting me up with one straight line after another. We should organize a comedy routine and take this show on the road."

"You should all take pity on the poor woman in the room who's not getting any action," Kendra offered. "And I'm not related to anyone, so I'm not going to get squicked out thinking about anybody doing the nasty."

"She's right," Lynn agreed. "It's got to be Kendra's turn for Prince Charming to come sweep her off her feet. Suz, you've got a billion brothers running around. Lay one on her for a while. Just to take the edge off."

Pepper stared in shock. "Who are you, and what have you done with my sweet nearly sister-in-law to be? That was a filthy comment."

"You said you didn't want to know, but I've got a damn good teacher." Lynn opened her eyes just so she

186

could give Pepper a wink. "And remember, looks can be deceiving."

"Innocent-looking packages sometimes hold the biggest secrets? I can believe that," Suz said. She lifted one foot out of the soaker tub and examined it for a moment before replacing it in the hot water. "All I know for sure is that I will not be acting as matchmaker for any of my brothers. If she'd like an introduction, Kendra will just have to go get herself arrested."

"Because that's the best way to meet a new man?" Lynn demanded. "Get arrested?"

"Hey, it got Pepper hooked up with Jack, in a roundabout way," Suz insisted. She held up fingers one after the other. "The way I see it, she got the parking ticket, icky kisses from icky dude, followed by Jack to the rescue."

"That's not how it worked." Lynn reached down, slipping her fingers into the water so she could flick droplets at her best friend. "Try this instead: Jack has the hots for her forever, Pepper shows up, and voilà, fate has its way."

"I thought you didn't believe in fate."

"Old dog, new trick."

"Woof," Pepper offered, and the room broke out in laughter again.

There was a momentary lull in conversation, the noises of the water basins underfoot the loudest thing in the room. Pepper sighed contentedly.

"He really is a pretty awesome guy, but a lot more alpha-dude than I thought *you'd* ever go for," Kendra offered, her expression still slightly confused. "I didn't expect Jack to be the type to have zero issues regarding you and the threesome."

A choking sound broke out from Pepper's left. She turned to see Suz tapping her chest and working on breathing properly. Lynn was staring as well, her amazing blue eyes filled with... Pepper wasn't sure if it was shock or horror.

"You okay?" she asked as Suz calmed herself.

"Honey, you have no idea." The blonde twirled toward her best friend and stuck out her hand. "I win. You owe me."

Lynn raised her middle finger.

"Did you two make a bet about me and my sex life?" Pepper demanded, more amused than pissed off.

Suz raised one delicately arched brow. "I make bets about everything, but this one I'm *very* happy to win. I told Lynn you were my kind of girl. Feet solidly on the ground but arms wide open to experience life to the fullest. Yada, yada, yada."

"I didn't actually have a threesome," Pepper confessed.

"But you wanted to." Suz snapped up a finger and stuck it in her face. "You wanted to, right?"

"Hey, now you're leading the witness," Lynn protested.

Pepper laughed. "You two are crazy. Yes, I wanted to try a threesome, but things went to hell, and it never happened, and that's fine. I am very happy with Jack. The man is talented enough in bed there could be two guys in there for all I know."

Suz clicked her tongue as her head moved from side to side. "I'm glad you're happy, and I know Jack's probably got all the moves and then some, but there is *nothing* like two guys taking care of business for you at the same time."

There was a flush on Lynn's cheeks that hadn't been there before. Pepper resisted asking *why* it was there, partly because if she found out Lynn had a threesome before Parker she'd wonder if he knew, and if she found out it was with Parker and someone else—

Nopeity, nope, nope. Awkward. Gross.

"Gee, look at the time," Kendra tossed out. "And how's the weather been lately?"

The women laughed as the spa workers returned to the room to continue with the next step of the pedicure. Conversation turned to more mundane things than sex.

She glanced over to discover Kendra staring off into space with a pensive expression.

Pepper wasn't a matchmaker either, but she really hoped her friend would find someone who would rock her world. Lynn was obviously head over heels in love with Parker, and Suz more than content with her hummingbird ways.

Maybe there was something to the old adage of wanting everyone to be settled happily in their nests. Pepper was having such a good time with Jack she wanted that same thing for her friend.

She reached over and caught Kendra's fingers in hers, giving them a momentary squeeze. Her friend blinked for a second before smiling back.

It was good to have a community of women around her that Pepper could lean on and trust. She never wanted to be without that ever again.

JACK THANKED the waitress as she placed a delicious-looking steak dinner in front of him, then unrolled the napkin containing his silverware. He picked up his knife and fork, about to cut into the juicy T-bone when he noticed his friend's bewildered eyes from the other side of the booth.

"What's the matter?" Jack arched a brow at Dean. "Steak's not big enough for you?"

"I need to ask you something." Dean awkwardly rested both elbows on the tabletop and leaned forward. He lowered his voice to a barely audible pitch as he said, "Is this a date?"

Jack wrinkled his brow. "Um. *What?*"

"Look around us, man." Dean swept a hand over their surroundings, gesturing to the expensive meals, the red linen tablecloth, the dim glow of the ornate light fixture above them. His gaze ended its tour on the single white candle at the edge of the booth before shifting back to Jack in dismay. "I think this might be a date, and I'm not sure how I feel about it. I mean, I'm not averse to the idea—if I was gay, I'd absolutely sleep with you. I'd even pick you over Parker, if someone held a gun to my head. But this is...weird."

Jack gaped at his friend. "What the hell are you babbling about? We're not on a date, Colter."

A groove appeared in Dean's forehead. "Then why did you want to meet *here*? This restaurant is way fancier than the usual wings-and-burgers joints we go to. There's a frickin' *candle* on the table, Jack."

"You said you were in the mood for steak. I Googled the closest place to the office that serves good steaks." He shook his head, his reasons for inviting Dean to dinner sliding to the backburner of his mind as he registered

190

what his buddy had said. "You'd fuck me over Parker? Really?"

Dean nodded fervently. "Hell yeah. Mofo's too intense. I want someone who'll smile and laugh when we're getting it on. And I have it on good authority that you like to have fun in bed."

"What authority? You know firsthand what I'm like in the sack."

"Exactly. Speaking as the person who's tag-teamed with both you and Parker, I'd much prefer going solo with you."

"Thanks?" Jack gave another shake of the head, wondering how on earth they were even having this conversation. On the other hand, he couldn't have asked for a better segue if he'd tried.

As Dean picked up his steak knife and sliced off a hefty piece of rib eye, Jack took a quick sip of beer before continuing. "I'm glad to hear you approve of my sex methods, because I actually wanted to talk to you about something." He folded his hands together. "Do you want to have sex with me and Pepper?"

Dean froze mid-swallow, then broke out in a fit of coughs that attracted the curious eyes of the other patrons occupying the restaurant's various booths and tables. The guy even pounded his own fist into his chest a couple of times to dislodge the piece of meat that had jammed in his windpipe, and the scene would have been comical if not for the utter seriousness of the request.

Jack didn't say a word as he waited for Dean to recover. But when his buddy finally spoke, it wasn't what he'd expected to hear.

"No." Swift and emphatic, zero hesitation.

"What do you mean, *no*?" When it came to sex, Dean Colter belonged to the *anything goes* camp. His turning down an opportunity to get kinky was unheard of.

"I mean no. As in, I'm not gonna do it."

A mocking note entered Jack's voice. "Are you telling me you're not even the least bit interested? Because a little birdie told me you seemed pretty damn into the idea the day you watched me spank Pepper's ass in my office."

Dean looked alarmed, as if he hadn't expected Jack to call him out on it. Three weeks had passed since that wicked scene in the office, but Jack hadn't raised the subject after Pepper confessed to seeing Dean in the adjoining doorway. Dean hadn't brought it up, either, which told Jack that his friend hadn't purposely been creeping on them. Most likely Dean had popped his head in Jack's office to talk business, stumbled upon them, and had chosen not to address it out of respect for both of them.

But there was no avoiding the matter now. Jack was a man on a mission, and if he wanted to succeed, he needed Dean. And *only* Dean.

Heat darkened Dean's eyes to a smoky silver as he drawled out a response. "Was wondering when you'd bring that up."

He shrugged. "Now seems as good a time as any."

Dean speared a roasted potato with his fork and popped it in his mouth, a thoughtful look on his face as he chewed slowly. "I'm not going to deny it was one of the hottest scenes I've seen in a long time, but…"

"But what? You're always down with three-ways. Why not this one?"

"Because it's your girlfriend!"

Jack raised his brows. "You and Parker slept with Lynn. And Lynn is Parker's girlfriend."

"So that means I'm down to sleep with *anyone*? What, you're pimping me out now? Snap your fingers and I pull out my dick and stick it wherever you want?" Dean sounded more amused than angry.

Jack swallowed his frustration. "Are you saying you're not attracted to Pepper?"

"Of course I am. She's smoking hot. But she's your girlfriend. And she's Parker's sister. In most threesomes, you only have to worry about one person potentially beating you up. It's a rare occasion when there's *two* people gunning for you."

"Nobody's gonna beat you up, dumbass," Jack said with a chuckle. "I'm *asking* you to do this. And as for Parker, he doesn't have to know. Actually, we'll make sure he *never* knows."

Dean slanted his head in challenge. "You're possessive as shit about her, man. You honestly expect me to believe you're okay with someone else worshipping at her sacred throne?"

"Not someone else. You."

Just Dean, and just once. Jack wouldn't even consider it with anybody else. He trusted Dean Colter with his life. The two of them had been to hell and back together, surviving two tours of duty, saving each other's asses more times than Jack could count. They were Rangers for life. *Brothers* for life.

If anyone was going to help him give Pepper her fantasy, it was going to be Dean.

Though a part of him still wasn't sure why he was so determined to make it happen. Pepper hadn't mentioned threesomes since Adam's scathing online tirade, but Jack knew her curiosity hadn't gone away. And he couldn't fault her for it. She wasn't as experienced as him when it came to sex. He'd indulged in his fair share of threesomes, experimented with kink that would make her blush. He understood that need to push the limits, to crave pleasure wherever and however you could get it, and he loved how eager she was to explore her sexuality.

The fact that she'd initiated a threesome with her two college buddies told him how badly she wanted to experiment. Well, he could help her do that. And so could Dean, the only man Jack trusted enough with something as intimate as Pepper's sexuality.

"Okay...let's pretend I'm saying yes," Dean started gruffly. "What kind of rules am I looking at here? Will you break my fingers if I touch her somewhere you don't want me to touch?"

"Nope." Jack spoke in a firm voice. "It'll be about her pleasure, not ours. If she asks you to touch her, then you touch her. Wherever she wants." A lump of jealousy rose in his throat as he imagined another man's hands on Pepper's delectable body, but he quickly choked it down.

Dean caught the reaction. "See?" he said triumphantly. "You're feeling possessive already."

"I'm not gonna lie. I get a little crazy thinking about it, but..." Jack swallowed, once again conjuring up the image of Dean touching Pepper. Only this time, he didn't focus on Dean's fingers, but the haze of ecstasy on Pepper's face as she rocked into that skillful touch. Her throaty moans. Her body trembling with pleasure.

Jack's cock instantly stirred, thickening as the need to please his woman surged through his blood.

His woman. Jeez. He'd played the field for so long it was strange to think about settling down with one woman. But Pepper was different.

Pepper was...

His.

"But?" Dean prompted.

"But all I have to do is think about how hot we're going to make her, and the possessive urges go away." He had to grin. "That day in the office? She knew you were watching and it turned her on like you wouldn't believe. That's all I care about."

Dean nodded slowly. "If I do this...you'd be calling the shots. From start to finish. I don't do anything unless you tell me to."

He nodded back. "Anything she wants, we give her. That's the only rule." When his friend suddenly looked stricken, Jack blinked in confusion. "What?"

"What if she wants you and me to...you know. Kiss or something."

Laughter bubbled in his throat. "Five minutes ago you were saying how you're dying to fuck me, and now you're shitting your pants at the thought of *kissing* me?"

"Dying? Uh-uh. Way to rewrite history, bro. Obviously you're vocalizing your own deep-seated desire for my fine ass." Dean primly picked up his knife and fork, then offered a magnanimous smile. "Fine. I'll kiss you if she asks."

Jack rolled his eyes. "That's a very generous offer. You're such a prince."

With that, the mood shifted from dead serious to lighthearted, and the two men dug into their food again. Once Dean had swallowed his last morsel of steak and polished off his beer, he glanced across the booth and said, "You're paying for dinner, right?"

A snicker flew out of Jack's mouth. "Cheap bastard."

"Hey, it's the chivalrous thing to do. *You're* the one who asked *me* out on this date—"

Their waitress chose that moment to check on them. Her smile faltered for a beat, then widened as she swept her gaze from one man to the other. "Are you gentlemen doing okay? Can I get you anything else?"

"We're great." Dean flashed a broad grin. "Can you bring us the dessert menu? My date's treating tonight, so I want to order the most expensive chocolate concoction you've got."

Her lips quivered with barely restrained laughter. "Right away, sir."

After she was gone, Jack scowled at his friend. "You're a jerk for toying with that poor woman."

"Toying with her? No way. I just made her night." Dean's expression turned smug. "Every woman on the planet fantasizes about two hot studs doing the nasty. Trust me, she'll make herself come a dozen times tonight and go to bed with a smile on her face."

Dean was probably right, but Jack wasn't too interested in putting a smile on their waitress's face. He was more concerned with putting one on *Pepper's*.

Yep, Pepper was the only woman who mattered, and by the time Jack was through, he'd make every single one of her fantasies come true.

Chapter Twelve

THE STEERING wheel under her hands responded like a dream as Pepper took the final corner, following Jack's directions into the hotel entrance way. "Damn, that was an awesome ride."

"Except for the bit when you decided to drag race on the 101, you did good," Jack teased.

"Drag race? Au contraire, I never even broke a hundred." Pepper slowed to take the turn, easing the Aston Martin down the narrow ramp into the underground parking area. "Thanks for letting me drive her."

"No problem."

She drove into an empty stall, put the vehicle in park and pulled out the keys. She dropped them into Jack's waiting hand, meeting his dark gaze with as much seriousness as her giddy happiness could allow. "Don't try to bullshit me. I know this car is your baby, and I don't expect to get to touch her again for a good long time."

His grin was slightly sheepish. "It's not that I don't trust you."

"Oh, I get it. Totally. I'm not letting you borrow my camera on a regular basis either. I mean, some things are sacred." She remembered to push back the seat so that he wouldn't be folded in two the next time he crawled behind the wheel, then accepted his hand as he magically appeared beside her door to help her out of the car. "I take it we've got some things to check for DreamMakers? The big gala in a couple of weeks?"

She didn't mention the evil Charlene's name, but somehow the woman still hovered in the back of Pepper's mind. The meetings between the two of them continued to be wrought with cordial antagonism. Pepper felt she was currently winning, though, because every time Charlene said something derogatory, Pepper would think back to the last time Jack had rocked her world, and her satisfied smirk would instantly silence the catty interplay.

Jack seemed distracted as he opened the trunk and pulled out a gym bag. "We made the bookings for the out-of-town guests, but I wanted to make sure the rooms they gave us are up to standard. I hope you don't mind."

"The night is young. We've got tons of time after we're done here. I thought we could try that new club on 9th and Howard."

He laced his fingers through hers, pulling her toward the elevator. "You feel like dancing tonight, do you?"

Pepper waited until the elevator doors closed behind them before she pressed against him, fingers linked behind his neck as she licked her lips in anticipation for the kiss she saw waiting for her. "I always feel like dancing with you. Slow, fast, dirty, naked..."

A flash of heat nearly incinerated her in the second before he wrapped his hand around her neck, the other dropping below her butt as he raised her in the air and took her lips as if he were starving.

The sound of his bag hitting the ground barely registered through the rush of blood roaring past her ears as his tongue slipped into her mouth and tangled with hers.

Screw it. If there were security cameras someone was about to get an eyeful. Pepper wrapped her legs around Jack's hips, clinging to him, soaking in every moment of the passion that flared so brightly between them.

Under her his erection was thick and solid, and she rotated her hips to rub their bodies together, triggering a low rumble as his arms tightened even more.

"Dammit, Pepper." He eased his mouth away, his gaze burning into her from only inches away. "I could fuck you right here," he growled.

Oh. Yes, please. Her heart pounded wildly, but she supposed the very rational and controlled move of him lowering her to the floor and picking up the gym bag was a better idea than having DreamMakers banned from the hotel altogether for breaking every one of the public displays of affection laws California had.

Still, her goals for the evening had totally changed. "Let's get this done so we can find a place where I can suck your cock."

It took Jack a second to recover from damn near tripping over his own feet. His hand on her arm tugged her to a stop beside one of the hotel doors, and then like some undercover ninja he had her inside the room and up against the wall in zero time flat.

His chocolate brown eyes held her trapped as he pinned her in place, one palm flat to the wall on either side of her shoulders. His blond hair was just messy enough she wanted to drag her fingers through it as he crawled over her and licked every inch of her body.

That wasn't the look of a man who planned on taking her dancing later. Pepper put his comments about the hotel together with the fact that he had a room key without them going to the front desk.

Fucking A. He'd rented them a place to go crazy?

She drew her fingers along the waistband of his jeans until she could play with the button, her exploration slipping lower to linger over the heavy bulge pushing forward. "Please sir, may I?"

Jack swallowed hard, his hips thrusting into her fingers. "I've got a surprise for you."

She stroked him again, pleased she'd played detective correctly. "I see you do."

The fire in his eyes only grew hotter. "Do you trust me?"

She rapidly went through a list of possible answers to that, but the only thing she could do was push his button through the opening and ease down the first part of his zipper. "Hell, yeah."

He pressed his lips to hers, just for a split second before working his way to the sensitive spot underneath her ear. The spot he'd discovered drove her crazy. Two could play at that game, though, and she snuck a hand

VIVIAN AREND & ELLE KENNEDY

under his briefs, wrapping her fingers around his thick erection.

"Playing with fire," Jack warned.

"Make me burn," she responded. But it was past time for games. "Tell me we're not just here to check out the room. Tell me we can actually check out the bedsprings—"

"Yes—"

The rest of what he planned to say was lost in a moan as she slid down the wall to her knees, tugging aside his jeans to free his cock. Pepper tipped her head back to look up at him as he leaned on the wall, braced on both elbows as she pulled out the tasty treat she was dying to savor.

"That's not what I planned for tonight," Jack muttered. "Tonight is supposed to be all about you. All the things you want to do."

"I want to suck you off, so we're good," Pepper retorted, extending her tongue to lick the head of his cock. She made that first contact while they were still staring at each other, and satisfaction hit in a rush.

Not only from the taste of the tiny drop of anticipation clinging to the narrow slit on his cock, but from the way his eyes damn near rolled back in his head when she licked him.

Whatever his big surprise was, she hadn't lied. Down on her knees before him, swirling her tongue over the hot surface of his fully aroused cock—this was what she wanted. She felt wild and incredibly powerful. Even as he slid one hand down the wall to thread his fingers into her hair, it didn't matter that with a single tug he could move her in any direction.

201

She'd made the choice, and that made the whole thing sexy as fuck.

"So damn beautiful," Jack whispered as he stroked her hair. "Never dye your hair again, baby. It's too damn pretty to hide."

Pleasure swarmed her chest. "You like the return of the red?"

"I love it." His fingers tightened slightly as he tilted her head so that the next time she wrapped her lips around him he could push forward. This was the moment when Pepper thanked whatever benevolent gods there were in the universe that she had no gag reflex.

The full length of his erection slid between her lips, her nose bumping briefly into his abs of steel before he cursed and withdrew, twisting himself away from her and dragging her to her feet.

"Pepper. God, you shatter my brain into a million pieces. Stop. I need to talk to you about something."

Talking, smocking. Pepper grabbed the bottom of her shirt and peeled it off overhead, tossing it aside as she paced after him. Jack retreated into the open living space. She undid her pants, stepped out of them, and joined him in the middle of the room.

"Talk fast," she demanded, lifting her hands to work on his shirt buttons. "I haven't had hotel sex with you yet, and I can't frickin' wait."

A knock sounded at the door, and Jack sighed. "So much for preparing you ahead of time."

"Oh, did you arrange some kind of naughty room service?" Pepper glanced at the abandoned clothes on the floor. "Want me to go hide in the bathroom?"

He turned on her, examining her carefully. Something in his eyes clicked, and she was suddenly aware she was dealing with a very determined man with an agenda she didn't fully comprehend.

"No hiding," Jack ordered. "I want you to stand right there, hands at your sides, and I don't want you to move an inch until I tell you to. Understand?"

Boy oh boy, this was kinkier than anything they'd done to date. Pepper widened her stance and upped the ante, placing her hands behind her and linking her fingers together. The position pulled her shoulders back and thrust her breasts forward, placing them on display behind her pale pink bra.

"How's this?" She breathed out the words slowly, but she already knew the answer. As soon as she had moved to follow his directions he'd gotten *that expression*. The one that said she was going to be a very happy girl, very soon.

Jack marched across the room, cupping her chin so he could kiss her breathless. Her lips were swollen by the time he broke away and turned without a backward glance to answer the door.

Pepper used the moment to try to calm her breathing. She shouldn't have bothered, because the instant Jack pulled the door open nothing worked properly anymore. She couldn't breathe, she couldn't move. Her heart was the only thing still going, and that was pounding hard enough to shake her entire body.

Her gaze met the incredible gray of Dean Colter's eyes, and just like weeks earlier, she was unable to protest, especially since Jack ushered him into the room.

She'd been ordered to stay motionless, but that was damn near impossible as every inch of her body was suddenly electrified with energy. It was one thing to think about pushing her boundaries, but this...

"Jack?"

He didn't say anything as he made his way back to her side. Dean stood near the door, his hands gripping the front of his jacket as if waiting for some sign.

Then Jack was there, his hands pressed to the sides of Pepper's face as he stared intently into her eyes. He hesitated for a moment before that sexy smile of his broke free. "This is your choice, baby. You say the word and Dean is out of here, and we'll never speak of it again. But if you want your fantasy, it's here. You can have it."

The electric sensation tingling over her had centered on her spine. It was the only thing still holding her vertical. "My fantasy?"

"You know what I'm talking about. I saw the way you looked that day when you told me your threesome attempt wasn't worth trying again. And I'm telling you even though this is only going to happen once, I want you to have a shot. I want to rock your world like no one's ever done before, so if you trust us, Dean and me, you can have anything you want tonight. Anything, and it's yours."

Pepper was sure the air in the room contained some kind of intoxicant. She was so lightheaded from breathing she couldn't imagine what it would be like when...

She glanced over Jack's shoulder at Dean. He was watching them cautiously, his entire body in that alert and ready-for-anything stance all military guys seemed to have built into them. Only he was smiling as well, the tip of his tongue sneaking out to wet his lips as his gaze dropped over her nearly naked body. The signs of his arousal were clear in the thickening length crowding the front of his jeans.

She spoke quietly, loud enough for only Jack to hear. "This isn't going to make things weird between you and Dean, is it?"

"Just going to make him jealous as hell that I get to have you every night after this, and he only gets one taste."

Instant shiver. "What kind of taste?"

She must've spoken louder than she'd thought because Dean's eyes sparked with interest as he stepped out of his shoes and shrugged out of his jacket. He tossed it over the back of a nearby chair. "You heard Jack. Anything you want."

Too many images were flashing through her brain to concentrate on anything. She should have felt something as Dean crossed the room to her side. Suddenly she was standing between two dangerously gorgeous men while wearing nothing but see-through underwear, and the only thing she could think?

"Hot diggity dog." She faced Jack again, shoving her fingers into his hair and pressing their mouths together for another explosive kiss. Whatever happened over the next hour or more, she knew only one thing. She stole her lips away from his, leaning their foreheads together intimately. "I want it all. I mean, I *think* I want it all. But I trust you. I trust Dean, too, but I don't know what to do. So do whatever you want. I know you'll make it good."

That steely glint returned to his eyes. "I'm in charge."

She snickered in spite of her excitement. "Yes, that's the illusion I grant you on a regular basis."

Dean laughed, the masculine tone reminding her there was a *third* person in the room. It was strange, and so freaking erotic Pepper was worried she was going to soak through her underwear and leave a puddle on the carpet where she stood.

Then it wasn't just his voice touching her, but his hand. Dean caressed her shoulder, his fingers tickling down the side of her arm as Jack carefully examined her reaction.

"You like it when he touches you?"

"Yes." Goosebumps were rising ahead of Dean's touch, every inch of her skin completely and vibrantly awake.

"Good." Jack backed away, watching for a moment before retrieving the gym bag from where it'd been abandoned. As he carried it to the coffee table and unzipped it, Dean continued to caress her. The mere ghost of a touch across her shoulder blades, along the dip of her waist, his palms ever so gentle over the bare skin at her hips and buttocks.

"I think it's time you got naked," Dean murmured. "What do you think?"

She was too turned on to answer, so she settled for a shaky nod.

Expert fingers undid her bra, straps nudged aside until they slipped from her body, the material falling from her to lie at her feet. Dean followed up immediately by tugging down the sides of her thong, holding her hand to support her as she stepped out from the scrap of fabric.

"Sweet mother of God, the carpet and the drapes match."

Dean's husky admiration made Pepper laugh, thankful all over for the night at the spa. She knew she looked good. Ready for anything, and man, oh man, this was *anything*.

His breath was warm on her back, and then the room was filled with the scent of the tropics. Floral aromas wafted up from where Jack had opened a couple of containers and placed them on the table.

He lifted his chin as if in challenge. "Wasn't lying about checking these rooms. We're putting out gift baskets. You get to approve the suppliers we selected."

"Body creams?"

Dean's hand slipped from her hip over her belly in a determined course. "And other things."

Then Jack was there, his hands on her breasts, plumping them in his palms, squeezing and rubbing as he moved his thumbs into position over her nipples. He dipped his head to take one into his mouth, and Pepper sighed contentedly before a gasp was pulled from her sharply.

Dean's hand had centered between her legs, his fingers delicately opening her sex to slip through her folds. Using the moisture there to pull up to her clit, he teased with tight circles over her most sensitive spot.

"Holy cannoli, this feels incredible." She breathed out slowly, working to keep vertical. The caresses weren't so different from what Jack had done before, multitalented man that he was, but there was an entirely different element to it. Jack continued to nip and suck, using his tongue and teeth then closing his lips around her and drawing tight until the sensation sang through her entire body.

"About to feel even better, baby," Dean drawled.

His hand vanished only to be replaced a second later with hot, wet pleasure.

Pepper's eyes flew open to discover him kneeling between her legs, hands holding her open so he could lash his tongue over her clit.

She was shaking now, the pleasure rippling through her body making her legs unsteady. She caught hold of Jack's shoulders, the crisp fabric of his shirt a cool contrast with the heated skin at his neckline.

She closed her eyes to better take in every sensation, every touch. Dean murmured happily, his hands skimming up her hips and around her butt as he moved her over him more firmly. Alternating his tongue between darting deep into her pussy and tormenting her clit.

Pleasure hovered like a live wire, just barely out of reach. "Oh my God, I'm going to come in like three seconds flat."

Jack's approval was clear as he went to work nibbling on the erogenous zone on her neck, his fingers expertly teasing her nipples. "Come now. Come later. You get everything tonight."

True, which meant there was no use fighting the violent need raking through her. Dean had taken charge of her clit as if he were prepared to work it without a pause for the next millennium, and with the attention to her breasts, and the sucking on her neck...

She clamped her teeth together to stop from screaming, but she still made enough noise to wake the dead as the tension in her core slammed up and broke apart, twisting through her like a miniature tornado and leaving her desperate for oxygen.

Jack caught her to his side as she shook, Dean still hungrily lapping until she reached down and shoved his head away, sucking for air like a deep-water diver.

"Move, bro," Jack ordered. "Take it to the bedroom."

"You expect me to walk?" Pepper complained, but she shouldn't have bothered. Dean simply picked her up in his arms and marched the short distance into the adjoining bedroom.

He laid her on the quilted cover with damn near reverence in his touch, his gray eyes dancing with laughter and a hell of a lot of heat. "No wonder I can't convince Jack to come out with me anymore. You're fucking delicious, woman."

"I didn't hear her scream," Jack pointed out. "Looks like you've lost a bit of your touch."

"I didn't want her to pass out and miss all the really fun stuff," Dean said as he leaned forward to press a kiss to her forehead.

Screw that. She got this one time to experience her fantasy? She was taking it all. Her arms shot up to snake around Dean's neck as she tugged him down, joining their lips in a brief invitation.

He accepted the challenge, damn near blowing her mind as he ravished her lips, tugging her higher on the mattress and crawling over her. His clothed body over her naked one was an erotically sensual tease, and she wiggled to enjoy it more fully. The soft cambric fabric of his shirt glided over her breasts, the coarser material of his jeans plus the heavy erection behind his zipper bumping her mound and driving her wild.

"I want to touch you," she blurted in frustration, her hands clawing at the pesky clothing serving as a barrier between them.

"Soon," he promised. Then he rolled off, and the mattress swayed as Jack took his place.

Amazing man. In the last ten seconds he'd stripped, and with every stitch of clothing gone, it was a naked man who pinned her to the mattress. The dusting of hair on his chest teased her nipples, the familiar weight of his cock trapped between their bellies as he lowered himself carefully, allowing his body to press her to the bed as he kissed her.

Oh yeah, she liked that as well.

Only he rolled, and she ended up on top, the air conditioning in the room cool on her skin.

She smiled down at him. "Hi."

"Hi." A brow cocked up. "So you want to touch Dean, huh?"

She hesitated for a beat, worried that might be off-limits, but Jack's expression conveyed nothing but heat and humor. "May I?"

A grin lifted his lips. "So polite. Who are you and what have you done to Pepper Wilson?"

Her eyes narrowed. "Excuse me for trying to figure out the rules—"

"Only one rule," he interrupted, his voice husky. "We do whatever you want. So if you want to put your hands all over our boy Dean, then that's what's gonna happen. Turn around, Candy Cane."

She twisted her head, gasping when she discovered that Dean had stripped during her and Jack's conversation. A virtual cornucopia of muscular man flesh assaulted her vision, so many yummy details to appreciate that her gaze went frantic trying to soak it all in.

"Sweet mother of Mercy, I've been a good girl all my life, I have," Pepper swore, staring at Dean's broad, golden chest. "To deserve such wonders."

"Dean? He's not much of a wonder," Jack teased.

"His tongue should be enshrined," she insisted. "And Lord Almighty, I love the ink. I really do."

Dean traced the tattoo over his left pec with one long finger, the faintest dusting of dark hair like a shadow over his skin. She followed the path of his fingertips, shivering when it swept over the Rangers banner before sliding up above it, where a majestic wolf was captured mid-pounce, as wild and dangerous as the man wearing the ink.

Pepper was tempted to make Jack roll over so she could admire his tattoo at the same time, that same waving military banner, only his deadly predator was a tiger. Her brother's lion was the third in the set, and she wondered if the three men had gotten them done on the same day.

"I want to get a tattoo sometime, too," she confessed.

Dean grinned as he stepped closer to the bed. "You'd better ask me to help you with that. Jack? Doesn't do tattoo parlors very well."

"Shut up, Dean," Jack ordered.

That earned him a rumble of laughter. "Oh, I plan on telling her the whole story, bro. Not tonight, though. Right now, I'm waiting for Pepper to put those beautiful hands all over me."

Pepper's breath hitched as she caught the smoldering gleam in his eyes.

"Don't keep the man waiting."

Jack's taunt hung in the air, prompting her to slide off his lap and crawl to the edge of the bed where Dean stood. She rose on her knees and pressed her palms to his chest, shivering at the hard, rippled muscles beneath her touch.

"You're shredded like a Ninja Turtle," she breathed.

Another laugh broke free, making those gray eyes sparkle. "That's the nicest thing anyone's ever said to me."

"He doesn't need to be showered with compliments," came Jack's gruff voice. "Touch his cock, Pepper."

Her pulse sped up. Lord. She never would've dreamed she'd hear those words coming out of Jack's mouth. He was a bossy alpha caveman to the core. He didn't like to share, and yet tonight he was giving new meaning to the phrase *sharing is caring*. That he cared about her enough to make this fantasy come true...she couldn't even wrap her head around it.

So she didn't try to. She just wrapped her fingers around Dean's cock instead.

He hissed in pleasure. "Oh yeah. That's what I want."

Her gaze locked with Dean's as she stroked his weighty erection, watching his expression to see what he liked.

"Faster," Jack ordered. "And harder. Dean likes it hard and fast."

She turned around to see Jack stroking his own cock with one large fist, his face taut with intensity as he eyed the scene in front of him.

"How do you know what he likes?" she challenged. "Given him a lot of handjobs, have you, Jackjack?"

Brown eyes gleamed at her. "Would it turn you on if I said yes?"

A rush of moisture flooded her core, and both men must have noticed the way she squirmed and clenched her thighs together, because they chuckled.

"Told ya, bro," Dean said. "Every woman fantasizes about it."

As Jack let out a rueful sigh, Pepper turned her attention back to Dean. Ignoring the relentless pressure between her legs, she scooted lower and brought the tip of his cock to her lips, her tongue darting out for a fleeting taste.

The answering male groan made her ego swell. "That's it," Dean mumbled in encouragement. "Tease me a bit."

She couldn't have denied him even if she'd tried. She was too desperate to explore, too eager to summon another one of those raspy groans from his mouth. As she dragged her tongue along the hard length of his shaft, she heard Jack's ragged breathing from behind them, his tortured moan as she took Dean fully into her mouth and sucked.

Holy Dolly Parton. She couldn't believe she was sucking Dean off while Jack watched. She never wanted to stop, but Dean only allowed her a few more languid licks before he thrust a hand in her hair and yanked her off him.

"Climb on top of Jack again," he commanded.

"I wasn't finished," she grumbled.

"Well, *I* almost was, and trust me, as sexy as your mouth is, there are more enticing places for me to come."

A thrill shot up her spine and closed up her throat. Without delay, she scrambled back onto Jack's lap, her thighs quivering as she straddled him.

"Did you like having his cock in your mouth?" Jack peered up at her, searing her flesh with his gaze.

She drew a deep breath, then nodded.

"You wanted to swallow his come, didn't you? You wanted to taste him."

The filthy words seized her lungs, trapping the oxygen she'd just inhaled.

Jack chuckled softly. "I'll let you taste him later, Candy Cane. Right now I've got something else in mind."

The mattress swayed as Dean joined them, and Pepper was too distracted to ask what he meant, too busy taking in every inch she could see, not only of Dean beside her but Jack beneath her. Muscular curves and dangerous strength surrounded her.

Dean cleared his throat. "Still game for more?" he asked her.

That shiver struck again—the one that made every inch of her hot and bothered. Jack watched her carefully, and he was the one who answered Dean's question.

"She's game for more." He brushed his fingertips over her thigh in a fleeting caress. "Lean forward."

With a shaky exhalation, Pepper followed his directions, the position making it all too clear what they had in mind. "Okay, I'm suddenly a little nervous."

Dean pressed against her back, every muscular inch sealing her tight to Jack. "I'll go slow, I promise. Jack said you guys have done this before."

She nodded. "Now I know why he seems to have such an obsession with my ass lately."

"Hmmm." Dean moved back, weaving his hands over her hips carefully before sliding a finger between her cheeks. "He probably has an obsession because you've got an amazing ass."

"It's a freaking amazing ass," Jack agreed.

Pepper leaned up on her elbows, staring down at Jack as Dean's hands moved over her, intimately touching the tight hole between her cheeks. The floral scent in the room increased, and a warm liquid slid down her butt.

She fought the urge to laugh. "Don't tell me you're putting lube in the gift baskets for the gala."

Jack grinned. "No lube, but the rest of the product line. You like?"

"Oh damn..." Pepper held her breath for a second as Dean slid a finger into her, the slippery lotion easing his way. It was still the strangest of sensations. She'd spend the first few minutes wondering if she actually did like anal play, until between one magical second and the next, the pressure would change, and she'd be going out of her mind with pleasure.

"Jesus, that's the hottest thing I've seen in forever," Dean muttered. "I'm going to go out of my fucking mind when I put my cock in you."

"Dirty talk just makes me wetter," Pepper warned.

He chuckled, moving his fingers slowly and teasing her. "That will make it even better when Jack puts his cock in your pussy."

The pressure increased. "Oh *God.*"

"Three fingers, baby. Nearly ready."

Dean seemed determined to draw out the moment as long as possible. "Hurry," she begged.

Her body was humming with pleasure, Jack's eyes on fire as she stared at him.

"Are you ready?" he asked.

"Maybe." A strange thought struck. "You guys don't mind how close this makes you? I mean, your cocks will be almost touching. And I don't know why I'm bringing that up because if you stop now I will never forgive you and I'll...don't know what I'd do, but...you'll be really close. Just saying."

"You're rambling, Candy Cane. You're nervous."

She pushed back carefully on Dean's hand, breathing easier as the pleasure shot skyward. "Nervous or not, I still want to know. You rub cocks often?"

Behind her, Dean laughed, his fingers slipping free and leaving her pulsing with anticipation as the sound of a condom wrapper hit her ears. "I warned you, Jack."

Jack only smiled, that flirty, dirty smile that drove her wild. "This is all about pleasure, and right now it's about your pleasure. The fact that we're both going to be in your body is just gonna make it that much better for all of us."

Dean took that moment to press forward, the solid head of his cock slowly pushing through her tight resistance. Pepper breathed carefully, trying not to move.

"So tight," Dean moaned. "Damn amazing. You're...fucking hell, so amazing."

Pepper looked down at Jack, concentrating on him as Dean worked his way in, the scent of lube heavy in the air around them. "Thank God you know what you're doing. I can't believe you're shoving that monster up there without it killing me."

Dean laughed. "Monster. Hmm, I like that. Godzilla?"

Below her, Jack's expression cracked into an enormous grin.

Pepper panted as she fought the urge to burst out laughing. "Please, tell me that's not what you named your cock."

"What?" Dean let out an utterly masculine sigh of satisfaction as his groin met her ass. "No. Only twelve-year-old boys name their cocks. Now, come here."

He wrapped his arms around her and pulled her into his lap, twisting on the mattress at the same time to end up seated at the edge, their feet hanging toward the floor.

The motion settled his monster cock deeper inside her, and she gasped. "Godzilla or not, holy mackerel I'm full. Full, full, full."

He turned her head toward him and kissed her for a moment, his tongue distracting her from the nearly uncomfortable feeling in her butt. Strong hands lifted her knees so her thighs were draped over Dean's, opening her pussy to the room. By the time Dean let her up for air she was ready to take deep, sucking drags into her lungs.

Jack had knelt between her legs and put his tongue to her clit, and all thoughts of being too full were wiped away by her indescribable need to come.

"That is the dirtiest thing... I've ever... Dammit, Jack... *Hell...*"

She couldn't seem to finish an entire sentence. She couldn't seem to finish an entire thought, not with another orgasm rushing up to meet her as Dean rocked his hips and Jack continued in his quest to blow her mind.

Hands were everywhere. Okay, not *everywhere*, but Dean had reached around to fondle her breasts while Jack not only tormented her clit, he'd snuck two fingers into her pussy.

"Now," she begged. "Fuck me *now*."

"Yes, now," Dean agreed. "She's squeezing the daylights out of my cock, and I'm not going to last more than two strokes if you don't get the hell in here, bro."

Jack moved without hesitation as Dean leaned back slightly and lifted his knees, opening Pepper fully. Jack rubbed the heavy head of his cock between her folds, nicking her clit with every pass. She whimpered, waiting for the moment when—

He pushed his hips forward ever so slightly, the two of them staring down at where they connected. His thick cock disappeared with difficulty into her tight passage, every inch of Dean's length felt even more fully as Jack stuffed into her.

"I'm going to explode," Pepper gasped. Her gaze shot up to meet Jack's as he worked his way in. All the way, every inch of pleasurable torment.

And then he fucked her. Thrusting forward hard, pulling back out as Dean joined in his limited way, but all three of them were moved on every rock. Jack's drives were hard enough to make groans of pleasure escape both Dean and Pepper's throats.

Through it all, Jack watched her. Dean was there— oh, there was no denying Dean was there—but *they* were together. *Pepper and Jack,* as he made her fantasy come true.

The orgasm hit as if every cell in her body wanted to melt, and Pepper leaned back on Dean's chest, letting the men hold her in position as she reveled in the sheer decadence.

Jack's eyes burned into her even as his face creased in pleasure and he came, he and Dean shouting as they found release as well.

Pepper found her arms wrapped around Jack as he nuzzled the side of her face. Behind her, Dean was doing the same to her opposite side, and she was surrounded and still filled.

"Holy Toledo, did I pass out?"

"I don't know," Dean muttered. "I just got back from an extended trip into outer space. Man, the stars are bright today."

She laughed, accepting the feather-light kisses Jack was dancing over her face. "That was fun," she said boldly. "What do you guys do for an encore?"

"Oh, I'm sure we can figure something out," Jack promised.

Pepper eyed the clock beside the bed and wondered exactly when the pleasure overload would hit.

Finding out was going to be an extraordinary experiment.

Dean

"ABOUT TIME you showed up, Jonesy." Dean tried to muster up some irritation, but he was so genuinely happy to see the traffic-stopping blonde who strolled up to his table that all he could do was grin.

Truth was, he looked forward to these regular get-togethers with Suz. For a man with enough notches to fill up a dozen belts, sex was a commonplace occurrence. A platonic friendship with a member of the female gender? That was a first for him. But Susanna Jones had quickly become one of his closest friends ever since she'd swept into his life like a hurricane. He'd first met her as his best friend's girlfriend's best friend, but these days he sometimes felt closer to Suz than he did to Parker, what with Lynn taking up most of Parker's free time.

220

"Hey you." Suz dropped a kiss on the top of his head before sinking into the chair across from him on the patio table of the bay-front restaurant. She slung her oversize purse over the back of her chair, then lifted the movie-starlet sunglasses that had been shielding her face.

Dean snickered when he saw her bloodshot eyes. "Ah, and the puzzle pieces slide together. Hungover, are we?"

Suz ran a hand through her wavy blonde hair and groaned softly. "You don't know the half of it. Note to self—never, ever let a total stranger talk you into a shooter contest. I got hustled, Colter. She drank me under the table."

"She?" His eyebrows soared in delight. "Oh, God, please, please tell me you took a walk on the girl side last night."

Red-blooded horndog that he was, he couldn't stop the naughty girl-on-girl images from flooding his mind. With the way his dick hardened painfully, you'd think he hadn't gotten laid in months, when a mere week ago he'd had a mind-blowing threesome resulting in too many orgasms to count.

"I did enough of that in college," Suz said in response to his remark. Or maybe *plea* was more accurate. "No, this was a nonsexual drinking fest. Last night was that fashion show I told you about a while ago. I was covering it for the paper, and a few of the designers invited me to the after party. I swear, you'd be *all over* this chick I met. She was a ton of fun. Smoking hot, too."

"I hope you told her all about your gorgeous best friend and how great he is in bed," Dean teased.

Suz rolled her eyes. "Sorry, babe, but no. We were too busy drinking and flirting with the non-gay designers at the party. All one-point-five of them."

Their waiter approached the table to take Suz's drink order, and Dean didn't miss the way the man's eyes lingered on her out-of-this-world rack, which was practically pouring out of the low-cut neckline of her shirt. Susanna Jones was sex personified. He would've hit that a long time ago, if the woman didn't remind him so much of himself. Somehow, sleeping with Suz would feel...weird. Obviously she agreed, because neither one of them had ever tried stepping out of the friend zone.

"Anyhoo, what have you been up to?" Suz asked once her vodka cranberry arrived. She took a dainty sip before toying with a strand of her hair. "I feel like it's been ages since we met."

"I know. We're in crunch time for that huge anniversary bash. I swear, when did we become party planners? I'm gonna tell Parker to keep me on recon for the next few jobs. It's way more fun than arranging for hotel rooms for out-of-town guests and helping Charlene go over the seating chart."

"Charlene...that's the chick Jack was sleeping with before Pepper came back to town?"

Dean nodded. "She's cute. But she strikes me as the high-maintenance type."

"Pepper's better for him," Suz agreed. "That girl is a firecracker."

Damn straight she was. But he didn't touch the remark—Suz was too perceptive for her own good, a master of reading between the lines, and if he said a single word about Pepper and how wild she was, Suz would pounce like a lioness.

Jack had threatened to break Dean's neck if he breathed a word about the threesome to anyone. Well, Suz went beyond the *anyone* category. She was Lynn's best friend, and Dean knew from experience those two didn't keep any secrets. If he told Suz, Lynn would be next to know, the truth would then reach Parker, and then Dean's head would be on the chopping block. Parker already wasn't crazy about the fact that *Jack* was sleeping with his little sister. If he knew that Dean had, too?

World war fucking three.

Fortunately, Suz reached into her purse before Dean was forced to switch to a safer, non-Pepper-related subject. "Speaking of firecrackers." She pulled out her vibrating phone and grinned. "My new BFF from last night just texted me a morning-after hangover pic." She clicked a button, then peered at the display. "Oh for Pete's sake. She thinks *this* is bad? Bitch."

Suz slid the phone across the table. "Check this out—girl still looks like a supermodel, even after downing ten shooters."

He picked up the phone mostly because he was curious to see the woman who'd out-drunk Suz, but the second his eyes focused on the screen, he froze.

No way.

No fucking way.

"She's stunning, huh?" Suz smirked. "Apparently she's half Chinese, half Native American. Look at that frickin' combination. God. I kinda wish I *did* play for the other team even now that there aren't pillows and college frat parties involved."

Dean blinked. Then blinked again. The woman in the picture was stunning, all right. With her dusky complexion, catlike dark eyes, and full, pouty lips, she belonged on the cover of a magazine.

Or at least, that's what he used to tease her...

"Earth to Dean Colter? Hello?"

He registered Suz's hand waving in front of his face. "What?"

Suz practically cackled, her green eyes sparkling. "Oh man. Looks like someone is in lust with Emma. Maybe I *should* introduce you."

His throat ran dry. "Emma?"

"That's her name. Emma—"

Emma Lee.

"—Lee. I think she's sticking around in town for a few more weeks. Should I ask her if I can give you her number?"

Swallowing was impossible—too much damn gravel in his mouth—so he swiped Suz's drink and took a hearty sip.

"Hey," she protested. "You have your own drink, you jerk."

"It's empty," he answered as he slid the glass back. "I drank it while I was waiting for your late ass." He pasted on a casual look, adding, "And naah. No need for any number exchanges. My roster's pretty full these days."

Luckily, she seemed to accept that at face value. "I know what you mean," Suz said, sighing loudly. "It's getting pretty hard to juggle all my suitors. So many men, so little time."

"Poor Jonesy. I feel for you, I really do."

But at that moment the only thing he really felt was stunned.

Emma Lee. Who the fuck could have guessed she'd ever cross his path again? Now the question remained...

Did he want to track down the only woman he'd ever given his heart? Or was he better off not poking into the ashes of the past?

Chapter Thirteen

HER FRIEND had been strangely quiet ever since Pepper had gone to rescue her. Kendra stared out the passenger window with an indecipherable expression, her fingers toying with one of her blonde pigtails.

"Penny for your thoughts."

Kendra snickered. "Penny. Hasn't she caused enough trouble already?"

"Hey, I think she did pretty damn good. At least, it was fun while it lasted," Pepper answered as she thought about her name decoy. Not having to constantly put up with the same jokes over and over again during college had been worth it.

But Pepper? That woman was living a pretty kickass life, and there was no way she wanted to miss a single second.

She gave her friend a sideways glance as she cautiously drove Jack's car into the parking lot behind DreamMakers. "Are you sure you don't want me to take you back to the apartment?"

"No, I'm okay. I don't want to get you in trouble with Jack. I can't believe he let you drive his car in the first place. But it was nice of you to come and pick me up." Kendra sighed. "It's crazy that I have to buy a whole new tire for my car! I thought it was just a regular old flat."

"Hey, at least the tire didn't blow out when you were on the freeway. I'm glad you're okay." Pepper shrugged. "Besides, it wasn't that far out of my way, and you did me a solid by helping me finish setting up all the equipment in the media room at the hotel. You've got some moves. I appreciate it."

"No prob." Kendra played her fingers over the stick shift as they sat facing the back door of the DreamMakers office. She looked as if she had something on her mind, but she'd been like that for the last couple of days, and Pepper didn't want to pry.

It was a different thing sharing an apartment. Surprisingly a lot different from living together in the dorm, and Pepper wasn't sure when—or why—the bit of unease had worked into their relationship.

Rather than voice her cryptic thoughts, Kendra suddenly brightened, turning to face Pepper with a grin.

"You wanna go out for dinner later? Maybe hit up a club?"

Pepper shook her head as the two women slid out of the car. "Jack's out on recon tonight with Dean, and they said they were heading to the office when they were done. I'm just gonna hang out here until he gets back. You sure you're okay cabbing it back to the mechanic and waiting for your tire?"

"Yeah, it'll be fine. I can flirt with all the sexy grease monkeys until my car is ready." Kendra grinned. "Trust me, I'll have a lot more fun than you will here. You've got that meeting with the barracuda, right?"

"Don't remind me." Pepper made a gagging noise as she punched in the passcode to the back-door security keypad. "I swear that woman does things just to piss me off."

"You took what she wanted. That would get anyone's back up," Kendra noted.

"Not my fault Jack's got good taste," Pepper said as she pushed through the door, glancing over her shoulder to smile at her friend. "You sure you don't want to come in and wait for the cab here?"

"Naah, I want to grab a coffee from Starbucks first. I'll call the taxi from there."

Pepper leaned in to give her friend a side hug, then said goodbye and headed to the conference room to prepare the final things she needed for this last dreaded meeting with Charlene. When she realized she'd left the connection wires she needed in the backseat of Jack's car, she sighed and rushed out to the lot to grab them.

She was just closing the car door when Charlene pulled into the parking space next to her, her tires damn near rolling over Pepper's toes.

Pepper adjusted her smile to maximum "you're a bitch, and we both know it, but I'm the bitch who got Jack" smile. "Well, hey, Charlene. So lovely to see you again."

This time Charlene didn't even pretend. She tossed off a dirty stare and led the way to the building. "I've got too much on my plate to make nice right now, little girl. Let's get this done, because we both know we don't want to be playing at being besties."

Oh, so it was going to be that way, was it? Pepper could go for the jugular just as hard. "Not a problem with me. The customer is always right."

Charlene paused before she went in the door. "Is Jack here?" she asked.

"No."

The woman hesitated in the doorframe. "But his car is here. Did he go out on a job?"

"Of course not," Pepper shared. "I drove it."

The expression on Charlene's face was a charming combination of admiration and disgust, with a touch of jealousy sprinkled on top like teeny blue, red, and pink candy confectionery. Pepper allowed a small moment of utter satisfaction to well up once more.

"She's a lovely ride," she said purposefully. "Handles the corners so well, don't you think?"

Charlene pushed past her with a soft sniff. "I have somewhere to be in a short while. Let's get this over with."

Bazinga.

During their brief meeting, however, Pepper became aware of an entirely new emotion tangling around the thoughts of Jack and the trust that he'd put in her.

Not only the fact that he let her drive his car, but that he'd trusted her with a whole lot of other things. She wasn't going to lie—the threesome with Dean had been freaking awesome, and something she had never imagined bossy, possessive Jack would ever do in a million years. But he had, for her. That was *huge*.

And even though she'd enjoyed herself immensely, the excitement of having the two guys showering her with attention had been spectacular only because Jack was there. Every touch, every joke, every interaction between them seemed to tug her heartstrings a little more.

By the time the meeting with Charlene finished, Pepper was eager to see the woman go. Charlene's presence only reminded her that Jack hadn't been living as a monk before they'd started dating, and she still felt a tad insecure in the face of Charlene's infuriating elegance.

As they rose from the table, Pepper had to remind herself that *she'd* gotten Jack. Charlene hadn't, except for a brief moment in time. "This media presentation better go exactly as we discussed," Charlene said coolly. "I don't want any snags or mistakes."

"I've got everything under control," Pepper replied, fighting the urge to grit her teeth. Or maybe snarl at the woman.

"You'd better. This is very important to my family. Please don't screw it up." With that, Charlene slid out the door with stiff shoulders and fast strides.

Once the woman was gone, Pepper made her way to Jack's office, the memories of entering the building in the pitch black nearly three months ago rushing into her mind. How things had changed. She wasn't the same woman anymore, she realized as she curled up on the corner of the couch, with Jack's soft blanket once again around her shoulders.

She stared into space. She still had some work to do, but right now she wanted to think harder about this idea. The one about how Jack trusted her.

It meant so much to her, especially since Parker still insisted on treating her like a little girl. And no matter how often Jack pointed out that it was because she was his younger sister, it didn't matter. Jeez. Would the ass still treat her like that when they were in their fifties?

Jack didn't treat her like a child. The thought made every bit of her warm and happy.

After several more minutes of basking in her Jack-centered thoughts, she got her act together, abandoning his office to the small workstation she'd set up near the staff room. Putting the final touches on the media display was satisfying, and she was nearly done when the door swung open. She lifted her head eagerly, but instead of Jack, she found her brother, storm clouds all over his face.

She shot to her feet. "What's wrong? Did something happen to Lynn?"

Parker jerked to a stop, his dark eyes narrowing as he took her in. "Are you the one responsible?"

Total confusion. "What?"

He strode forward another two paces, towering over her. "Were you the one driving Jack's car when it happened?"

"When what happened...?"

"Jeez, Pepper. How could you be so careless?" Parker's entire body tensed with emotion. "Jack freaking loves that car."

"What the hell is your problem?" Pepper demanded. "You've got some kind of enormous stick up your ass."

"Seriously, you're telling me you have no idea what I'm talking about?" Parker folded his arms over his chest and looked at her in disgust. "You're not ten years old anymore. I would've thought by now you'd learn to own up to your mistakes."

"What mistake?" She shook her head indignantly. "I've been in the damn office for the last hour and a half, working my ass off, I might add. Where do you get off coming in here and telling me—" She took a deep breath then let it out slowly. Obviously something was wrong, and yelling at him was not getting them anywhere, so she tried again. "*What* are you talking about?"

"Come on," Parker muttered. "See for yourself."

They headed outside, and it didn't take a rocket scientist to figure out exactly what Parker wanted to show her. She gasped when she rounded Jack's sleek black car and spotted the rear bumper. The tail of the classic car had been crumpled, as if someone had backed into a fire hydrant or a barrier.

Pepper moved forward in a panic to examine the damage. "Dammit, Parker. This wasn't here when I parked the car. I swear it wasn't."

"So what, we have car-bashing fairies in the parking lot now? Just like we had perfume-tossing fairies before?"

She glared at him. "That wasn't my fault either, so don't start with that one again."

Parker shot out a hand at the car. "No, it's not like the perfume because if this happened after you parked it, then where's the glass? If someone bumped the car right here, the glass would've fallen to the ground underneath, and there's nothing there, Pepper."

She felt sick to her stomach, but mostly because she hated the fact that she was going to have to explain what she didn't know how to explain.

"I didn't do it," she insisted. A jolt of triumph suddenly shot through her. "Go and check the security tape! You'll *see* that the car was fine when I drove into the lot."

"The system is still down," Parker mumbled.

Her jaw fell open. "Are you *kidding* me? It's been weeks since I pointed out how outdated that piece of junk is! How have you not fixed it yet?" It was her turn to shake her head in disgust. "You should be on top of this stuff. You were an *Army Ranger*, Parker!"

"Exactly," he snapped back. "And so were Jack and Dean and Colby. And don't get me started on how deadly Gillian is. The five of us can protect this building in our sleep. We don't need goddamn cameras to tell us when there's a threat."

Pepper's gaze shifted back to the damaged car. "Well, the camera could have told you that I *didn't fucking do this*."

"Sure, little sis. If you say so."

Anger bubbled in her gut. "Don't you dare use that condescending tone with me, *big* brother. I didn't hit anything, but damn it, believe what you want, okay? I'll pay to have it fixed regardless."

Parker shook his head in irritation. "Why don't you go home? I'll talk to Jack when he gets back from his job and take care of the damages."

"I'll talk to him myself. He's my boyfriend."

"And he's my best friend."

They stared each other down, tensions rising as their heated gazes clashed.

"Go home, Pepper," Parker said in an ominous voice.

"No way." She scowled hard at him. "I'm not going anywhere."

JACK COULD almost see the thunder clouds brewing over them as the siblings stood together in the parking lot. Pepper had both fists planted on her hips, and Parker's arms were folded into a wall. Jack had seen them in that position a hundred times over the years, and the aggressive standoff raised his hackles.

"They never fucking stop," he muttered to Dean.

"They're both too stubborn." Dean's tone was absentminded as he backed the car into a parking space, setting up like he usually did for a quick getaway.

Jack glanced at his friend. "You've been awfully quiet tonight. Something on your mind?"

The other man shook his head, then let loose a cocky grin. "Are you ready to go rescue your girlfriend from her overbearing big brother?"

Jack sighed. "Hey, we both know Parker's not that bad."

"I'd still fuck you first."

Jack snickered as they made their way across the parking lot, but the humor faded fast when Parker turned on him with a grave expression.

"Something wrong?" Jack said warily.

His friend hesitated.

"I need to talk to you," Pepper interjected.

Jack moved toward her, pausing for a second before figuring, screw it. He wanted to kiss his girlfriend hello,

VIVIAN AREND & ELLE KENNEDY

and Parker would have to get used to the fact that his little sister and his best friend were going to—

He'd just reached for her when he noticed the crumpled back end of the car. A single curse escaped before he slammed his lips together.

"I swear I didn't do it," Pepper blurted out. "Someone must've driven into the parking lot and hit the corner turning around, but I'll pay for it to be fixed. I know it looks bad, but really, it's not my fault."

It was a hollow pit in his stomach as he moved to examine the damages. *It was just a car.* Even if Pepper had totaled it while driving, it wasn't as if it were the end of the world. A wild mishmash of thoughts raced through his brain, but he couldn't seem to spit the words out.

All he could think of were the hours spent with his dad. Restoring and painting and working on the car. The only memories he had from his youth that were at all happy, and it didn't matter that it was *just* a car. Somehow family was wrapped up in it.

Pepper was back, threading her arms around him as she pressed her head to his chest, her voice soft. "I'm so sorry."

"You don't have to pay for anything," Parker said, stepping in and laying a hand on Jack's shoulder. "We'll cover the repairs out of DreamMakers' expenses."

Jack frowned. "I have insurance. I'll fix it myself."

Parker stiffened, the disapproving gaze he let fall on Pepper all too clearly stating what he thought. The man obviously believed his sister was to blame.

Jack shook his head. "It's okay. Don't worry about it," he insisted.

"I'll take care of it," Parker replied firmly.

235

Jack tensed as the whirlwind woman made of fire and passion who he'd become so attached to lifted her head and glared evilly at her brother. "Do you think I'm stupid as well as everything else? Why don't you just come out and tell Jack you think I'm a liar?"

"Pepper," Jack said in warning. His brain and heart hurt too much to deal with another round of bickering at the moment.

She took a half step away from him, looking at him in disbelief. "Are you taking his side? Again? Like all the other times when he thinks I've done something childish?"

"No one is saying you've done anything," Parker began. "But right now you're *acting* damn childish."

"Screw you, too," Pepper snapped. She caught her hands in the front of Jack's shirt, staring up at him pleadingly. "Jack. Tell my brother that you trust me. That you don't think I'm being childish, and that you believe I didn't mess up your car."

"Pepper, give me ten damn seconds to do something without ordering me around," Jack snapped, aware that he was out of line, but he was tired, and the entire situation had put his nerves on edge.

Her face went completely white. "I'll get it fixed," she whispered. "I promise."

"It's just a car," he said through clenched teeth.

"But I know it means a lot to you."

When Parker muttered something in the background, Pepper whirled on her brother again. "Would you fucking stop that?"

"What? I didn't do anything."

As their voices once again rose in anger and accusation, Jack resisted the urge to slam his fist in the already crumpled back end of his car. He was no stranger to screaming matches—his parents had engaged in plenty of them before his mom had packed up and walked right out the door.

Jack threw his hands in the air, his frustration boiling over. "Would you two just shut the hell up?"

The siblings froze.

"Jack—" Parker started.

"Seriously, just *shut up*," he growled. "Do you two not realize how good you have it? How lucky you are to have each other? I see you going at each other's throats and I want to slap some fucking sense into you! You have no goddamn idea what it's like to..." He stopped abruptly, his throat closing up as the memories closed in.

His gaze drifted back to his dad's car, the only measly possession, other than the couch in his office, that his father had bothered giving to him.

Pepper followed his gaze, speaking in a cautious tone. "Jack, I promise, I didn't mess up your car. I—"

"Jesus Christ!" he interrupted. "Not everything is about you, Pepper! Or you—" He shot an angry look at Parker. "Fuck the car. Fuck your bullshit fighting. Fuck. *This*."

Breathing hard, he pushed past both of them, nearly slamming into Dean, who'd been lingering on the sidelines, his eyes wide. Jack didn't blame his buddy for looking shocked. He didn't normally lose his shit like this, but he'd reached his breaking point, and at the moment, he needed to be as far away as he could from Pepper and Parker's arguing, and the car, and most of all the goddamn memories.

Ignoring the concerned voices behind him, he squared his shoulders and stormed around the building. Fuck everything.

He hailed a cab and headed home.

Chapter Fourteen

PEPPER STARED at Jack's retreating back. Stricken. And absolutely stunned by what had happened. She'd never heard Jack raise his voice in anger before. Never seen him this upset.

She slowly turned her head back to Jack's Aston Martin, but it was becoming increasingly obvious that his fit of temper had nothing to do with the car.

Oh no, it was about so much more.

"I'll go talk to him," Parker said quietly, all of his bluster faded.

Her hand flew up to stop her brother from taking another step. "No," she told him. "*I* will. And if you argue with me right now, so help me God—"

239

To her surprise, Parker instantly backed down. The shame flickering in his eyes was unmistakable. "You're right. You go."

She didn't bother dwelling on her brother's sudden one-eighty—or the fact that he'd actually uttered the words *you're right* for the first time in...well, ever. She was too worried about Jack at the moment. Her laidback, flirty Jack, whose face had held such devastation before he'd raced off that her heart was aching for him.

Dean jogged back to their side just as Pepper prepared to dash into the building to track Jack down. "He's headed home. Just heard him catch a cab."

"You didn't try to stop him?" Parker asked.

The look Dean gave Parker could have flash frozen a year's supply of fish. "You really think I was about to order him around when he's already over the edge?"

Her need to go comfort and confront Jack grew by the moment, along with her helplessness.

Then Parker shocked the hell out of her. He caught her by the hand and tugged her toward his car. "Come on, I'll drop you at his place."

The ride was silent for the first couple minutes, nothing but the faint buzz of wheels spinning under the car.

Parker let out a huge sigh. "I keep screwing up, don't I?"

"It takes two to tango," she admitted. "I'm not the easiest person to get along with at times."

"Actually, you're pretty easygoing. I..." He clutched the wheel tighter, the platinum ring Lynn had given him shining like a bit of moonlight in the glow of the streetlights. "When you were gone it was easier to think of you as a grown-up. Having you around—I just want

240

the best for you, and I forget you can take care of yourself. It's wrong. I'm sorry."

More heart-aching revelation. Pepper swallowed around the knot in her throat. "I'm sorry, too. I push too hard. You're a great big brother when you're not smothering me. And you chose the most awesome woman to fall in love with, so I know not all hope is lost."

He snorted. "Lynn *is* awesome. And she's going to kick my butt for being an idiot."

"She'll have to go through me," Pepper said as she laid her hand over his for a moment and squeezed tight, blinking hard to keep tears from filling her eyes.

He dropped her in front of the apartment doors, flashing her a thumbs-up before he pulled away and left her.

Pepper grabbed the hidden key Jack had shown her all those months ago when she'd crashed at his apartment for the week. She let herself in and found him sprawled on the couch, one hand absently running over the dark gray cushions.

He lifted his head at her entrance, a tired look in his eyes. "I'm not in the mood to talk about that damned car, Pepper."

"Screw the car." She was at his side in a nanosecond, nudging until he sat up and made room for her to settle next to him. She put her arms around him and hugged him tight. "That's not why I'm here. Tell me what's wrong, Jackjack."

She felt his answering sigh travel through his whole body. His chin fell on her shoulder, his breath tickling the side of her neck as he spoke. "It's nothing. Don't worry about it."

"Bullshit." She eased back and gripped his cheeks with her hands. "It's *not* nothing, and I *am* worried. I saw the look on your face when Parker and I were arguing. I know it annoys you when we fight, but it was different this time. It was like you were..." She searched for the right words. "Seeing a ghost, maybe?"

"I may as well have." His voice cracked slightly. "Watching people fight isn't exactly new to me."

She hesitated, sweeping her fingers over the strong line of his jaw. "Your parents?"

He nodded. But he didn't elaborate.

"You've never talked about them, for as long as I've known you," she said cautiously.

A derisive sound left his mouth. "Wasn't much to talk about. My parents fought. My mother left. End of story."

Pepper gently touched his cheek. "We both know there's more to it than that."

"What the hell else is there to say?" The vehemence in his tone startled her. "There was a reason I spent every waking hour at your place when I was growing up. Your house was my salvation, Pepper. Just being around you and Parker and your parents..." He breathed heavily. "It was everything I wished I had, okay? And when I was there, it meant that I didn't have to see..."

He trailed off, but she didn't let him stop. "To see what?"

"My goddamn zombie of a father!" he burst out.

Pepper's eyes widened as Jack shot to his feet, raking both hands through his hair as he paced to the window, staring into the darkness. "It was like living with a coma patient," he mumbled, anguish etched into his voice. "After Mom left, he barely said a word to me.

242

VIVIAN AREND & ELLE KENNEDY

Barely looked at me. I was a living, breathing reminder of the woman he loved—the woman he'd frickin' *forced* into marriage."

She couldn't stop the gasp that escaped. The only detail she'd known about Jack's background was that his mother had walked out on him and his dad, but this revelation...it sent a spike of agony to her heart.

Jack caught her shocked look and laughed harshly. "Oh yeah, you heard me right. My dad knocked her up when they were nineteen. She didn't want to keep me but he talked her into it. And then he pretty much strong-armed her into marrying him."

Pepper's heart split in two. She rose from the couch and marched up to him, stilling his frantic pacing by planting both hands on his chest. "Oh God. Jack."

"She didn't want to be a mother. Didn't want to be a wife." His eyes darkened. "My dad was desperate to make a good life for her, but she couldn't keep on pretending. I used to sit in my room and hear them screaming at each other. Dad would beg her to try harder, she'd yell at him for making her be there."

Tears pricked Pepper's eyes, her hands trembling as she stroked his chest, which was heaving with each ragged breath he sucked into his lungs. "I'm so sorry, baby."

Jack didn't seem to hear her. He kept talking in a faraway tone. "Eventually she had enough. I came home from school one day to find her packing her bags." His voice shook again, harder, ringing with torment. "She didn't even kiss me goodbye. You know what she did?"

Pepper wasn't sure she wanted to hear it, but she forced herself to whisper, "What?"

243

"She *shook my hand*. I was seven years old, Pepper. She got on her knees so we were at eye level, and she shook my fucking hand and told me to mind my dad. That's it. Then she walked out the door, and I never saw or heard from her again."

The tears spilled over. No stopping them, either. From the way Jack kept gulping repeatedly, she knew he was fighting back tears of his own, but he was too damn macho to give in to them, and so she cried instead. She cried for *him*. For the young boy he'd been when his own mother abandoned him and his dad mentally and emotionally checked out of his life. For the man he was now, strong and smart and living his life as if he hadn't a care in the world.

She suddenly realized exactly how difficult it was for him to witness her and Parker's shouting matches. She and Parker loved each other, and they would never abandon each other. *Ever.* But how often had their frequently negative interactions struck a chord with Jack? How many times had he seen them argue and been reminded of his parents' volatile relationship?

"I'm so sorry," she said again. She leaned up and pressed a kiss to the center of his throat, feeling the rapid hammering of his pulse against her lips. "I didn't realize how hard it would be for you to see me and Parker fight. I didn't realize...that your mom...and your dad..."

Jack swallowed again. "It wasn't the worst childhood. I mean, other people have it a lot worse than I did."

"Doesn't matter," she said firmly. "It still affected you, and you're allowed to be upset about it. There's no list that says you have to endure XYZ for your situation to qualify as shitty."

"I know. It's just..." His brown eyes shifted to the picture on the wall, one taken during a Wilson barbecue once upon a time. Glasses and hands were raised in the air as smiling faces turned to the camera, immortalized forever. "You don't get how lonely it was, how frustrating it was. I'd come over to your house and your family was so damn perfect, you know? And then I'd go home and my dad would look right through me. The only time, in all the years after Mom left, that he ever paid any attention to me was when we were fixing up that stupid car."

Guilt rippled through her as she remembered the dented bumper, even though she hadn't been the one to cause the destruction. "He left you the car when he died?"

Jack nodded, then shook his head abruptly. "And the couch in my office. That's it. Did I get love? Forget it. Or support, or advice, or freaking *conversation*? He couldn't be bothered." Bitterness streaked across his face. "A couch and a car. That's all my father deemed important enough to leave as a legacy."

"I'm sorry." She seemed to be saying that a lot, but she couldn't stop herself. "Not just about your dad, but about everything. I'm sorry I got mad that you didn't back me up out there. I get why you don't want to take sides." Pepper took a breath. "I promise I will never put you in that position again. And I *will* pay for the car repairs. You trusted me with your car, and I screwed up, even if I wasn't the one who busted it. I should have parked it somewhere safer, maybe, or—"

"Enough with the damn car already!" But Jack was smiling, and she could see in his eyes that he wasn't angry with her. He opened his arms, and she crawled right in, clinging to him tightly. Somehow she needed to show him exactly how much more he deserved, not just today, but all those years ago.

She pressed a palm to his chest, right over his pounding heart. "Let me take care of you?"

BETWEEN ONE moment and the next, the atmosphere in the room changed. The woman in his arms was soft and strong, all at the same time, and she didn't bother waiting for his answer. Jack concentrated on breathing out all of his frustrations and anger, and all of the hurtful memories that had flooded into him over the past hour, while Pepper pressed her lips to his chest as if she could kiss everything better.

A reluctant smile hit his lips. "You like my T-shirt?" he teased.

"I *love* your T-shirt," she confessed breathlessly, kissing him again and again as she worked her way across his chest. "It's the most gorgeous T-shirt I've ever seen in my life, and I demand you give it to me this instant."

She helped tug the fabric free from his jeans, but Jack was the one who grabbed the bottom of the shirt, peeling it over his head and abandoning it on the couch. Pepper returned in an instant, her warm lips back to tease him. Little flicks of her tongue accompanied the heated kisses, her hands stroking the sides of his abdomen.

He rarely gave her control when they fooled around, mostly because he was too impatient to let her play. Or because he was a bossy bastard and could never hold back for long enough.

But today was different. Today it didn't seem to be about sex. It was connection, and caring. When she dragged her nails along the ridges of his six-pack, his body reacted in a very predictable way, his cock rising eagerly. But the touch—

Tender. Giving. As if Pepper were using her fingers and lips to deliver some new kind of language, passing on a wordless message strictly with touch.

She jerked open his button, sliding the zipper down just far enough that she could ease her hands under the fabric of his jeans and cup his butt in both hands. Fingers massaging strongly as she continued to dance kisses over his torso.

She licked one of his nipples, grazing it with her teeth for a second, and Jack shuddered. "Are you going to eat me alive?"

"You're giving me ideas," she murmured, pushing the fabric off his hips and toward the floor. She moved with the clothing, waiting until he stepped out of his jeans. Tugging his socks off as he laughed. He was naked, and she was fully dressed.

"I don't think this happens often," he pointed out, swinging a finger between them.

Pepper caught his hands and pulled him with her down the hallway to his bedroom, walking backwards as her gaze ate him up. "Jackjack, you should live in a clothing-optional climate at all times."

"I think you should join me."

She pointed at the bed. "I still have plans."

"And you can't do those plans while you're naked? Sad plans."

"You're so bad," she whispered, pushing on his shoulders to get him to roll on his stomach.

Jack would've complained about the position except she was stripping off her clothing and crawling on top of him, a bottle of lotion appearing out of nowhere.

And then her hands were on him working magic. Rubbing and pressing, her strong thumbs digging into the muscles he'd clenched tight enough to leave knots.

"You know I'm never going to let you leave this room again," Jack warned. "Morning to night all you're going to do is give me massages."

A sharp nip to his butt cheek sent an electric pulse raging through his system. "Is that all you want me to do?" she asked, innuendo dripping from her tone.

"Let me roll over, and I think you might find a few new things to massage."

"In a minute."

Complaints vanished, because even though he was lying on a cock sorely wanting attention, she'd turned around and focused on his feet. Never in a million years could he have believed how freaking awesome it felt to have someone else work out the aches.

He figured she would get tired eventually, but he'd forgotten how determined Pepper was. Every bit of him got thorough attention. His calves, the backs of his thighs, his butt muscles—and suddenly he wasn't simply lying on top of a thick cock, he had to change position before he passed out.

Jack rolled, reaching down to capture Pepper before she could decide to try anything else. "You need to take care of me now."

"That's what I've been doing."

He caught hold of her hand and lowered it to his groin, wrapping her fingers around his cock. "This bit."

Her lips twitched as she pressed her breasts against his torso, wiggling in tight and slowly stroking him. The sadness was still there in the depths of her eyes, but the mischief was never far away. Not when they were together.

She licked her lips.

He tilted his head and leaned in so he could lick them, too.

A burst of laughter escaped her. "Jack?"

"Pepper?"

"Jack."

This time she'd spoken in such a sultry, lust-filled tone, that with the accompanying hand motion it was damn near enough to make him spill uncontrollably over her fingers.

It'd been long enough. He dropped her to the mattress under him, pulling his fingers between her legs and testing her quickly. Fingertips soaking wet showed him she was just as turned on as he was.

He brought his fingers to his mouth and licked them clean, humming happily. "Mmmm, Pepper. My favorite flavor."

She stared up at him, wrapping one leg around his hip as he settled between her legs. It was so perfect, and so familiar, and completely brand-new as he tilted his hips and pushed into her welcoming heat.

Those emerald-green eyes pinned him in place, passion-filled and dancing with life as he buried himself completely.

He wanted to go slow. To savor every moment as the rich connection between them continued to grow. Her fingertips skimmed over his shoulders and stroked the back of his neck, and he leaned down and captured her lips in a scorching-hot kiss. Bodies joined, rocking together with a growing fervor until there was nowhere to go. Nothing to do except become one.

Her eyelids fluttered as her body tightened around him, but she refused to look away. Refused to break the connection.

And Jack understood just a little bit more exactly what love was. He might not have been taught it by the people who had brought him into the world. But he'd learned it from his neighbors—a family kind of love. And he'd learned it from Parker and Dean—a brotherly love that would go to their deaths. He knew about sexual love in spades.

But staring into Pepper's eyes he realized there was an entirely new kind of love that he was experiencing for the first time in his life. The kind of love he would give anything for, give up everything to have.

A forever kind of love.

As they lay wrapped in each other's arms, the warm glow of sexual satisfaction painting everything, it wasn't the sex that made him press a kiss to her temple. It was that other sensation deep in his heart.

The words trembled on his tongue, but he wasn't ready to let go yet. He needed a little more practice just thinking them first. But as she fell asleep in his arms with a smile on her face, Jack couldn't resist giving them one test run.

"I love you, Pepper."

Chapter Fifteen

"YOU'RE LATE." Charlene's flat observation greeted Pepper as she hurried into the media room on the first floor of the Grande Hotel.

She'd sprinted through the lobby carting her heavy messenger bag, so her breathing flew out in quick pants as she skidded to a stop near the table laden with monitors and audio equipment. On the other side of the cramped room, Charlene stood with her slender arms folded over the front of her silky blue dress. The party wasn't starting for another three hours, yet the woman already looked like the belle of the ball.

"I'm sorry," Pepper said breathlessly, setting down her bag. "I don't have a car, so I had to cab it over here, and my driver was ten minutes late to pick me up."

Charlene's perfect nose turned up. "You don't have a car."

A thinly veiled judgment, but Pepper decided to treat it like a question. "Haven't gotten around to buying one yet." She looked the woman up and down, opting to try and be nice for a change. "You look fantastic. Everyone at the party is going to love that dress."

"What? No." Looking frazzled, Charlene adjusted one of her spaghetti straps. "This isn't what I'm wearing tonight. It's just a day dress."

A day dress? What the hell was that? And...*seriously?*

Pepper made another wise decision not to voice a smart-aleck remark. She unzipped her bag and pulled out her laptop. "I got your email about the changes you wanted for the photo collage. I fixed it this morning, but I want to get your official approval before I finalize the file."

"Get to it then." Charlene flung a hand at the computer. "I still need to get my hair done and then head to the airport to pick up my brother and sister-in-law."

The woman sounded so stressed that Pepper was willing to cut her some slack. She snapped to action, plugging in her laptop and shoving the flash drive into its slot. A moment later, she clicked on the file, glancing over at Charlene as she waited for it to load. "So I didn't alter any of the older photographs, but I did play around with the contrast like you asked, so the images are clearer. And for those last-minute wedding photos you found, I—huh. This is weird."

An icon had appeared on the screen, informing her of a file error.

"Why is it saying that?" Charlene leaned over Pepper's shoulder as she voiced the demand.

She pursed her lips. "I have no idea. Hold on." She closed the box and went into the hard drive menu to load the file from there. Again, the error message popped up.

Pepper bit her lip and attempted another solution, ejecting the drive, then sliding it back in, using the digital program to try to open the project. This time, the message was different, informing her that the file was corrupted and couldn't be opened.

"What the hell?" she mumbled under her breath.

Behind her, Charlene cursed loudly. "Why isn't it working? What did you do?"

"I didn't do anything," Pepper protested. "The file was working this morning."

"Well, it's not working *now*! So *fix it*!"

She ignored the woman's shrill yells and refocused on the screen. None of her troubleshooting paid off, and by the time she admitted defeat, Charlene was spitting mad, her high heels clicking on the floor as she rage-paced.

"I can't believe this is happening!" the older woman hissed. "I should have known better than to trust a *child* with something so important!"

Pepper wearily rose from the chair. "Relax. I'm not sure what's wrong with the file, but I have—"

Charlene cut her off. "Of course you're not sure! You're incompetent, Pepper!" She made a sound of disgust. "Pepper. What kind of moronic parents name their kid *Pepper*?"

"*Hey*," she said sharply. "Leave my parents out of this. It's not their fault."

"You're right. It's *your* fault. Do you know how much money my brother and I spent on this fucking party? Tens of thousands of dollars! Oh God, I can't believe you screwed everything up!" Charlene's breathing became shallow. "Actually, no, I *can* believe it. I'm *not* surprised you screwed up. The only reason Parker hired you was because you're family. Or maybe Jack was the one who convinced him—we both know what a horny bastard that man is. He probably wanted easy access to you."

Anger rose in Pepper's throat. "Enough. Stop bringing other people into this. I have everything under control—"

But Charlene wasn't listening. She just kept spitting out nasty words and accusations. "You really think Jack is going to stick around, little girl? He'll get bored of you in no time and dump your immature ass." The woman jabbed a finger in the direction of the computer. "Go get Parker. *Now*. At least your brother knows how to get things done. I want *him* to fix this."

Fury and panic warred in Pepper's gut, twisting her insides until her entire body felt tight and cold. No way was she bringing Parker into this messed-up situation. They'd only called a ceasefire the other day, with Parker admitting that he treated her like a child. Pepper refused to give her brother another opportunity to chew her out, especially since, as she kept trying to tell the aggravating woman, she really did have everything under control.

"Parker knows shit-all about this level of computer work," Pepper replied, trying to keep her voice as calm as possible. "I, on the other hand, have not one, but two backups of the project at my apartment."

Charlene blinked. "You do?"

"Yes, and you would've known that already if you had let me finish." Pepper clenched her teeth. "So right now, I'm going to pretend you didn't say all those nasty things, and I'm going to fix this error. Which, by the way, was not a result of anything I did. Files get corrupted sometimes. It happens. I'll go home and grab the extra drives, and we'll be good to go."

The other woman still didn't look happy, but her cheeks lost some of their crimson red flush. "Fine," she snapped. "Go get them. I'll be done at the salon in an hour."

"Fine," Pepper mimicked. "I'll meet you back here and we'll get everything taken care of."

Without another word, Charlene marched out the door, leaving Pepper to gather her equipment in stony silence. God. This was the last thing she needed. She'd stayed up half the night adding the newly found pictures to the stupid project in an attempt to impress Charlene, and instead of receiving a thank-you for all her hard work, she'd gotten a scathing verbal assault instead.

But she refused to let her mind linger on the hurtful words Charlene had hurled her way. She *wasn't* a child. She was smart and mature and fully capable of handling this gig without running to Parker or Jack for assistance. In fact, she had no intention of telling them about the corrupted file. They had enough on their plates at the moment.

Slinging her bag over her shoulder, Pepper reached for her cell phone and quickly pulled up Kendra's number as she hurried to the hotel lobby. "Hey," she blurted when her friend answered. "I really, really need your help right now!"

Kendra's voice was laced with concern. "What's wrong?"

"Did you end up going to that shoe store on 23rd? The one down the road from the Grande Hotel?"

"Yeah, I'm there now. Why—?"

"Can you come pick me up from the hotel? I desperately need a ride back to our place. Like *right now.*"

"Sure, but what's going on—?"

"I'll tell you everything when you get here," Pepper interrupted. "Just hurry."

A beat. Then Kendra spoke briskly. "I'm on my way."

Like a true friend, Kendra not only burned rubber into the parking lot, she burned rubber out, after Pepper leapt into the moving vehicle. She strapped herself in while pressed against the door.

"I am so glad you were in the area. I'm having the most incredibly shitty morning ever, but you're a lifesaver."

"You sound frazzled. Take a couple deep breaths, and we'll get you home as soon as possible," Kendra soothed. "But what the heck happened?"

"Technology sucks." Pepper leaned her head back and took the advice, breathing slowly and trying to calm her rapidly beating heart. "I had a file failure, and to make it worse, Princess Charlene had to be there to witness my faux pas, so now I'm playing catch-up. I've got maybe fifty minutes left before I have to prove myself."

"You have what you need at the apartment?"

Pepper nodded. "I was smart enough to make backups. Of course, I could have been even smarter and stuck the damn things in my pocket instead of leaving them on my desk."

"Don't beat yourself up over it," Kendra said as they closed in on the apartment. "Only, you should probably double-check your files before you leave."

"Definitely. I'm so paranoid it will totally be worth the extra two minutes to make sure everything is in order." She glanced over at her friend, who was concentrating on pulling into one of the few parking stalls along the road. "Wait here for me?"

Kendra shook her head. "I have to run upstairs, too. I forgot a couple of things I need for later tonight."

The two of them raced through the security at the front door and into the elevator, the slow ride leaving Pepper feeling as if there weren't enough air in the teeny box. Gears above them clicked like a countdown timer.

Tick.

Tick.

Tick.

But even when they burst into the apartment, she wasn't going to be a fool and simply accept the other drives were ready. Maybe the set she'd bought were damaged to begin with.

She dropped behind her computer and hurriedly checked her work.

Behind her, Kendra was moving around in the kitchen. "I know we're in a rush, but when you've got what you need, you might want to touch up your makeup. You look like you've seen a ghost. A little bit of armor when you face Charlene might be a good thing."

Dammit. Pepper jammed the media sticks into her pocket and rushed into her bedroom, slipping into the bathroom to examine her face carefully for a moment.

She didn't think she looked pale. If anything, all the rushing around had brought a flush to her cheeks, and her eyes were bright. The only thing she could think of was dragging a brush through her hair and grabbing a colored lip balm so when she told Charlene to kiss her ass, she'd do it in style.

She had both hands raised in the air when out of the corner of her eye she noticed the bathroom door swinging closed. She jerked around and grabbed for the doorknob, but it was too late. An ominous click rang through the miniscule room. "Fuck. *No.* Not now."

Even with two hands on the knob and twisting as hard as she could, the door refused to budge. Frantically, Pepper placed her palms on the door and banged. "Kendra. Help, I'm trapped in this damn room again."

Her friend's anxious reply came a couple moments later. "Pepper? What are you doing?"

"The portal to hell closed on me. Get me out." God. Why now?

The scrambling noises from the other side of the door weren't very reassuring. Since they'd moved into the apartment, Pepper had gotten stuck in the bathroom two more times after that initial adventure. She'd taken to leaving the door propped open for a reason.

"It's not moving," Kendra moaned. "I'll get the supe. Be back right away."

"Wait," Pepper called, but this time there was no answer.

She stared at the solid barrier between her and freedom for all of two seconds before twirling toward the window. Screw this. The last time it had taken nearly an hour to track down the maintenance dude, and Pepper didn't have anywhere near that amount of time. She jerked open the window and stuck her head out, examining the fire escape.

There had to be laws against this, but she didn't give a damn. Pepper made her way onto the rickety metal platform outside her bathroom, clutching the railing tightly as she stayed as close to the wall as possible.

She reached for her phone to tell Kendra to meet her down at the car, but the check came up empty. Her phone—

Of course. She could picture it, lying beside her computer where she'd dropped it in her frantic rush to check the flash drives.

One cautious step after the other, Pepper made her way down the fire escape, metal creaking around her. Bits of paint flaked off and left her hands covered with a light dusting of black metallic flecks.

Lowering the final section of ladder caused a loud screeching noise like a dragon calling out its dismay at intruders invading its territory. Pepper was far more worried about the final drop from the bottom of the ladder to the ground in the back alley. She took a deep breath and worked her way down until she was clinging to the bottom rung.

Why did she have to be so short?

She let go, timing it the best she could and using her knees to absorb the shock of the final five or six feet as she free fell. Momentum sent her all the way to her ass, but as she gingerly brought herself back to her feet it was to find she'd made it in one piece.

"Holy crap, maybe I should join the guys when they do recon." She gave a fist pump then raced to the front of the building. She could use the intercom to get ahold of Kendra. Or maybe the phone at the—

Kendra's car was gone.

Moving slowly toward the mysteriously empty space didn't give her any more clues as to why it was empty. "Where the hell…?"

"Penny?"

Could this day get any weirder? She whirled toward the voice.

"Adam?"

Her former classmate stood to the side of the front entrance, clutching his hands awkwardly. He wore jeans and a faded green T-shirt, and his black hair had grown out since she'd last seen him, curling under his ears. He was a handsome guy, but the sight of him only made her angry.

"I need to talk to you," Adam said, sounding distressed. "I want to explain—"

"I really don't have time for this right now." The panic she'd felt earlier was back, and a whole lot stronger. "I have work to do, and there isn't anything that I want to talk to you about, you shit."

"I didn't post about you," he burst out. "I swear I didn't. My Facebook page was hacked, and the next thing I know someone posted stuff that I never would've dreamed of sharing, and I had no way of getting rid of it or changing it."

There were way too many questions she needed answered, but at least he had her attention. "You know, that's fascinating, but this is *not* a good time. I need to be somewhere else five minutes ago."

"I can drive you," he offered eagerly before cringing. "I know, I'm probably one of the last people you would trust, but I swear, anything you need and I promise I'll do what I can to help you. I feel so awful about—"

"Give me your driver's license," she demanded. Along with the mystery of Kendra's missing car, the media sticks were burning a hole in her pocket. She needed to get back to the gala this instant.

Adam fumbled in his wallet then handed the card to her.

She pointed at him, backing toward the coffee shop to the side of the apartment doors. "I'm leaving your info with my friend. If *anything* happens to me, they will know exactly who to track down."

He nodded. "I'll grab the Jeep."

She was walking a fool's path, but Pepper had no choice. After doing what she needed to be safe by leaving Adam's information with Timothy the barista, Adam could take her back to the hotel, and maybe during the drive he could explain what the heck he was talking about.

A SEA of happy faces surrounded Jack, the grand foyer of the hotel filled with people greeting each other enthusiastically. A festive mood hovered in the air along with the hum of voices.

"I've checked the perimeter, sir. Other than the actual guests of honor, most of the gala attendees are trickling in at a steady pace." Gillian stood at ease beside him, her dark brown eyes taking in every inch of the room as she reported in. "Looks like another successful mission completed."

Jack fought the urge to snap off a salute. "You do know this is a party we set up, not a military coup."

Gillian looked sheepish for a moment, before letting out a sigh. "You guys think I'm a total stick-in-the-mud, huh?"

"That's not true," he protested.

"I'm not, you know," she said as if he hadn't spoken. "I can be a lot of fun."

He'd seen enough humor twinkling in her eyes to know she wasn't lying, but he couldn't help but make a cautious remark. "You *could* stand to lighten up sometimes."

"I know." Something indecipherable crossed her expression. "I'm just trying to be professional. The last time I let my guard down..." She didn't finish the sentence, just shrugged instead. "I appreciate this job, Jack. I really do."

He smiled, realizing it was the first time she'd used his name instead of *sir.* "Good. We're glad to have you on board."

They turned together to face the hallway leading to the grand ballroom where the festivities would start in just a few hours' time. "I'm going to go check on Pepper. You need anything?"

Gillian shook her head. "Dean and I leave at seventeen hundred hours for that last-minute recon assignment. Everything else is in order, and with Colby as backup, you should be fine."

The woman was right. There really wasn't that much for DreamMakers to do at this point anymore. Most of their work was over once they'd dealt with the timing and coordination of getting people to the event.

Except for Pepper. She had a job to complete, and he was primed to cheer her on as she showed off her stuff.

He found himself grinning as he took the stairs two at a time up to the room where she'd organized her computer equipment. After the incredible evening they'd shared, there hadn't been a chance yet for him to do the next thing. He wasn't about to simply blurt out in front of everyone exactly how he felt. But once they were finished with this gala, Jack had plans to steal her away. Head up the coast and rock her socks off at some classy resort.

Tell her he was crazy about her. Crazier than she might even have guessed, smart woman that she was.

He cautiously stuck his head through the doorway, not wanting to interrupt her if she was busy.

There was no one behind the computer desk.

"That little bitch. I bet she did this on purpose."

Jack spun around at the outraged feminine cry. Charlene stood in the doorway, her hair artfully arranged in an elegant updo, her blue eyes bright with anger. "What?"

The anger turned on him. "If she's not back in time, I'm holding you responsible. What were you thinking, giving your girlfriend a pity job like that? Don't you realize how important this is to me?"

"I have no idea what you're talking about," he said evenly. "Where's Pepper?"

"Gallivanting around the countryside—how the hell should I know? She said she had a backup dick or something she would go and get, but she was probably lying." Charlene planted her fists on her hips and hit him with a quivering lip on top of the anger and frustration. "My parents are scheduled to arrive in less than thirty minutes. I don't have time to track down your fuck buddy and get her to do her damn job."

It was easy to deduce there'd been some sort of snag with the media display, though Jack tensed at Charlene's words—backup *dick*. The nasty insinuation only pissed him off, but he swallowed his irritation as he pulled out his cell phone and quickly brought up Pepper's number. "Let me see where she is," he told Charlene in the most polite tone he could muster.

But all he got was ring after ring, before Pepper's phone switched over to voicemail. Worry tugged his insides. "She's not answering."

"Of course she's not answering. She's probably off somewhere laughing her ass off that she's pulled a fast one on me. Immature little brat."

His hand shot up in warning. "Stop. Whatever your opinion on my relationship with Pepper, she's still a professional, and if she said she's coming back, then she's coming back." He stepped to the door. "I'll go check the parking lot. Maybe she's just pulling in."

Charlene followed hard on his heels. "I want to know what you're going to do if she doesn't show up. Surely you didn't trust this entire portion of the program to some wet-behind-the-ears unproven employee."

Jack didn't answer. Truth was, they didn't have a Plan B, and he didn't think they'd need one. Pepper was a lot of things, but she took her work seriously. If she wasn't here, then that meant something was wrong.

With concern squeezing his chest, he hurried to the stairwell and dashed down to the lobby, moving slightly slower to avoid attracting attention as he crossed the floor to the front door. Incredibly, even in her spiky high heels, Charlene hit the exit on his heels, rushing outside in a flurry of frilly green satin and lace. She stomped her way toward the parking lot, head dipping from side to side like a bobblehead toy.

She whirled, brow raised, complete disgust in her expression. "Well?"

Jack's heart plummeted to his stomach like a brick. Pepper was nowhere in sight. Shit.

He glanced at his phone to check if she'd called back, but no luck. "Let me try calling her again."

Her phone sent him to voice mail just as he spotted Parker marching up. Charlene noticed as well, squaring her shoulders as if preparing for battle.

"Jack, do you need help?" Parker's wary green eyes shifted from Jack to Charlene. "Gillian said there seemed to be some commotion. Is something wrong?"

"Damn right there is!" Charlene fumed. "Your *sister*—" she said the word as if it carried a deadly virus, "—just screwed up everything!"

Parker's body language was all too easy to read. He stiffened like a board, his total annoyance screaming out, and Jack wondered if he was going to have to defend Pepper all over again. Instead his friend turned on Charlene. "I'm sorry you're upset. Give me a moment, and I'm sure we can straighten this out."

"We don't have any time. Your precious Pepper ran off to get some supposed backup file, and if she's not here in the next—"

As if a higher power had heard her, the sound of a car engine roared through the parking lot. Jack swiveled his head, relief soaring through him when he glimpsed Kendra's junker speed through the parking lot gates. The little sedan squealed to a stop in a nearby space, and then the driver's door swung open.

Jack's relief drained from his chest. It wasn't Pepper. Just Kendra.

With tracks of tears rolling down her cheeks.

Chapter Sixteen

OF ALL the unbelievable situations Pepper could have pictured for that day, she was living the most impossible. Technological disasters, being abandoned by her best friend—which was the only freaking explanation she could think of for Kendra's car being gone—and now add in Adam?

She wasn't that much of a drinker, but at the end of this day, she was going to tie one on so hard she'd be incoherent for the next week.

Pepper took a deep breath and braced herself. "So. First up, how did you find me? No—first, what the hell were you thinking storming in on me and the guys and swinging your fucking—"

She jerked to a stop. She couldn't decide what to grill him about first. Rational thought was not working well right now.

In the driver's seat, Adam drummed nervous fingers on the steering wheel as he stopped at a red light. He glanced over, embarrassment reddening his cheeks. "I've been calling and texting you for weeks, Penny. Trying to apologize for it."

"That's called stalking, dude. You should have gotten the message I didn't want to hear from or see you ever again."

"I did. I mean, I thought I did. But Kendra—" He stopped abruptly.

Shit. "Kendra, *what?*"

Her roommate's mysterious disappearance was annoying, but having Adam bring her up sent Pepper's spidey senses tingling.

"She told me you wanted to talk to me but you were too embarrassed about the whole thing that happened during the road trip." He looked upset now. "You know me, Pen, I don't harass chicks who aren't into me. But we're friends, and Kendra said you felt bad about everything. You know, because you had a crush on me all year, and then—"

Pepper could feel her brows rising higher and higher the longer Adam spoke. At this rate, they'd be bumping the ceiling of the car, and she still wouldn't have registered all the "what the fuck?" she was feeling. "I need a moment to—*are you out of your goddamn mind?* I had a crush on you?"

"Yes."

"And Kendra told you this?"

"Yeah, right before we left Chicago."

Add another point to the list of oh-hell-we-need-to-have-a-come-to-Jesus-talk. What was Kendra doing? Had she flipped her frickin' lid?

"Adam, I never had a crush on you. Plus you walked into a private situation and ended up punching me in the face. Not to mention writing crap on your Facebook, and going through my suitcases and stealing my clothes, and—"

"*What?*" he interrupted, his face going whiter than mayo. "I didn't go through your stuff. What kind of sicko do you think I am?" The car shuddered, as if Adam's foot was shaking on the gas pedal.

"Well, it's not like I stole things from my own damn suitcases. And there was only you and Kendra who could..." Oh Lord. Another teeny flash of panic struck her. Adam had access.

So had Kendra.

Adam couldn't hear her internal ramblings. He went right on answering her other accusations. "I thought I was protecting you that night, Pen. Kendra said the other guys were wasted and trying to coax you into three-way sex. And I told you before, I didn't post that shit on Facebook. Someone hacked into my account."

Someone...or Kendra?

Pepper couldn't deny that her friend had the skills to do something like that. Kendra had studied computer technology and game design in college. But... *why?* None of it made sense when Pepper thought about it one thing at a time, but connected together, the only thing that every shitty occurrence had in common...

The only *person...*

"Why?" Pepper glanced over at Adam, who was still white-knuckling the wheel. "Why would Kendra do any of this? I mean, she straight-out lied to you."

"I don't know." He sighed heavily. "I really didn't mean to hurt you. And if you need me to help you deal with Kendra, I will, no strings attached. She called me about thirty minutes ago, by the way—that's why I was at your apartment."

What Pepper needed right now was to get back to the damn hotel and deal with the media emergency first. After that crisis was over, she'd figure out what alien creature had possessed the person she'd thought was her best friend.

IF THERE was one thing guaranteed to get Jack tense and uncomfortable, it was a female's tears. They reminded him too much of his mother crying in frustration during his parents' fights, and he had to smother the urge to turn away from Kendra and her visible distress.

But this was Pepper's best friend, and with Pepper AWOL, Kendra might be the only person who could provide some answers.

He hurried forward, leaving Parker to deal with Charlene's furious ramblings, and met Kendra halfway.

"What's wrong?" he said instantly. "Where's Pepper?"

Moisture clung to Kendra's blonde eyelashes, a whirl of emotions swimming in her eyes. It was the angry glint that caught him off guard.

"What's wrong?" he demanded again.

The petite blonde took her sweet-ass time responding, playing with the strap of her purse, glancing down at her open-toed sandals, biting her bottom lip.

"For fuck's sake, tell me," he snapped, unconcerned with his harsh tone, because damn it, he was seriously worried now.

"I don't know how." Kendra's voice was small and tired.

Impatience roared through his body. "Take a deep breath and say the words, Kendra. We don't have time to stand around. We're trying to track down Pepper and—"

"She's at the apartment," Kendra cut in.

Some of his concern ebbed, but the revelation only brought a dose of confusion. "Is she getting the backup files?"

Kendra slowly shook her head, while he fought the urge to shake *her*. "There are no backup files," she revealed.

Jack narrowed his eyes. "What are you talking about?"

"She screwed up the project on purpose." Bitterness flashed in her eyes. "I tried convincing her that it was a terrible idea, but she wanted to get back at Charlene. She was jealous that you and Charlene used to...you know..."

His shoulders went rigid, a queasy sense of disbelief mingled with doubt floating through him. "Pepper wouldn't do that."

"She did," Kendra insisted. "She sabotaged your party, and now she's back at our place—" Her mouth slammed shut.

"Finish that sentence," Jack said in an ominous tone.

271

Kendra looked him square in the eye. "She's back at our place having sex with another man."

The ground beneath Jack's feet swayed. Bullshit. Bull. Shit. His mind was only capable of producing those two syllables. He didn't know what kind of game Kendra was playing, but he didn't believe a single word coming out of her mouth. Pepper would never sabotage a DreamMakers event, nor would she hop into bed with someone else a mere two days after tending to Jack so damn lovingly.

Whatever was going on right now, he suspected it had nothing to do with Pepper and everything to do with the woman in front of him, who was now crying in earnest.

"I'm so sorry, Jack," she wailed. "Why did you have to make me tell you? You deserve *so* much better than her. I hate seeing you get hurt."

She'd mistaken his silence for acceptance, apparently. But Jack had known enough liars in his life to see through every choked word, every crocodile tear.

Hardening his jaw, he reached for Kendra, intending on gripping her chin to force her to own up to what she was doing, but the damned woman mistook the gesture for one of comfort, and the next thing he knew, she dove into his arms. Slender arms wrapped around his neck and held him tight as she buried her head in the crook of his neck.

Her tears soaked his collarbone and triggered a burst of annoyance. "Stop," he muttered, attempting to push her away.

She clung on like a spider monkey hugging a tree. Loud sobs echoed between them, but not loud enough to cover up the sound of a car engine. Jack gripped Kendra's slender hips, trying to pry her off him, while his gaze moved beyond her shoulders to rest on the black Jeep that had driven into the lot.

Still holding on for dear life, Kendra twisted her head to follow his gaze. When both the driver and passenger doors flew open, the blonde gasped. Then her sharp intake of breath rushed out in what could only be considered a jubilant noise. "Oh my God, *see*? She was with *him*. I walked in on them right before I came here."

Jack managed to unhook her hands from his shoulders just as Pepper skidded to a stop, a dark-haired young man in tow.

"What the *hell*?" Pepper burst out when she caught sight of their too-close bodies. "Get your hands off him, Kendra."

Jack could have sworn he saw a gleam of triumph in Kendra's eyes before she finally let him go, taking a step to the side.

"Don't bother denying it," Kendra told Pepper, her singsong voice raising Jack's hackles. "We all know what you and Adam were doing."

Pepper's cheeks were bright red, her shoulders trembling with fury, but to Jack's surprise, she didn't explode. She simply flashed her friend a cool look before glancing beyond her to the redheaded woman marching toward them.

"It's about time you showed up!" Charlene snapped.

"I told you I would," Pepper replied, sounding so calm Jack couldn't help but be impressed.

The only way to describe what was happening at the moment was *clusterfuck*. A big ol' clusterfuck of monstrous proportions, with accusations flying and tempers high. And yet he'd never seen Pepper look more controlled.

Parker came up beside him, warily glancing from Kendra's tear-streaked face to Charlene's furious eyes to Adam's bewildered expression, and finally at Pepper's unruffled presence.

"Okay, everyone needs to chill out," Parker started.

Jack hid a smile as Pepper cut her brother off by raising her hand. "I've got this under control, Parker." She turned to Charlene and held up the small flash drive in her hand. "I have the backup right here. I checked it myself and it works fine. I also brought a third copy in case we need it." Her voice tightened as her gaze shifted to Kendra. "And you...I have no idea what you're up to, but I don't have time to deal with this cuckoo-craziness right now. I have a job to do."

The burst of pride that filled Jack's chest nearly sent him soaring off his feet.

"Come on, Charlene," Pepper said firmly. "Let's go load this up so we can give your parents a walk down memory lane they'll never forget."

To Jack's surprise, Charlene nodded, flashing Pepper a look of deep gratitude. "Thank you. That's the first rational thing I've heard in a while."

Pepper squeezed Jack's arm as she moved to follow Charlene. "Don't kill Adam, and don't believe a word she says," Pepper murmured. "We'll get to the bottom of it later."

Good heads-up on the Adam business, and Jack didn't need to ask who *she* was. He gave a quick nod. "Go. I'll find you when you're done."

Jack had never been prouder as he watched Pepper walk off with her shoulders held high. He noticed Parker

274

wearing an indulgent expression, and shot his friend a smile as if to say, *see, your little sister is all grown up.*

Then both men turned to Kendra, Parker beating Jack to the punch. "You're not welcome here. I suggest you go home," he said coolly. "I'm sure my sister will track you down later."

Kendra had the decency to keep her mouth shut. With a curt nod, she headed back to her car, speeding out of the lot a moment later.

Only the dark-haired young man remained, shifting uneasily on his feet as Jack focused on him.

"Adam, right?" Jack said lightly. "I'm Jack."

He nodded, slightly stricken. "I recognize your voice. You know, from when you told me on the phone that you'd shatter every bone in my body and turn me into a mass of blood and pain."

A loud snicker came from Parker's vicinity. "Word-for-word recitation. Must have sunk in hard."

Jack ignored him, genuinely contrite. From the sound of it there were a bunch of new developments he needed to be informed about. "Uh. Right. Sorry about that."

"It's okay," the guy said ruefully. "You thought I wrote that stuff on Facebook. I get it."

Jack sighed, then glanced at Parker. "Can you and the others handle everything, or do you still need me?"

"Naah, we've got it covered," his friend said.

"Good." Jack turned back to Adam, gesturing to the hotel entrance. "C'mon, let's go have a drink."

Adam's lips twitched before a smile broke free. "Best idea I've heard all day."

Chapter Seventeen

SHE WAS damn near bouncing, the adrenaline still racing through her system leaving her with a head rush Pepper would be happy to kill with a massive order of something drenched in butter.

But she had one final task before she was free.

The systems check had gone perfectly this time. Charlene excitedly grabbed her and squeezed her in an unexpected hug before racing off to go meet her parents. Pepper leaned back in the sudden quiet of the room, preparing everything for the final moment.

She had about thirty minutes to kill according to the master schedule that Parker had given her. Impressive, that her brother wasn't *so* bad at handling details. In

276

fact, as she sat and got a chance to calm down, there were a lot of things that struck her as unexpectedly good in her life.

Although how she could be thinking that right now seemed simply mental. It must be the eye of the tornado. That moment of calm before everything would hit the fan one more time.

From Adam to Kendra to Jack to Parker to Charlene—

—and *always* back to Jack. He had become the center she wanted to be with in the middle of any storm. Not to cling to him, not to have him rescue her. But to be with her as they faced situations together.

Strangely enough, the chaos of the day had helped her see so clearly what was important in her life. Family, friends...

Jack.

The room below her filled with party guests, excited voices rising up to her level as brightly colored dresses and formal suits drifted in random patterns. People milled around, searching for their seats at the massive round tables covering the ballroom floor.

A head table had been set up like at a wedding, the faint sounds of background music swirling around everything and bringing a festive air as people took their places.

The door opened beside her, and the soundman returned. "You've got everything under control for your part?"

"Piece of cake," Pepper drawled, lips lifting in a smile, but she refused to elaborate.

"Rock on." He leaned toward her slightly, whispering conspiratorially, "You're lucky. Once you're done, you get to leave. I get to play golden oldies until I'm twitchy."

"Every job has its burdens." Pepper kept a straight face, watching with interest as a flurry of activity started on the floor below.

"And that's my cue," Daniel said. He flicked a bunch of switches, and the opening strains of a wedding march began. Pepper watched Charlene's parents stroll down the center aisle, waving enthusiastically to their friends and family who all rose to their feet to cheer them into the room.

Pepper found herself grinning like a fool without even realizing it. There was just so much joy happening before her, and she was so into observing everything that she missed the moment when Jack slipped into the room behind her.

He draped an arm over the back of her chair, leaning in to press his lips against her cheek. "Almost your time to shine."

She caught hold of his fingers with her left hand, trapping him in place. He dragged over a chair and sat close, gently caressing the back of her neck as the welcome speech down on the podium finished, and everyone turned expectantly to the massive screens arranged on the walls.

One flick of a button started the media montage, and as the room lights dimmed, images of years shared flashed out bigger than life accompanied by the couple's favorite songs. Friends and laughter, a growing family. Ageless beauty recorded in every smile, and it was Pepper's skill that had made the entire thing possible.

It was her turn to shine indeed.

"Damn, Pepper, this is amazing." Jack's cheek brushed hers as they watched together. Live-action video merged with shots donated by family and friends—it must've looked like magic to someone who didn't know the process.

But the amazing thing was the man nestled so close to her side that his body heat wrapped around her like a blanket, his fingers casually linked through hers as if he couldn't get enough of touching her.

Whatever magic was happening on the screen, there was more magic happening in her heart.

The moment it was done everything became a blur. She heard voices offering congratulations, along with thunderous applause from down on the ballroom floor. She got a thumbs-up from Parker in passing, but none of that registered beyond a momentary flash.

Jack had her by the hand, dragging her to his car.

His rush to leave suddenly struck her as hilarious, and she started giggling. Maybe it was the tension, maybe it was sheer relief, but she couldn't stop laughing for long enough to draw a full breath. She clutched his arm and fought for balance as he turned her carefully, grinning at her.

"You are incredible."

"I am so ready to crash, you wouldn't believe it." She draped her hands around his neck, leaning back on the car door as she stared up into his gorgeous eyes. "I'm glad that's over with."

His expression grew more serious. "There's still something we need to deal with."

Ugh. Kendra.

Pepper nodded slowly. "By the way, I really do hope you didn't do anything drastic to Adam."

"He's still alive. We had a discussion about the difference between defending a woman and being a creep, and I think he's got it solid now." Jack closed the distance between them and planted a fiery kiss on her lips. Like a branding, one hand holding their lips together, the other pressed to her lower back to seal their bodies so tight she could feel every muscular inch of him.

Pepper wasn't sure what had set him off, but she really didn't care. She liked this side of Jack very much.

When he finally let her breathe, she glanced up at him from under her lashes. "You know nothing happened between me and Adam. Never did, never will."

"Damn right."

He said it with such conviction, Pepper laughed again. Her amusement faded as he pulled open the car door for her. "Kendra."

"We'll deal with her." Jack lowered himself so their eyes were on the same level. "Not that I don't think you're capable, but you don't have to do this alone. I want to be there for you, at your side."

There was nowhere she would rather have him.

Letting herself into the apartment felt eerily like entering a tomb. A mess of boxes lay scattered in the living room, items pouring out of the top of them as if they'd been hastily filled.

Jack moved in front of her defensively, and Pepper didn't bother to protest. She called out a warning. "Kendra. I'm home. We need to talk."

A loud crash rang from the back bedroom that Kendra had claimed. "There's nothing to talk about."

"Well, she's a fucking dreamer if she thinks that's all it will take," Jack muttered.

Pepper agreed, but none of it made sense. "Sit down. I'll go get her."

He hesitated then reluctantly shifted toward the couch, perching gingerly on the armrest as if ready to leap to her defense at a moment's notice.

She wasn't going to do anything stupid, but this had to get cleared up here and now. She cautiously stuck her head around the corner into Kendra's room to discover her friend had most of her stuff packed into suitcases. "Going somewhere?"

Kendra glanced up, her eyes puffy and red from crying. "Don't be a smartass."

Fighting back a retort that wouldn't get them anywhere, Pepper moved farther into the door opening. "Obviously you're packing, but I think I deserve a little more information. I'm going back to the living room, and I expect you to join me there when you're ready."

She didn't bother to wait for a response, just stomped back to Jack's side. She leaned into his body and breathed slowly, trying to calm her rapidly beating heart. If Kendra didn't come out this was going to get even more awkward.

But the petite blonde joined them not even two minutes later, dropping the suitcases she carried in either hand by the front door before turning back to face them, arms crossed, face pulled into a sullen pout. "What?"

Not this again. Pepper was ready to scream. "How about you explain what the heck happened today. You straight-up lied to me, to Jack. Heck, I found out that you lied to Adam, too."

"Doesn't matter." Kendra's gaze darted to take in Jack before returning to Pepper. "You got it all in the end, just like always. Everything you *ever* want you get. It's just no damn fair."

This was like some bizarre Picasso painting where everything started to melt and droop and made no sense at all. "You lied to me because I get everything I want—Kendra, are you *high*?"

Kendra snapped her head in anger. "You have no idea what I'm talking about, do you?"

Obviously not, but just in case she'd missed something blatant, Pepper thought back for anything the woman could be referring to. She shook her head slowly. "As far as I know, I've been operating under the assumption that you were my friend. Now I find out you've been lying to me ever since we left school, maybe even before—"

"Friends don't steal the guys their friends are interested in," Kendra snapped.

"You can't steal a guy who's not interested in you," Jack interjected, his arm around Pepper a solid base for her to lean against.

Kendra made a face. "You *were* interested in me, but you're not the one I was talking about. You're just another example of *exactly* how little Pepper cares about anyone but herself."

Now Pepper was completely lost. "Who are you talking about?"

"Ben." The word shot out like a bullet from a gun. "He and I were friends, and maybe about to become more, then suddenly you show up and you're all la-di-da-di-da, and he's not only got the hots for you, he's willing to fool around with you *and* another guy just to make you happy!"

Kendra stepped forward a couple of paces. At Pepper's side Jack tensed, ready to protect her. Only, the other girl stopped far enough away, her eyes flashing with anger as she glared daggers at Pepper.

"You didn't even once notice what you were doing. And then we got here, and I thought maybe it would be better, but no. As soon as you find out I'm interested in Jack you had to swing your hips and seduce him. So fuck you. I'm gone."

Pepper's head was reeling from trying to take in the outpouring of venom, even as Jack swung up a hand to stop Kendra from stomping off.

"You are one misguided little girl, but you're welcome to your delusions," he said flatly. "Before you get the hell out of here, I want you to know if you *ever* come near Pepper again, you will regret it."

Kendra sniffed, the threat rolling over her without much impact. "You wouldn't do anything to me. You wouldn't dare."

"He wouldn't have to." Pepper stepped in front of Jack, nudging away his warning hand. "He's not threatening to physically harm you. There are laws about harassment, and even though I feel sorry for you, I have no objection to using the law to its fullest extent."

"So high and mighty," Kendra muttered. "I hope you're happy. You took all the good things I tried to give you as a friend, and you just ground them underfoot. You're a terrible person."

With that, Kendra vanished into the back corridor, and Pepper gasped for air. She must've been holding her breath because she felt lightheaded.

"It's not true." Jack spoke softly, one arm coming around her as he pulled her against his body. "You are one of the best people I know. Whatever her issues are, they're hers."

Pepper nodded, her chin cradled in his fingers as he caressed her cheek gently. "Still sucks to think I've been living with a crazy woman."

"You're safe. That's all that counts."

It was stupid, but at that moment Pepper noticed a familiar shirt hanging out of one of the boxes. "That...*bitch.*"

She slipped from Jack's arms to pull the fabric free. So. That answered the question of who had gone through her suitcases.

Something else dawned on her. "Oh my God. Jack."

He tensed. "What is it?"

"The perfume..." Pepper's breath caught in dismay. "She took it from my suitcase—it must have been Kendra who threw the bottle in the parking lot." Another thought struck, this one even more horrifying. "And your car. Oh God. She was there that day. Do you think...would she really..."

All words escaped her. She couldn't speak properly. Couldn't think clearly.

She'd gone numb.

OF ALL the crazy, mixed-up, *fucked*-up things Jack had ever dealt with, the double-cross of Pepper's supposed best friend had to rank right near the top of his seriously-shitty-moves list.

Pepper's face had gone ashen, and even he couldn't hide the shock and fury that pounded him in the gut. It had cost him a lot of money to fix his father's car after the insurance company informed him his premium would skyrocket if he filed a claim, since he couldn't prove he hadn't caused the accident himself. But it wasn't the cash that boiled his blood—it was the thought that Pepper could have been *in* the car when the damage was done. That she could have been hurt.

He opened his mouth to respond, but Pepper stepped away from the boxes, letting go of the shirt and bra she'd been holding. She whirled around to the doorway, where Kendra had just appeared.

"Did you do it?" Pepper said coldly. "Did you bust up Jack's car?"

Kendra met Jack's eyes, and he was overcome with blind rage when he noticed the tiny smirk on her face. "So what if I did?"

"You...*lunatic!*" Pepper charged forward, two steps from lunging at her ex-best friend before Jack hauled her backward. His entire body shook with anger, but he refused to give Kendra the satisfaction of seeing him lose it.

"Stop," he told Pepper, locking his hands on her waist. He felt her shaking, too, her shoulders trembling so wildly she was swaying on her feet. "She's not worth it."

"Your car, Jack!" Pepper shouted. "Your father's car!"

"It's just a car, Candy Cane. And it's fixed. It's over." His frigid gaze traveled back to Kendra. "What I said stands—you come near either one of us again and we'll slap a harassment charge on you. Understood?"

"Oh, spare me the macho posturing," Kendra muttered. "I never want to see either of your faces ever again." The blonde shifted her grip on her two suitcases and took a step to the front hall. "I've arranged to have my stuff shipped to my parents' house. Have a nice life— you two assholes deserve each other."

Ten seconds later, the door slammed and Kendra was gone.

"I can't believe she damaged your car," Pepper whispered. "God, Jack, how crazy and vengeful does someone have to be to *do* something like that?"

"Pretty crazy and vengeful." He swallowed before meeting her distressed eyes. "She's right, you know."

Alarm skittered across Pepper's face. "What do you mean?"

"We *do* deserve each other," he said softly. "But not in the negative way she meant. We're perfect for each other, Candy Cane. I hope you know that."

A ghost of a smile lifted her lips. "Of course I know, Jackjack."

"Yeah?" He brushed his fingertips over the soft edge of her jaw line. "What else do you know?"

The cloud of hostility and betrayal hanging in the air slowly dissipated like a puff of steam, something sweet and tender rolling in to take its place.

"I know a lot of things, actually." Pepper leaned in to his touch, sighing when his thumb teased her lower lip. "I know that I've taken so much for granted."

He blinked in surprise, but she hurried on before he could argue. "I've griped and complained about my family so many times, without once stopping to think about how good I have it, how lucky I am to have them."

Jack ignored the pain that constricted his chest. She was right—she *hadn't* realized how incredible it was to be surrounded by family who loved and supported her, and for some reason, hearing her admit the error of her ways lightened the heavy weight pressing on his heart.

"I also know that I work well under pressure," Pepper said with a smile. "I know that I can handle my own with women like Charlene, who, by the way, I was so damn jealous of. Not only because she's older and prettier and more sophisticated, but because she had you first."

He had to smile. "I'm gonna call bullshit on the 'prettier' part. She doesn't hold a candle to you, not just in the looks department, but in *every* department."

"Aw, that's sweet of you to say. But I'm not jealous of her anymore." Pepper shrugged. "Because I know something else."

He tipped his head. "Yeah, what's that?"

"That you love me."

The grin returned to his lips. "Oh, really?"

"Definitely." The confidence ringing in her voice was a major turn-on. "You love me." She flashed a smirk. "And you're in luck—I just happen to love you, too."

Pure joy soared inside him, and he gave himself a mental fist bump, tempted to do a little victory dance. Other women in his life had dropped the L-bomb before, but he'd never said it back. Hearing those words leave the mouth of the woman he was absolutely fucking crazy about was...a fucking amazing feeling.

"You love me, huh?" He couldn't seem to wipe the goofy grin off his face.

"Sure do."

"Even though I'm bossy?"

"I'm bossier, so it's not like I can hold that against you."

A laugh flew out. God, he loved her. With all his frickin' heart.

"Now say it back so I can know for sure," Pepper ordered.

"Say what?" he asked innocently.

"Jack."

He cocked a brow. "Pepper."

"*Jack.*" Exasperation darkened her eyes.

"*Fine.*" With an exaggerated sigh, he crossed his arms over his chest and said, "I love you."

"Good. Now once more with feeling."

His shoulders shook with laughter as he cupped her cheeks and gazed into her emerald-green eyes. "I love you, Pepper Wilson. I love you so much it hurts. I love you so much I can't sleep at night. I love you so much I—"

Her lips were on his before he could finish. She kissed him so greedily he was gasping for air by the time she released him, but the dizziness didn't leave him, because now she was tearing at her clothes, pieces of fabric whipping in front of his eyes and landing on the floor. Until she was gloriously naked. Naked and beautiful and *his*.

All his.

"Wait."

Pepper froze at his command, complete perplexity on her face. "What?"

He was a crazy stupid bastard for stopping them, but he didn't want this to happen right there, where the shouting and anger and betrayal was still fresh and raw.

He jerked his T-shirt off, dragging the fabric forward over his head. Her eyes flashed with interest until he handed it to her. "Put it on."

"You're…" Her nose wrinkled in that adorable way he loved. "Why?"

He snuck the neck over her head and she slipped her arms into place in spite of her confusion. Once she was covered, he caught her by the hand, pulling her toward the door. "We're going out."

She snorted, but slipped her feet into sandals. "Crazy man."

"I have this apartment I need you to check out."

"Sure. No problem." She stood in the elevator next to him, one hip cocked to the side and mischief all over her face. Fingers stroked his bare chest as they waited to arrive at the parking level. "I have no underwear on, you know."

Jack chuckled. "Hold that thought."

Pepper was astonishingly silent during the entire drive to his place, and the trip to his door. Once she was through the entrance, though, her curiosity obviously couldn't be contained any longer. "Jackjack, you're a nut. We were like three seconds away from having sex."

He stepped up to her, reaching down to cup her ass and lift her in the air against his body. She tangled around him like a vine, arms to his neck, legs around his hips. All of them connected and so nearly skin-to-skin his cock was ready to explode.

But he looked into those big eyes and saw a hell of a lot more than just freaking awesome sex.

He touched his lips to hers. One second. Pulled back just enough that when he spoke their mouths still touched, like they were breathing the same air. "And now I'm going to make love to you. And then we're going to talk about where we want to live."

Pepper grinned. "You were hopelessly romantic for a second, dude, and then you lost it."

He didn't fucking care. "I love you, Pepper."

She smiled at him. A full-out Pepper heart-on-her-sleeve smile. "I love you, too, Jack. Now let me have Big Jac—"

He drowned out the rest of her words with his lips.

Emma

THE MORNING sun spilled over the tenth-floor hotel room, and like a cat, Emma was curled up in the corner of the couch, steaming cup of tea in her hand. Her third of the day—the one trouble with being on the West Coast. Even now at not-quite seven a.m. she'd needed to be up for hours to keep in touch with the rest of the team back in New York.

What was supposed to be a two-week trip had extended for a bit longer, but she was enjoying the change of pace. There was nothing quite like New York, but then there was nothing like Paris or London—all of the places she'd lived over the years had their own unique flavor with wonderful things to enjoy.

She stared out the windows of the corner suite, gazing down at the beach and the paved boardwalk running along the entire length of the hotel. A long dock extended from the beach, the water simmering around the solid structure. The trip had been a great way to break up her routine, coming out to San Francisco for the charity benefit.

A reluctant smile tugged her lips. Not that she could call anything in her world *routine*. The trip had turned out far more interesting than she'd expected.

There were still two wine glasses on the coffee table, an empty bottle on the small bar counter. Not as many as a week ago. Partying that hard wasn't something she did very often anymore, but her new friend Suz had brought out the devil inside.

Last night they'd simply shared a bottle of wine and chatted. That was something sorely missing in her life. Friends who weren't part of the industry, or models trying to get ahead as they showed off the latest fashions. The world of design was glamorous and star-making, and both exciting and tedious at times, but Emma loved every second of it. At least the way she worked the industry.

Secrets. She had them, and as long as she did, things should continue to be amazing.

Down on the boardwalk, a solidly built male figure jogged into sight, and she watched in admiration as his legs turned over again and again, thick thigh muscles supporting a trim body with broad shoulders and well-formed biceps. She was high enough up that the details of his face and whatever logo graced his pale green shirt were just a blur, but there was enough to see to keep her interested as he slowed to a walk in front of her hotel.

Something about the way he moved seemed familiar, and Emma found herself on her feet, one hand pressed to the floor-to-ceiling glass as she tried to ease the strange sensation that she'd seen him before. The man turned toward the beach, stepping off the path and moving to a bench surrounded by grayish white sand. When he propped a leg on the bench, Emma got to admire his butt as that niggling feeling at the back of her brain continued to grow.

She must have seen a million people over the past year. Why should one admittedly fine man make her heart start to pound?

She watched him while he watched the birds, a crowd of them swooping in as he pulled something from his pocket and scattered food in front of him.

Another memory struck, and it was crazy, but she abandoned her perch at the window, rushing back through the suite to slip her feet into a pair of sandals, pulling a cover-up around her shoulders, and grabbing her room key before dashing for the elevator.

The mirrored wall in the elevator gave her plenty of time to tell herself she was crazy. Her hair lay loosely braided over one shoulder, she didn't have a stitch of makeup on, and here she was, racing down to the beach so she could casually spy on some stranger.

Her own dark brown eyes mocked her. She stuck out her tongue and made a face, jerking back to attention as the elevator dinged and the door slid open.

She strolled as casually as possible through the foyer, heading for the entrance that opened onto the beach. The warm air outside struck her skin like a caress, the scent of the ocean filling her nose. She twisted, trying to orient herself, moving confidently to her right and up onto the boardwalk.

No need for subterfuge. The bench was empty, the birds still fluttering around it. As she approached, they scattered, only a few of the bolder ones returning to peck at the breadcrumbs littering the sand.

A sense of sadness struck. Emma leaned her hands on the back of the bench and wondered—

On the arm of the bench a little pile of bread crumbs still remained. The birds hadn't managed to eat enough yet to destroy what was a distinctly heart-shaped pattern. She pressed her hand to her chest as a wave of memory rushed through her.

Fingers linked with hers. Fumbling kisses in the dark that set her heart fluttering. The freshness and wonder of first love.

Emma whirled, searching the boardwalk for another sign of the dark-haired stranger, wondering if what she was imagining was possible, or if she'd seen a ghost. Dean Colter had been everything to her before their paths had separated. That had been a long time ago, and yet the thought of him was enough to make her simultaneously furious and thrilled.

Whoever the man was, he was long gone, but her curiosity was at an all-time high. She turned back to the hotel, striding quickly.

There was nothing to say she couldn't take a stroll down memory lane with the help of Google. Maybe she'd find out Dean was back in the south, married and with half a dozen kids.

But then again, maybe not. Life didn't always follow the expected path. It certainly hadn't for her.

Although she wasn't sure what she would do if she found out that after all this time they were both in the same city.

Chapter Eighteen

THE MARGARITAS were getting stronger.

Pepper eyed the almost-empty glass in her hand, then glanced up at Suz with suspicion. "Did you have a shaking fit while pouring the vodka into the blender? Sweet sombreros, this is strong enough to peel paint."

"We're drinking them, not applying to walls," Suz said, happily raising her glass in the air and letting the afternoon sunshine sparkle off the ice. "Of course, they'd taste better if we could have them delivered by well-oiled, nearly-naked cabana boys, but that's probably out of the question."

"Yeah, Parker would cut off the fingers of any man who tried to deliver me a drink," Lynn spoke up with a sigh.

"Jack wouldn't be as nice," Pepper told her almost sister-in-law. "He'd go for the cabana boy's ding-dong."

Suz and Lynn hooted, while Gillian, who'd been silently sipping her margarita, cracked a smile.

"What? You pull them, they make noise," Pepper insisted.

"The cabana boys, or the ding-dongs?" Suz laughed harder. "Oh, baby, you are one of a kind. Never change."

Pepper wasn't quite sure if that was a compliment or a subtle insult, but even insults from Suz were right up there on her "okay by me because it just means you love me" list.

A list that kept getting longer the more Pepper thought about it.

A wave of laughter wafted over from the patio, where most of the men had congregated to discuss the upcoming football season. The Sunday barbecue wasn't as crowded as last time. Pepper's parents had kept it to immediate family and close friends, though there was one notable absence Pepper was trying not to dwell on. She hadn't heard from Kendra since the woman moved out, and she didn't expect to. But Lord, her heart still clenched when she thought about her former best friend.

Or had they ever *really* been best friends? Pepper wasn't so sure anymore.

"What's the next big thing on the agenda?" Gillian asked, prompting a round of groans from the rest of the women.

Suz held out the pitcher toward Gillian's empty glass. "You. You need to stop working so hard. You need a date? I'll set you up with someone. Because, lady, you are too fine to spend so much time thinking about work."

Gillian grinned. "Be careful, or I'll think you're hitting on me."

"*Pshaw.* If I were hitting on you, you'd know. I'd have you so hot and bothered that the two of us would be writhing by the pool using up a year's supply of baby oil."

A male throat cleared.

Pepper choked on a laugh when she glimpsed the glazed look on Dean's face. He'd appeared behind them, clad in a white tee that stretched over his broad chest and board shorts riding low on his trim hips. As usual, he looked sexy as hell, and he flashed Pepper a secretive wink before turning to Suz.

"Sorry to interrupt—actually no, I'm not sorry at all," Dean drawled, his gaze shifting from Suz to Gillian. "Baby oil, huh?"

"You know it, hon. Wanna be there to help us out with the hard-to-reach spots?" Suz grinned.

"You know it," he mimicked. "But first, let me use your phone, Jonesy. I forgot mine in the car."

Lynn snickered, a surprisingly unladylike sound. "Is there something special about Suz's phone? You could have grabbed Parker's. You were right there next to him."

Dean flashed another deadly smile, this one straight at Lynn. "He said I couldn't. Something about 'inappropriate pictures' he still needs to delete. You two kids getting kinky in public, were you?"

"Shut up, Dean." Lynn's cheeks were brilliant red, but she smiled.

"That's not a denial," he pointed out, accepting the phone from Suz.

As he strode off toward the gazebo, Pepper picked up the conversation thread and changed the topic. "So, I did make a decision before the alcohol outweighed the blood in my veins. I'll keep working at DreamMakers, but I'll also be freelancing. Parker and I talked it through, and he doesn't think there'll be enough work for me full time."

"Your first freelance project should be a hundred-photograph essay of Jack. Naked, of course," Suz said helpfully.

"I heard that," came Jack's voice.

"You were supposed to," Suz replied as he walked up to the group. "I never throw out the word *naked* unless I know a hot man is there to hear it."

"It's true," Lynn piped up. "She doesn't."

Rolling his eyes, Jack touched Pepper's arm. "Your mom insists you're the only one who knows how to put the potato salad together 'right'. You've been summoned to the kitchen."

Pepper accepted his hand, thankful for the support as the lawn shifted underfoot. "She's never seen me make a batch after drinking Suz's ZombieMakers. Holy spamole."

Jack tucked an arm around her, chuckling as he guided her toward the house. "You're drunk as a skunk."

"Nope," she denied. "I don't stink. I'm drunk as a wino after a five-day bender and I need you to take me into the house and strip off all my clothes and fuc—"

Jack's hand clamped over her mouth. "And we'll just hold that thought for a little longer. Since we're all of five steps away from your dad and Parker."

"Oops?"

Pepper made a supreme effort to walk in a straight line as they climbed the patio steps, but her sharp-as-a-hawk pain-in-the-ass brother didn't miss a thing.

"Dad, Pepper's drunk," Parker announced the second she and Jack reached the deck.

Pepper opened her mouth to blast him with a good comeback, but then it just didn't seem worth the effort. "I love you, too, Spidey."

His eyes narrowed. Pepper giggled. Ha. He was probably shocked she wasn't fighting back.

This could be fun. More fun than fighting. Hopefully she'd still remember this interesting tidbit when she wasn't high on lemony goodness.

"As long as she can still make the potato salad." Pamela Wilson motioned from the kitchen door. "You still sober enough to give your mom a helping hand?"

"For you? I'd peel potatoes even if I were in a coma." Pepper smacked a kiss on Jack's cheek. "Be right back, Jackjack. My mommy needs me."

JACK STOOD aside, another layer of contentment rolling in as Pepper paused to wrap her arms around her mother and squeeze her tight. The easy affection and the sheer-out love was so blatant it shook him to his core.

That was Pepper. Living life large, and these days she was hauling him along with her, and he fucking loved every second.

As the two women disappeared into the house, Parker drifted off to find Lynn, leaving Jack alone with Patrick Wilson. The older man flipped the row of burgers on the grill, then glanced at Jack with a warm smile.

"Come keep me company, son."

Never in a million years would that get old. Jack settled on top of the tall stool beside Patrick, soaking in the sheer sense of belonging. "You think the ladies will ever return, or will they stay inside all night making plans to torment us?"

"Of course they'll be back. Right in time to make sure I don't burn anything."

Jack laughed.

"Yep. Over forty years together, and she's still checking to make sure I put my shoes on the right feet every morning." Patrick's expression softened. "And you know what? Sometimes I think I'd get it wrong if I didn't have her challenging me all the time. Keeps me on my toes. You'll see what I mean—you got yourself a Wilson woman now, too."

Forty years. It sounded like an astronomical amount of time to Jack. Hell, his parents had barely made it eight years. Wouldn't have even been that long if his father hadn't hammered his mother into sticking around.

But damn, it sounded nice. Forty years with Pepper. Forty years of her contagious laughter and thrilling spontaneity and lust for life.

He had himself a Wilson woman, all right, and he was never giving her up.

In the end he was the one who snuck away from Patrick after receiving a final body-jarring back-pounding—the older man was damn powerful for someone who drew comics all day long. Jack slipped into the house, discovering Pepper alone at the island counter, staring in dismay at a pile of cooked cubed potatoes.

He stepped behind her, arms automatically pulling her body to his as he rested his chin on her shoulder.

"Whatcha thinking about with such a serious expression?"

She leaned against him, the connection so perfect— so right. Then she spoke in barely a whisper. "They're staring at me."

Jack struggled to push down the laughter that wanted to escape. He glanced at the pile but saw nothing there that would freak her out. "You go ahead and put those mean ol' potatoes into the salad. I'll be right here to defend you."

A giggle escaped her. "You making fun of me, Jackjack?"

"Maybe a little," he confessed.

She twisted in his arms and smiled up at him. "I like you."

"I like you, too, even when you're tipsy."

"I'm not tipsy," she insisted seriously before cracking a huge grin. "I'm *drunk*. Two very different things."

"Ah. Good to know."

She tilted her head to the side, shining red hair tumbling over her shoulders as she examined his face. "I'm not too drunk to tell you something very, very, *very* important."

Jack grinned. "But will you remember what you told me tomorrow?"

She shrugged. "Doesn't matter, because it's never going to change. I love you today when I'm pissed, and I'll still love you tomorrow. I'll love you when I'm pissed off, and when I'm pissing, and—" She stopped and frowned. "Maybe not that last one."

He lost it, laughter bubbling up and escaping. "You are going to have one hell of a headache tomorrow, baby."

She swayed again, green eyes blinking brightly at him. "You'll take care of me, though, because you love me, too. Right? Always?"

Jack brushed a kiss over her mouth, then pulled back. "Always and forever," he promised.

New York Times Bestselling Authors

Vivian Arend
&
Elle Kennedy

DreamMakers

All Fired Up
Love is a Battlefield
Don't Walk Away

Vivian Arend has been around North America, through parts of Europe, and into Central and South America, often with no running water. When challenged to write a book, she gave it a shot, and discovered creating worlds to play in was nearly as addictive as traveling the real one.

Now a New York Times and USA Today bestselling author of both contemporary and paranormal stories, Vivian continues to explore, write and otherwise keep herself well entertained.

A RITA-award nominated author, Elle Kennedy grew up in the suburbs of Toronto, Ontario, and holds a B.A. in English from York University. From an early age, she knew she wanted to be a writer, and actively began pursuing that dream when she was a teenager.

Elle currently publishes with Signet Eclipse, Harlequin Romantic Suspense, and Samhain Publishing. She loves strong heroines and sexy alpha heroes, and just enough heat and danger to keep things interesting!

Printed in Great Britain
by Amazon

17569719R00175